CRUCIFIXION CREEK

ALSO BY BARRY MAITLAND

THE BELLTREE TRILOGY
Crucifixion Creek

THE BROCK AND KOLLA SERIES
The Marx Sisters
The Malcontenta
All My Enemies
The Chalon Heads
Silvermeadow
Babel
The Verge Practice
No Trace
Spider Trap
Dark Mirror
Chelsea Mansions
The Raven's Eye

CRUCIFIXION
CREEK

A Belltree Mystery

BARRY MAITLAND

MINOTAUR BOOKS
NEW YORK

This is a work of fiction. All of the characters, organizations, and events portrayed in this novel are either products of the author's imagination or are used fictitiously.

CRUCIFIXION CREEK. Copyright © 2014 by Barry Maitland. All rights reserved. Printed in the United States of America. For information, address St. Martin's Press, 175 Fifth Avenue, New York, N.Y. 10010.

www.minotaurbooks.com

The Library of Congress Cataloging-in-Publication Data is available upon request.

ISBN 978-1-250-07214-6 (hardcover)
ISBN 978-1-4668-8354-3 (e-book)

Our books may be purchased in bulk for promotional, educational, or business use. Please contact your local bookseller or the Macmillan Corporate and Premium Sales Department at (800) 221-7945, extension 5442, or by e-mail at MacmillanSpecialMarkets@macmillan.com.

First published in Australia in 2014 by The Text Publishing Company

First U.S. Edition: November 2015

10 9 8 7 6 5 4 3 2 1

For Margaret

CRUCIFIXION CREEK

ONE

IN SOUTH-WESTERN SYDNEY, ON a chilly winter's night, a siege is in progress. The street is very ordinary—suburban, brick veneer and tiled roofs—and the only thing a stranger might notice is the number of houses that have steel roller-shutters on their windows. They're all closed now.

Two neighbours have reported a man's shouts, a woman's screams and a burst of gunfire. Now everyone is here—ambulance and fire brigade, local area command uniforms and detectives, scene of crime, and Harry Belltree and Deb Velasco from homicide. And the Tactical Operations Unit, the black ninjas, who have parked their big black American armoured Lenco truck, bristling with menace, in the driveway of the house. This has surely given the occupants something to think about.

Nothing is known about the man apart from a neighbour's hazy description of the female resident's new boyfriend: bulky, pony-tailed, bearded, tattooed. The TOU negotiators got a single grunt from him before he disabled the house phone, and now they are using the loudhailer, trying to "engage" him. The house backs on to rough ground in the area known locally as Crucifixion Creek, and there are marksmen out there and in the gardens on either side.

"This could go on for ever," Deb mutters. When Harry doesn't reply she starts the engine again to warm them up. Outside two uniforms are crouched behind their patrol car, blowing into their hands with misty breath. Deb takes a sip from her takeaway cup. "And why do we need to be here? Nobody's dead, far as we know."

She wants conversation and Harry rouses himself, picking up his own cup. She is five years older than him and more experienced. This is the first time they've been sent out together.

"Not yet, but when it happens we'll be right here."

"Does this remind you of Afghanistan?"

"In a way." He doesn't really want to respond but knows he should. Sharing confidences is an important part of team-building, apparently. "Sydney is very like Afghanistan, only here the Taliban wear Armani."

She gives a croaky laugh and lights up again. The whole car stinks of it. "Not in this neighbourhood."

"No."

Another long pause, sipping as the coffee cools. "They say you died over there."

Oh dear. He likes Deb, what he's heard of her—fierce, thorough. But she wants to talk. And smoke. He thinks of Carmen in the tobacco factory and tries to picture Deb dancing flamenco.

"Who does?"

"Oh, you know, some of the blokes were talking. Is it true?"

He nods.

"Seriously? How long?"

"Eighteen minutes."

"Shit. Didn't that—?" She stops.

"Leave me brain-damaged?" He smiles and she ducks her head, embarrassed. "No, I was like this before. We had much better A&E than you get around here."

"Did you . . . see stuff, like they say?"

"You mean a bright light? Someone dressed in white beckoning at the end of a tunnel? No, nothing like that. Nothing at all. Maybe I was going," he grins at her, "elsewhere."

At that moment a bright light from the TOU truck blazes on the front door which is opening slowly. A woman stands there looking blinded and disoriented, clutching a bundle to her chest, perhaps a baby. One of the men in black calls to her, urging her to walk forward. She puts a hand to her eyes against the glare and begins to move, painfully slowly, towards the light. After she has taken four or five steps there is a sharp noise, muffled inside the car, like the branch of a tree cracking, and the woman falls. Then several more shots, and they get a glimpse of a figure in the doorway toppling backwards into the house. "Fuck." Deb grinding her cigarette out. Black figures are running forward.

They get out of the car and wait. Watch the TOU secure the scene and call the ambos to the victims. Scene of crime join in, filming, and when the last black figure has cleared the house the white overalls move inside. The last one waves from the doorway and Harry and Deb move forward to look at the bodies.

The woman, shot in the back, has fresh bruising all over her face and arms. The bundle she was carrying is a white woollen jacket. In the hallway, stretched out on the floor, lies her killer. They have an ID now. Stefan Ganis: known to police as an armed robber and dealer in methamphetamine. Deb opens his lips to expose the blackened and missing teeth of the meth user. She pulls back an eyelid and looks at the pupil. "High as a kite." She seems enthusiastic about poking about in the corpse and Harry turns away—not squeamish, God knows, just a feeling, close to superstition, that the dead are out of it and deserve to be left alone.

The TOU men (they are all men) have put two bullets in him, and Harry is thinking ahead. Police shooting, a Critical Incident Investigation Team from another command brought in quickly. When that happens they'll most likely all be cleared out and interviewed, and he's impatient to have a look around the house before then. He begins to move off. Deb says, "What's this?"

She has rolled up the man's sleeve to inspect his tattoos, and she points to a solid block of black cross-hatching on his left biceps. Harry squats down and makes out a pattern faintly visible beneath the hatching. "He's inked over another tattoo."

"Old girlfriend's name?"

"No, an emblem of some kind, probably a biker logo. Looks like he got kicked out of one of the gangs. You don't get to keep the colours. Come on."

They begin to work quickly through the rooms, all of them in chaos as if the place has been trashed. Almost all of the stuff tossed around seems to be hers, except for one small corner with T-shirts and a pair of heavy biker boots. Above them, he has haphazardly taped a spread of photographs to the wall, a little shrine above the Harley boots. There are several pictures of him with some hairy, beefy blokes, all grinning at the lens; a faded old snap of a middle-aged woman, arms folded, perhaps his mother; a photo of a white tow truck.

Harry studies the pictures carefully, making his own record of them with his phone. He can just make out the name painted in vivid letters on the truck door—*13 Auto Smash*. He peels the photo off the wall and slips it into an evidence bag.

Deb looks over his shoulder. "What's that?"

Reluctantly he offers her the plastic pouch and she examines the photo inside. "Important?"

He shrugs.

She peers more closely. "Why 13?"

"The thirteenth letter of the alphabet is M. Short for meth."

"Really? The tow truck from hell. Just the sort of thing you'd want in an emergency. Can't see the rego."

"I'll see if the techs can bring it up."

She starts to ask him why, but he turns and moves on to the mess in the kitchen.

Crime scene will have bagged and removed any drugs, cash and weaponry, and taken 3D laser scans of all the rooms, which will have recorded every dent and scratch and bloodstain. The two of them sift through the debris anyway, without result.

It is after 5:00 a.m. when they are told to leave by the Critical Incident Team. Outside they see the TV cameras and reporters at the barriers, waiting for the local area commander to give a media briefing.

Harry's phone rings: Superintendent Marshall. Bob the Job. He pictures the old man in his pyjamas, pacing around his living room with his phone at his ear, grey hair awry, his big frame looming over the tiny porcelain ornaments his wife liked to collect. "Sir?"

"Harry, I've just had Wagstaff in my ear. What's the latest?"

Harry fills him in.

The superintendent grunts unhappily. "Deb Velasco with you?"

"Sir."

"Getting along all right?"

"Of course."

"Good. She's a fine officer, Harry."

Harry wonders why he needs to say that. Is she under some kind of cloud? As he turns to look at her he sees her face illuminated by the flame beneath her cigarette.

By the time the CIT officers release them, a bright clear day has dawned. The TOU tank has gone, as have the reporters and the TV crews and the sense of menace. Metal shutters are being raised in the windows of one or two of the neighbouring houses. As Harry makes his way to the car a woman, a wild-haired redhead, bursts out in front of him, coat flapping, listing under the weight of a large bag slung from her shoulder.

"Harry!" she cries, as if they are old friends. He tries to place her. Forensics? Domestic violence liaison?

"Kelly Pool, *Bankstown Chronicle*." She thrusts out a hand which he ignores.

"You've missed the fun," he says. "They've all buggered off."

"That's okay, I was at the briefing. Same old speech—tragic death, detectives investigating, appeal for help from the public blah blah. But this is my patch, see. Crucifixion Creek. So what was the guy's name?" She snatches out a notepad and pen, standing poised as if she seriously expects him to tell her.

"Piss off, Kelly Pool."

"Oh, Harry. That's not nice."

"And how the hell do you know my name?"

"I never reveal my sources. And a very famous name too, Harry Belltree. Son of the judge, right?"

"No comment." Harry pushes past her and reaches for the car door handle.

"I know this neighbourhood, Harry," she calls after him. "Maybe I can help you."

Deb has been listening to this exchange with interest. As she tugs at her seatbelt she looks across at him. "What was that all about? What judge?" And then her eyes go wide and her jaw drops. "Belltree? Belltree! Oh fuck—Danny Belltree! 'First Aboriginal judge of the New South Wales Supreme Court!' He was your dad?"

"Just drive the car, Deb."

"How could I have missed that? Nobody told me! How come nobody told me?"

He wonders about that.

TWO

FIVE HOURS LATER AND twenty-two kilometres away,
across the city to the north-east, an elderly woman puffs
her way down the hill towards the bay. Phoebe Bulwer-
Knight missed her bus and now she's hurrying in case
they give up on her and go home. The three of them have
been meeting for brunch every Friday for over twenty
years, ever since she retired from being Charlie's secretary and bookkeeper, but she has missed the last four
Fridays with her hip and the problems with the drains.
Now she's worried that the tradition may be broken. She
should have phoned, of course she should, but she was
already late.

She reaches The Esplanade at last, and the curve of
Balmoral Beach lies before her. The pale sand, the sweep
of water across Middle Harbour, the little white figure
of Grotto Point Lighthouse on the far headland, a ferry
making its way up to Manly. The café on the corner and,
yes, they are there, Grace and Charlie at their usual table,
and she breathes a sigh of relief. They're very still, she

thinks as she gets closer. Concentrating on the ferry? Perhaps they're having a bet on how long it will take to cross the bay. But no, their heads are bowed. They're surely asleep, dozing as they wait for her to join them.

When she does, she hesitates, a flutter of alarm rising in her chest. At the same moment the young waitress steps out onto the terrace and smiles at her. "They have a little sleep," she laughs, "for an hour now. Maybe more. I don't want to wake them."

Phoebe is suddenly struck by their clothes. Both are wrapped in heavy coats that seem too big for them now, as if they've shrunk inside them. Charlie is almost smothered in his orange scarf—*my muffler*, he calls it—and though it is a mid-winter's day, the sky is a brilliant blue and here in the sun it's quite warm. And the state of Grace's hair! An unruly tangle beneath a hat that looks as if it's been in an accident. And their clothes are filthy. There is what looks like a soup stain down the front of Charlie's good coat, and a tear in his sleeve. "Oh, Charlie," she whispers. "What happened to the Manly Dandy?"

She reaches out and touches Charlie's cheek. It is so cold she recoils as his head drops forward. "You must call an ambulance," she says to the waitress.

"What? He is not well?"

"I believe he's dead."

"Oh my God! He has passed away? The lady will be so upset when she wakes."

"I think she's dead too."

The girl shakes her head, eyes wide. "Both together . . . ? Is that possible? Oh, that is so sad, but also . . ." she struggles to find the right word, ". . . so beautiful. They go everywhere together. I have seen them, holding hands. And now they pass away together."

"Please just phone for an ambulance."

"Sure, sure." The girl takes a mobile from her pocket and makes the call, then points the phone at the old couple, and it makes a loud click. The girl starts jabbing away at it with her thumbs.

"What are you doing?"

"I'm sending to my friends. So sad, so beautiful."

"No . . ." but Phoebe's eyes blur, her knees buckle, and the waitress keeps tapping at her phone as she yells to her boss to come and help.

THREE

HARRY DROPS HIS GEAR off in his locker and signs out. He walks to Parramatta station and catches a train packed with commuters in to Central. A twenty-minute walk up into Surry Hills takes him to his street, to the plane tree at the mouth of the laneway, bare of leaves. He can smell baking, hear the sound of an orchestra.

She comes to the door as he steps inside, hugs him, says, "Oh, you stink."

"Sorry. My new partner. Smoker." He gazes at her face, the smudge of flour on her forehead, the smile on her lips and frown across her eyebrows, and his heart aches.

"They said on the news there was a siege again last night. Were you called out?"

"Yes. But we were just onlookers. The nasties did all the work."

He wipes Jenny's forehead and she says, "What was that?"

"Just flour. Any problems?"

"I can't find my good oven gloves. They must be somewhere in there."

"Let's take a look."

They are in the middle of the kitchen table. He picks them up and puts them in her hands.

"Thanks. Are you hungry?"

"Yeah, but dirty. I'll have a shower."

"You haven't forgotten about lunch?"

"No." It's the anniversary. How could he forget?

"Poor you. You probably just want to sleep."

LUNCH IS AT JENNY'S sister's house, which is thirty minutes away on a good day. Her husband, a builder, once came across Frank Lloyd Wright's advice to a house client to buy the cheapest site in a good neighbourhood because it would be difficult to build on, and therefore a bargain and a challenge and an opportunity for the great architect to do his stuff. Greg found a narrow and precipitous site on a gully overlooking a reserve, which the agent privately considered unbuildable, and paid a modest price for such a good suburb. The design that his architect devised was highly ingenious, with seven different floor levels tumbling down the slope and taking advantage of every angle of view and opportunity for sunshine and breeze. Unfortunately the engineering works, largely invisible beneath the ground, consumed most of the budget, and the house is still unfinished, limping slowly towards completion whenever Greg can scrape up the cash and spare his men from other jobs. It has, however, earned him a reputation as a builder for challenging small projects, and has brought him in a fair amount of work.

But it is a nightmare for Harry, with its multitude of cascading steps, its unexpected shifts of direction, its jagged corners. He follows Jenny through the obstacles, tensing to leap forward to snatch her from danger. She seems oblivious to the risks, accepting the unreliable guidance of her two nieces and the remembered images in her head. But Greg is always making changes, and she can't see those.

They are nearing the difficult descent to the family room when Nicole rushes out of a bedroom, fiddling with her hair, hugs her sister and guides her down to safety. Harry hands over the chocolate cake that Jenny has baked for dessert and thankfully accepts a beer from Greg. Greg has already had a few, Harry judges, his gestures sweeping, verging on belligerent. He fetches a tray of meat from the kitchen and marches out to the barbecue on the deck with barely a word. Nicole notices and gives Harry an apologetic little smile. "It's been a bad week," she whispers. "You know, people letting him down."

"Sure." He goes out onto the deck, where Greg is stabbing the meat. "How's it going?"

"Great." Greg spins around and yells through the door, "Nicole, where did you get this steak?"

Harry doesn't hear the reply. He goes over to the rail and looks down at the rock shelf far below. Something vanishes under a bush. Possum maybe.

"Yeah, sorry, what?" Greg is at his elbow. "Were you at that siege last night?"

"Yes."

"Cops killed another poor bastard, didn't they? Jeez mate, why do they even bother giving 'em tasers?"

"He was high on ice and he'd just shot his girlfriend dead while we watched."

"Christ." Greg deflates all at once, the aggression abruptly gone. "Sorry, mate," he mumbles. "I don't know how you do that stuff." He shakes his head. "How *do* you do it? Because of your mum and dad?"

"Eh?"

"Nicole has this theory you went into homicide because . . ." He shrugs.

"Because what?"

"You don't really still think it was murder, do you?"

"Someone ran them off the road. Either it was deliberate or they were criminally negligent. If it was an accident they should have stopped, tried to help, called triple-O."

"No evidence, Harry." Greg is almost pleading now. "The cops, the coroner, the press . . . No one found any real evidence of another vehicle."

"The paint scrape on the bodywork."

"From the fence post."

"No, wrong kind of paint."

Greg shakes his head. "I just . . . it can't be good for Jenny, knowing you still think it was deliberate, having to live with that thought."

Harry says nothing.

Greg hesitates, then presses on. His words are becoming a little slurred. "Nicole said Jenny's been back to the specialists. Anything?"

"Not really. No change. Not much they can do. We've got her name down for a dog."

"Oh." Greg runs out of steam again. He turns to the barbecue and lights up the burners.

"I read about a case the other day," Harry goes on. "Bloke in America, same thing as Jenny—blindness arising from traumatic brain injury in a car smash. Nine years he was blind. Then one day he was struck by lightning, and his sight came back, just like that."

Greg stares at him, perhaps wondering if this is some kind of terrible joke. "Truly?"

"Yes. That's how it is. The problem's in the brain, you see, not the eyes. They don't understand how it works."

"Shit. I just think . . . Put it to bed, Harry, eh? All this raking in the past. It's three years now. I mean, today, the anniversary thing, every year . . ."

"And every day and every minute," Harry says quietly. "I'm going to get the bastards, Greg. Sooner or later, I'm going to get them."

Greg suddenly lurches to the rail and throws up. Harry hopes the possum got clear.

On the drive back home Harry says, "So what's the problem with Greg? Did Nicole say?"

"It's to do with work. She's worried about him. He keeps it all to himself, and things get on top of him. She said I should try to persuade you to leave the force and join Greg and run the business side, let him concentrate on the building work. Could be a brilliant partnership, she said."

"Oh yes?" Nicole once confessed to him, after a few wines, that she thought he was selfish to do the work he did. What if he got hurt in the line of duty, where would that leave Jenny?

He says, "What do you think?"

"Maybe. When you've had enough of what you're doing now." Then, after a pause, "I overheard a bit of what Greg was saying to you about tracking down whoever caused the accident. I think he's right, Harry. It's not something you need to do. It wouldn't bring your mum and dad back, and it wouldn't help me to see again."

He thinks, is that how other people see me? A shell-shocked obsessive, compulsively scratching away at old wounds? Does Bob the Job believe that? The other guys in the squad?

FOUR

AT TIMES LIKE THIS Kelly Pool tends to brood on the past. When she was twenty-three, a hundred years ago, she managed to break a murder case while working for a small suburban newspaper. It was a combination of persistence and local knowledge—she unearthed the evidence police needed to crack the grieving husband's alibi. In return, the cops gave the paper first lead on the story and acknowledged Kelly's crucial role. For a dizzy, unbelievable spell she was a star.

After a fortnight of record sales and international exposure, the paper's owners threw a party for her at a top hotel in the city, where she drank a large amount of champagne and fell into conversation with a charming man who congratulated her and told her that she obviously had a huge future in front of her with one of the big nationals.

"As long as it's not one of Murdoch's," she said, and began a rant about what rubbish they all were and how the editor of the Sydney paper was a total moron and sleazy scumbag. Full of her new self as beacon of journalistic integrity, she became more and more expansive. "I wouldn't accept a job from him if he crawled across hot coals," she said, and the man smiled. "Oh, I don't think there's much chance of that," and bade her good night. A friend immediately appeared at her elbow, eyes bright with excitement. "How did it go?" she asked.

"What?"

"With—" She mentioned the name of the Murdoch editor. "That you were just talking to. Did he offer you the job?"

She is still working for the small suburban newspaper. And at times like this, being sent out to interview some little old lady who's lost her cat, or in this case her friends, Kelly lacerates herself with the bitter memory of the moment when her brilliant career crashed. It wasn't fate, she tells herself. Fate guided her to the one big chance of a lifetime. It was a character flaw that made her blow it.

And what kind of a name is Phoebe Bulwer-Knight anyway? What is she doing living here, among the Mahmoods and Cheongs and Krishnamurthis, the last survivor of a vanished Anglo-Saxon tribe? In Crucifixion Creek of all places.

She leaves her car on the main road that forms the eastern boundary of the Creek because she's not sure about taking it into Mortimer Street, which is narrow and has a reputation. The street sign has another hand-painted sign mounted on the pole beneath it, Crow Country. What Mrs. Bulwer-Knight is doing here really is a puzzle, but not one Kelly has any wish to solve.

As she makes her way along a line of tiny period villas, looking for number eleven, she is suddenly paralysed by a shattering noise. A gleaming Harley-Davidson with extravagant handlebars roars up alongside her and sidles past. Its rider turns his head to her, black helmet, black shades, ominous. Steroids, she thinks, from the bulging flesh of his tattooed neck and arms, and there's a large red and orange logo on the back of his black leathers. She stares back, defiant. Fucking middle-aged teenager.

"Grow up," she says, but he can't hear over the Harley. He twists the throttle to a devastating pitch and speeds off.

A little way down the street an elderly lady standing at the kerb gives a stately wave to the biker as he roars past, and he waves back. Phoebe, Kelly realises. She approaches and shakes the lady's hand. At the far end of the street the biker is disappearing into what looks like a fortress—high steel walls, a watchtower, cameras, razor wire.

"They must be afraid you might break in, Mrs. Bulwer-Knight," Kelly says, and the old lady chuckles and invites her in for tea. When they are settled among plump flowery cushions, sipping Earl Grey from Wedgwood, Kelly says, "I recognised you from Facebook. And YouTube, you're very big on YouTube."

Phoebe clearly has no idea what she's talking about.

"At Balmoral Beach. The waitress filmed you, with your friends."

"Yes, and I told her to stop. Don't you find it rather ghoulish?"

"Yes." Kelly goes on quickly, "It must have been a terrible shock for you."

"Oh very much so. Mind you, I've seen a good few dead bodies in my time. I was a nurse during the war, you know." The war? As Kelly tries to calculate how old she must be, Phoebe begins a meandering account of how long she knew Charlie and Grace Waterford, and how much they meant to her.

"And such an extraordinary coincidence," Kelly prompts, "for them to pass away together like that."

"Oh hardly."

Kelly stops writing and looks up at her. "How do you mean?"

"I saw the ambulance man take two pill bottles from Charlie's coat pocket, and frown when he read the labels. When I asked him he was evasive, and later he showed them to the police officers, and they had a very serious conversation."

"So . . . what are you saying? Do you think they killed themselves?"

"Oh yes. And I wouldn't blame them for that, sitting there at their favourite table in the sun, a final glass of wine, holding hands. But I think they felt that they had no other choice."

"How do you mean?"

"Well, the state they were in. Filthy dirty, clothes ruined, and so thin, as if they hadn't had a square meal in weeks. If you knew Grace and Charlie, how fastidious they were, how *spoilt*, you'd hardly believe it. It was as if they'd become street people, beggars."

"But you said just now that he was a successful businessman."

"Oh very. I should know—I kept his books. He was a

millionaire when that meant something, and they owned a number of properties around here—this house, for example. When I retired from the business Charlie gave me free tenancy for life, as part of my retirement package."

"So what happened?"

"I've no idea. As soon as the ambulance left and I'd given my statement to the police I went back up to the bus stop and set off to see their son Justin over in Rose Bay. It took me some time to get there, and when I finally arrived someone from the police had already called and broken the news to him and Jade." She frowned, shook her head. "I thought I was doing the right thing."

"How do you mean?"

"They were so rude. Didn't even offer me a cup of tea. Couldn't wait to push me out the door."

"They'd be upset, I suppose?"

Phoebe sniffs. "I've known Justin since he was born. I know that sneaky evasive look he gets when he's been up to something naughty."

"Like what?"

"I don't know, but when I mentioned that the last time I'd seen his parents I'd overheard them arguing about someone—a man called Crosstitch—Justin got positively aggressive with me, told me to mind my own business—he actually used the f-word to me!"

As the old woman continues, it occurs to Kelly that it is Phoebe, not herself, who is leading this conversation. In fact, it feels as if she is being assessed for a task. Finally Phoebe comes out with it. "So I think you should go and talk to Justin. I believe he'll be a little more open if he's confronted by a member of the press."

Kelly thinks about that. It's a story anyway, the old couple passing away in their favourite café. And if there is more to it, a scandal of some kind, a failure of the social services, a suggestion of fraud?

"Crosstitch, did you say?"

"That's what it sounded like. Justin certainly reacted when I mentioned the name."

Kelly writes down the son's address and phone number and promises to think about it. On the way out she takes a photograph of Phoebe at her front door. "How long have you been here, Phoebe?"

"Forty years. Charlie bought the house from an Italian family. There were lots of Italians around here then, with market gardens in the land behind. Charlie built factories on the fields and made a lot of money. He was a very smart businessman. That's what makes it so hard to understand what happened."

"And then the Crows moved in?"

"About ten years ago. They're not bad boys really. They sometimes give me a lift back from the shops."

"On their motorbikes?" Kelly tries to imagine it.

Phoebe laughs. "No, no. They have a big black four-wheel-drive too."

FIVE

HARRY IS WORKING AT his desk, typing and scanning his notes into the e@gle.i database. It's a routine chore, but the army taught him the usefulness of routine chores as a corrective to the moments of chaos. He's been hoping to get through tonight without chaos, but Deb Velasco shatters that hope.

"Harry?" She's out of her seat as if she's been tasered. It's a killing, over by Crucifixion Creek again.

She drives fast while he gets on the phone for more information. Unidentified white male, stabbed to death in the street. No phone or wallet, no witnesses.

The ambulance is drawing away as they arrive, leaving the victim in a pool of blood and the uniforms securing the scene. Harry and Deb move in, Harry shining his torch at the body. He stops dead. He swears softly and Deb says, "What? You know him?"

"Yes," he says. "His name's Greg March. He's my brother-in-law."

"Sheez. He live around here?"

"No . . ." Harry shakes his head, fighting off the sense of disorientation. "No, miles away, northern suburbs. But his yard is around here somewhere. He's a builder." He turns to the uniforms. "Car keys?"

"No."

Harry runs back to their car and pulls up Greg's car number on the computer, then puts out an alert. Within seconds a report comes in of a chase in the inner west, a vehicle driving at speed to evade a patrol car. The number matches Greg's blue Ford.

Deb joins him and he says, "Give me the keys."

She hesitates. "We should leave this to the uniforms, Harry."

"Deb!"

"I'll go. You stay here."

But as she starts the car he jumps in the passenger seat and buckles up.

The Ford appears to be circling back towards the south-west, fast enough that the patrol car is ordered to abandon the pursuit. Other cars and Pol Air are being called in. As Deb turns onto Liverpool Road they see the traffic parting up ahead and then the blue car barrelling through towards them. She switches on her warning lights and the approaching car makes a sudden wild skidding turn to the left into a side street. She follows while Harry talks into the radio. The road ahead is deserted and she slows down, then jerks her head over to the right. The sound of a crash. She turns into a residential street and they see the car up ahead, smoking, reared up against a tilting power pole.

Deb pulls in across the street and they run over. There is a girl in the front passenger seat, face pressed against the blood-smeared window, eyes open, lifeless. No one in the back or the driver's side, banknotes spilled all over the seats. While Deb calls in their location, Harry draws his gun and sets off down the footpath, following a trail of black spots on the concrete. Deb shouts after him, but he's already disappeared into an overgrown front garden. He sees feet sticking out from beneath a bush and pulls the foliage aside, gun raised, but the figure is slumped like a doll, hands empty. Harry crouches and reaches for his throat, and the boy's head jerks and his eyes open. He stares at Harry, then says something. It's hard to make out, but it sounds like, "He wana me do it." Then he closes his eyes and the head flops to one side.

Deb races up behind him, takes in the scene and cries, "Oh fuck, Harry, what have you done?"

He looks up at her. "I haven't done anything, Deb. He's dead. I was just feeling for a pulse."

He gets to his feet and holsters his pistol.

"You should have let me, Harry. You should have stayed at the car."

"I'm just doing my job, Deb."

They return to the car as headlights converge from both ends of the street, and he asks her again for the car keys.

"What now?" she says.

"I need to be the one to tell Nicole. I don't want some flatfoot barging in on her in the middle of the night."

"Oh . . . right. But this is a critical incident. Are

you sure you're okay? You should wait for them to clear you."

He nods and takes the keys.

ON THE WAY HE phones Jenny and tells her to get dressed. He imagines her getting up and taking a shower in the dark, and opening her wardrobe, every item of clothing in its designated place. When he arrives at the end of the lane she is waiting, wrapped up against the cold. She smells fresh and he doesn't like to kiss her, feeling contaminated. He explains about Greg and she gasps.

"He phoned me tonight," she says. "It was a mistake—he meant to ring Nicole, hit the wrong number on his phone."

"Did he say anything?"

"Just that he was sorry for bothering me. He sounded flustered. He said it twice, that he was sorry, really sorry, then he hung up."

"What time was this?"

"About ten-thirty. I was still on the computer."

Three hours before he was murdered. "He didn't say where he was?"

"No." She thought for a moment. "I think he was in a lobby of somewhere—an office building or a hotel. I heard a lift chime. It happened a couple of times . . . Poor Nicole, and the girls. What was he doing out there?"

"I don't know. It wasn't far from his depot, but at that time of night?"

"Maybe there was a break-in. Maybe the security firm called him out."

"Yes." But he was half a kilometre away from the yard.

THEY STOP OUTSIDE THE house and Jenny phones Nicole to say they have to speak to her and not to wake the girls. She looks tousled and frightened seeing them standing there at the door, and the first thing she says is, "It's Greg."

They sit in the little sitting room just inside the front door, an odd, in-between kind of space that nobody uses, the women on the sofa, Jenny's arm around her sister. Nicole is in shock. Finally she looks at Harry and says, "Was it a robbery? At the depot?"

He knows this mental process: if only she can find a simple answer to this, Harry might realise it's all a mistake, and Greg will walk through the door.

"We don't know," he says gently. "Did he tell you it might be?"

She frowns, forcing herself to think. "He rang. I was just going to bed. He said he had to go out there and not to wait up. He didn't say why."

"Do you know where he rang from?"

She shakes her head. "He went out after dinner, to see a client." She puts a hand to her eyes, whispers, "Oh, Greg," and begins to weep.

WHEN HE GETS BACK to the car he turns his phone on and finds a string of messages, from Deb and from the duty inspector at homicide, all containing the word URGENT.

At Parramatta he senses heads turning as he walks

through the open-plan office. He doesn't see Deb and reports to the office of the duty inspector, Toby Wagstaff, who gives him a bollocking for not answering his phone.

"Sorry, sir. I turned it off—I was breaking the news to the widow."

Wagstaff, a plump, rosy-cheeked man with curly blond hair and an Ulster accent, gives a sigh. "Aye, well Harry, you have my sympathy, but you're in deep shit." He reaches for the phone and murmurs into it, "He's here, sir," and after an uncomfortable minute Detective Superintendent Marshall marches in. Wagstaff gets up and leaves, closing the door firmly behind him.

Marshall turns on Harry. "What the bloody hell are you playing at?"

"Sir?"

"You attend the murder scene of your close relative, involve yourself in the pursuit of his killer, and end up alone with your hands around the bloke's neck."

"I was feeling for a pulse, sir, like we're trained to do."

"Then you leave the scene of a critical incident, switch off your phone and pay a visit to the victim's wife. What was going through your mind?"

"I was trying to do the right thing, sir."

"No you weren't. The right thing would have been to step back as soon as you recognised the victim and let others get on with it. You were involved, compromised, and you knew it but you kept on doing the wrong thing, and compromised a fellow officer, until you finally ended up compromising the whole bloody investigation."

"Sir, I don't think . . ."

"Shut up! I shouldn't even be talking to you. The critical incident team are downstairs waiting to crucify you. Before you go down you will surrender your weapon to Inspector Wagstaff." Marshall leans forward and lowers his voice. "You've disappointed me, Harry. I was a great admirer of your father. That's why I supported your transfer to homicide. I wanted you to shine as he shone, and I feel let down. Most of the time your performance is exemplary, then a personal issue intrudes and you're off—you throw your training and judgment to the winds, and you do your own thing. And it makes you a menace, Harry, a menace to your colleagues."

"Sir, I responded as I believed the circumstances demanded."

"Really?" Marshall sits back, staring at Harry, then gets to his feet and snatches up a plastic pouch from Wagstaff's desk. "What's this?"

The photograph of the tow truck he took from the siege house. He opens his mouth but Marshall cuts him off. "Yes, I know where you got it. Why did you ask for tech support to follow it up?"

"I thought it might tell us more of what the guy was up to."

"You're disappointing me again, Harry. I expect honesty from you. You asked them to find out where the truck is now, yes?"

"Yes."

"Because?"

Harry is silent, and after a pause Marshall continues. "Because you want to take a scraping of the paint and test it against the marks on your folks' car, right?"

Harry nods.

"You see? Secretive and obsessive. Three years and you're still diverting police resources to your personal quest."

"It's still an unsolved case, sir." He is thinking of Greg telling him much the same thing.

"Get out, Harry. Think about what I've said. And tomorrow, if the critical incident boys have finished with you, you'll report to the police medical officer and the police psychologist for a fitness for duty assessment. That's an order."

"Sir."

He does as he's told, surrenders his pistol and heads downstairs, where he gets an extended grilling from the CIT. When they're finished with him he finds a note on his desk with the time of his appointment with the workforce safety psychologist. In the locker room there is a second padlock on his locker door. It is the public symbol of his humiliation—this man cannot be trusted with his gun. The others frown at the two padlocks, looking uncomfortable as they pass by.

Deb, on her way home, puts her head round the corner. "Sheez, Harry, I'm sorry."

"Yeah, well. I asked for it, I guess. You warned me."

"Yes."

"Though you didn't have to tell them I had my hands round the bloke's throat."

"I never said that! I said you were feeling for a pulse."

"Well, maybe forensics and the PM will put them right."

He goes home to the empty house feeling filthy,

stained with aggression and death. He doesn't want death, he wants life, he wants Jenny. As he moves through the house there are reminders of her everywhere and of how she has to live: a little patch of dirt and grease missed on a worktop that she has scrubbed clean, a towel abandoned in an otherwise spotless bathroom. Most telling of all, her best friend sitting in the corner of the living room.

Before the crash she was a researcher for a big law firm in the city. Her work mostly involved computer searches, and she was very good at it. She'd done a part-time computer science course and developed programs and search tools of her own. For over a year after the crash she was unable to access her beloved computer, until a friend from the course put her on to a new voice interface. For six months she worked at it until she was almost as proficient as she had once been, whispering to the machine, listening attentively in conversations that were incomprehensible to Harry. The law firm has started giving her work again, which she does at home, with her electronic best friend over there in the corner. She is slower than before, but she claims that now she has to visualise the data in her head instead of seeing it on the screen, her thinking is clearer and more creative.

Harry would like to believe it, because he feels guilty about what happened too. It was his suggestion that she go with his mother and father on their trip up to New England. They took the scenic route north of Newcastle across the Barrington Tops on Thunderbolt's Way to Uralla. It was on that beautiful road, winding and lightly trafficked, that the crash occurred.

SIX

KELLY MISSED THE STABBING and police chase last night. The young lad who normally listens in to the ambulance and fire brigade radios (not the police since they went digital) was sick and didn't pick it up. She hasn't got anywhere with the son of Phoebe Bulwer-Knight's friends either, but she has left a message on his phone saying she hopes she can meet him to check a few facts before she publishes her story about his parents' tragic ending and their relationship with Mr. Crosstitch. Perhaps that'll get a response.

And now she's daydreaming through three hours of local council planning committee tedium. She misses the beginning of Councillor Potgeiter's item but when she does tune in she is startled. Apparently he is proposing a new sculpture to celebrate Aboriginal reconciliation in the civic precinct. A replacement for the old monument in Bidjigal Park, which is in a bad way and rarely visited. Kelly blinks. Hearing Councillor Potgeiter showing an interest in Indigenous affairs is like listening to Genghis

Khan making an appeal for the widows and orphans. Kelly wonders if she can use that line in her column. She's never heard of Bidjigal Park or its substandard monument, and when she checks on her phone she finds that it is a small pocket in the north-west corner of Crucifixion Creek, not far from the siege house. The Creek seems to be cropping up a bit these days, and she wonders if she could do a piece on it. When she leaves the council chamber she calls in to the library next door, the local heritage section, where she finds a slim monograph, *The Grim History of Crucifixion Creek*.

The name comes from the activities of a Lieutenant Walter Perch, she reads, sent out from the settlement at Sydney Cove in December 1790 at the head of a company of marines on a punitive expedition, carrying hatchets and sacks with which to collect the heads of five adult Aboriginal men, following a series of attacks on settlers.

After several days sweating through the bush in their thick uniforms, they finally saw smoke rising from a wooded knoll in the middle of a low-lying area of reeds and ferns. It turned out to be a swamp, into which the heavily laden redcoats began to sink. A number of Aboriginal men carrying spears appeared on the knoll to watch them struggle, and Perch ordered his men to open fire. When they finally floundered up onto the knoll, covered in stinking mud, they discovered the bodies of three men and Perch ordered their heads to be cut off and their spears broken, and declared that that would have to do. On the marines' return to Sydney Cove a rumour spread that they had also nailed the three victims to the trees, and despite Perch's denials the name stuck. Crucifixion Creek.

That's a good start, Kelly thinks—murder then and now. She flips forward. Forty years after Perch's expedition an Englishman called Roger Grange bought the land around Crucifixion Creek with a view to farming sheep. Cleared the bush, drained the swamp, built a house on the knoll. Then the price of wool collapsed and Grange, ruined, took to drink. In 1842 he and his family perished in a fire that consumed their house. He'd tried to change the name of the place to Grangeville, but it didn't take.

During the 1870s a family of Chinese immigrants turned the Creek hollow into a flourishing market garden, but in 1888, during the racial panic that engulfed the country, a mob attacked and hanged them from the trees on the knoll.

Kelly begins to feel depressed.

In 1919 a builder returned from the Great War and laid out Mortimer Street in the eastern part of the Creek, and began to build modest villas. He was wiped out by the Great Depression, the street only half-built. After the Second World War Italian migrants moved into Mortimer Street and restored the market gardens, until drought in the mid-1960s dried up the stream that had fed the Creek. Their crops failed and they moved away, giving Phoebe Bulwer-Knight's benefactor Charlie his first big break with his light industrial development which, for a while, went quite well. In the 1980s a group of local citizens persuaded the council to turn the undeveloped north-west corner of the Creek into a small public park, and raised some money to build a memorial to the victims of Lieutenant Perch's little massacre. By the turn of the century, however, the area was run down, the poorly built concrete roads of the industrial estate cracked and broken on the unstable ground. Then the Crows moved in.

Kelly, finished with her notes for the article she has in mind, feels she needs a drink. She drives around the perimeter of the Creek on her way back to the office. Takes photographs of the park and its monument and of the industrial estate, seeing with fresh eyes just how derelict the whole place has become. She turns into Mortimer Street and takes pictures of the little villas, still in reasonable shape, and of the most modern and well-maintained structure in the whole area—the Crows' clubhouse.

As she is leaving she sees Phoebe walk slowly into the street, a shopping bag hanging from each hand. Kelly stops and gets out to say hello, and the old woman looks startled, then accusing.

"I got into trouble for talking to you."

"Did you?"

"Yes. Justin telephoned me. He said a reporter had contacted him about Charlie and Grace, and threatened to say bad things about what happened to them, and it was all my fault and I had no right to talk to you."

"I left a message on their answering machine. I'm sorry he took it that way. He hasn't got back to me."

Phoebe drops her bags to the ground and wipes her brow.

"He's probably right. I am an interfering old fool. I

think it upset me more than I realised, discovering them like that. I expect Justin's ashamed of what they did. The young don't understand."

Kelly carries Phoebe's bags to her front door. The sun has come out and she notices for the first time the profusion of pot plants, flowers, shrubs and herbs. She makes a comment and Phoebe says, "They grow better on this side of the house. I love them all. They're so optimistic. Soon the jonquils will be out, and the bluebells."

As she gets back into her car, Kelly's phone rings. Justin Waterford, sounding stiff and formal. He says he can't imagine why his parents' death could be of any interest to her, but if she is thinking of publishing anything she should certainly come and talk to him first. She says she'll be right over.

The apartment has a wonderful outlook over Rose Bay. It is very modern, very stylish, with no signs of children, pets or clutter. Justin and Jade are dressed in weekend clothes, and Kelly wonders why they aren't at work. They sit, Jade very alert and focused, Justin wearing an air of puzzled indifference.

"We're extremely distressed by the deaths of Mum and Dad," Justin says, "and frankly find your interest inappropriate and intrusive." He has an educated drawl. Jade, leaning forward, is giving Kelly the death stare. Kelly has taken an immediate dislike to both of them, but is trying not to let that influence her.

"I'm sorry, Mr. Waterford. I do appreciate what you're saying. The thing is, their unusual deaths have aroused a lot of public interest and sympathy, and also a good deal of misinformed speculation. I just want to set the record straight."

"Look." Justin sighs wearily. "My parents were both suffering from dementia. Now, is that the sort of thing that you would like to see published in the newspapers about your parents? I think not. It developed very rapidly in the last couple of months, and much more severely than any of us realised. I was shocked, actually, to see the state they were in when they were found, truly shocked."

"Oh dear." Kelly scribbles her notes. "And is that why they had no money? I understand they had no money at all on them, not even enough to pay for the glasses of wine they ordered at the café."

Justin eases himself upright at the word "money."

"And presumably they would have been in no fit state to enter into financial arrangements with Mr. Crosstitch?"

Justin and Jade both begin to speak at once, then stop abruptly. Justin starts again. "What do you know about him?"

The truth is that Kelly knows nothing; her searches have thrown up no one of that name. "What can you tell me?" she asks blandly.

Justin stares at her, no longer laid-back. "Not a thing. All we know is what Phoebe told us, and that seemed pretty vague. But if you know something—anything at all about my parents' financial affairs, you'd better tell me right now."

He is lying, Kelly is almost sure of it; there is only one thing she needs to be certain.

"And our lawyers have advised me to tell you," he goes on, "that if you publish one word that isn't true, or misrepresents us in any way, we will sue you and your paper for every penny you have."

And that's it, the threat.

"Well," she says, "let me give you my card. If there's anything more you can tell me about your parents, do please get in touch."

She gets to her feet. At the front door she says, "Who is your lawyer, by the way?"

He gives her a nasty smile. "Let's hope you don't have to find out."

SEVEN

HARRY WAKES AFTER A couple of hours, thinking about Jenny in that difficult house, banging her knees against unfamiliar obstacles. She hates him being overprotective, but what else can he be? He wonders about her dreams. Have the images become more vivid, now that her waking life has none to feed on? Does her sleeping mind work overtime, creating the scenes and faces she can no longer see? And will it one day remember the last moments before the crash, when she must have seen the unknown vehicle that tipped them down that hillside?

He gets up and makes coffee, and goes to his own computer—he doesn't like to touch hers. He logs on to the police intranet and his appointment with the police psychologist that afternoon is flashed up. His access to the e@gle.i case files has been blocked.

He phones Jenny. She tells him she's hungover; she and Nicole sat up drinking, and she is now making something to eat. Nicole is still asleep. Harry's heart thumps. "You're in that kitchen alone?" He imagines her pouring boiling water on herself or straightening up suddenly and cracking her head on an open cupboard door.

"Don't fuss, darling," she says. "Anyway, the girls are helping me."

"How are they doing?"

"Oh, you know, in shock, like we all are. It still doesn't seem quite real."

"I know."

"Anyway, Mum's coming over. She'll stay here for as long as Nicole needs her. A couple of weeks anyway."

"Good." Bronwyn is a capable, sensible woman, just what they need.

"She'll be here in time to look after the girls while we're out." Jenny doesn't say where.

He gives them a couple of hours to get ready, then goes over to pick up the two women. They drive in silence to the mortuary at Glebe, where Jenny and Nicole are taken to see Greg.

While they're away he asks if Dr. Roberts can spare him a couple of minutes. They know each other from the post-mortems Harry has attended, and the pathologist puts his head around a door and waves him into a small office. He is dressed for his next case. They shake hands.

"Sorry about your brother-in-law, mate."

Harry nods. "Just wondered if you could fill me in."

"Not a lot to tell. Two clean, deep stabs to the heart. Death instantaneous. He would hardly have felt a thing. Banged his head on the concrete when he fell, but that was post-mortem."

"Defence wounds?"

"No. No bruises or cuts to his hands. No traces under his fingernails."

"Nothing else?"

"He'd had a fair bit to drink. Whisky. A big slug just before he died."

Harry thanks him and collects the women to take them back to Nicole's. Bronwyn gathers them in and he leaves for his appointment at the Sydney Police Centre in Surry Hills, not far from home.

HE HAS HAD A couple of meetings with the psychologist there before, at his annual weapons tests, but they had seemed like a formality. This time it's different, his credibility on the line, his fitness for duty.

She shows him in with a friendly smile, making out like it's no big deal.

"Harry," she begins, "I'm so sorry about your brother-in-law. That must have been a terrible blow."

"Well, yes. But for his wife obviously."

"Your wife's sister," she prompts. She seems well informed. "How is she?"

And suddenly, despite his earlier warnings to himself to say no more than necessary, he finds himself telling her about the visit to the mortuary, and his mother-in-law coming to help.

The psych nods sympathetically, letting him finish. "If you feel she needs professional help I can suggest some people. And your poor wife, how is she?"

Jenny would hate being talked about that way. "She's been great."

"This was your second homicide in two nights."

"Yes."

"That first night you saw someone shot dead in front of you."

"It wasn't the first time."

"In Afghanistan, do you mean?"

He nods.

"Want to tell me about that?"

"Not really." Pause. "It's not relevant."

"Was it someone you knew well?"

"Someone in my platoon, yes."

She seems reluctant to let it go, but decides not to press him. "So with that in your mind from the previous night, you're then called to another murder scene where you go to examine the victim and realise that it's your brother-in-law. Can you tell me about it?"

"It's not such a freak experience," he says.

She looks surprised. "How do you mean?"

"When I was at school, one of the other guys did work experience at a funeral director's, and one day his girl-friend's body was brought in. It's the sort of thing we're warned about, trained for. That you might know the victim."

"But still . . . When did you last see him—Greg, was that his name?"

"Yes." He clears his throat. "Saturday. There was a family barbecue at his house."

"A special event?"

He looks at her. How would she know that? Did Marshall tell her? How would *he* know? "An anniversary."

She waits, sympathetic, and it works. "Of my parents' death."

"And of your wife losing her sight. I noticed the date on your file. Is it possible do you think that with these traumatic things coming on top of each other, that you've linked the two things, your parents' and your brother-in-law's deaths?"

"What? No, of course not."

"The mind does funny things under pressure, trying to make sense of coincidence."

"Did Superintendent Marshall suggest that to you?"

She has the grace to look embarrassed. "He's concerned about you, and so am I. I know you're a very resilient person, used to handling stress, but anyone experiencing what you've just gone through would need time to absorb and deal with it. I want you to take leave on health grounds—one week to begin with, then we'll see. How do you feel about that?"

"Okay."

"You don't look happy."

He shrugs.

"I can give you some CDs to help you relax, sleep better. What do you do to unwind?"

"I go running. And I help my wife with the cooking. Most of the time she doesn't really need help, but I get nervous with her and knives, and the food processor, and the, umm, julienne thing."

He leaves after making an appointment for the following week.

When he's clear of the building he puts in a call to

43

Deb. She'll be awake now, getting ready for the night shift that he should be on. He tells her he's taking some leave, but would like to be kept up to date with any developments in Greg's murder.

"Are you okay about that, Deb?"

"Yes, sure, Harry."

"He made two calls from his mobile about three hours before he died, to his wife and my wife. These are the numbers . . . I'd really like to know where he was when he made those calls. Also, I'd be interested in any other calls he made in the twenty-four hours before his death."

"The investigators will be getting all that stuff, Harry, but I don't know if I can access it."

"Who's doing it?"

"I don't know, but I'll find out."

"I don't want you to do anything you're uncomfortable with. I'm a bit on the nose at the moment."

"That's okay. I'll do what I can."

"Thanks. I appreciate it."

After dinner he switches the lights off in the house so that it's the same for both of them and they dance together, he and Jenny in the dark. He remembers he didn't tell the psych about the dancing. Over in the corner Jenny's computer glows like a jealous lover waiting for its blind date.

"Could you hack into Greg's email account?"

"Of course."

EIGHT

A COUPLE OF YEARS ago Greg asked Harry to be his executor along with Nicole, and the following day Harry picks her up and takes her to a meeting with the solicitor. Her doctor has given her something; she seems groggy and passive. The will is straightforward—Greg has left everything to Nicole—but the solicitor passes on a message from Greg's accountant asking that the executors get in touch with him. Harry calls him and arranges to go straight over there. When they get to the car Nicole yawns and says she just wants to go to bed, so Harry drops her home and goes on alone.

The accountant's office is in a suburban shopping centre, above a fast food outlet. Sam Peck is a small, rotund, cheery man and he has a bag of golf clubs sitting in the corner of his office, like a promise to himself. This, together with the smell of old grease that seems to have saturated everything, does little to fill Harry with confidence. He apologises for Nicole's absence and Peck smiles his sympathy and says actually it's a relief.

"A relief?" Harry queries.

"Well, to be frank, Greg was pretty hopeless with his business finances, and I really don't know what I could tell her about where she stands. He was a great builder— I know because he did the extension on our house—but hopeless with the accounts. End of year was always a nightmare, chaotic records, all at the last minute. Building's a rollercoaster business at the best of times, but Greg made it that much harder."

"But you were his accountant."

Peck waves a hand airily. "He didn't confide in me, Harry. Nor in anyone else as far as I can tell. Have you met his manager? Peter Rizzo. He organises the building side, the sub-contractors and suppliers and so on, but not the financial side."

"You think there's a problem?"

"He always sailed close to the wind, living on credit, not chasing up debts. A few years ago he was on the verge of bankruptcy—some local council very nearly tipped him over, holding back on payments, Greg didn't force the issue, got in deeper and deeper—came very close to going under."

"And you think that's happening now?"

"I don't know, but there have been worrying signs. Earlier this year—February, March—he ran out of cash again. Bank refused to extend his loans and he asked me to find him another source of credit in a hurry. I ran into problems with that, then he said he'd found someone. Company called Bluereef Financial Services, good address in the city, Bligh Street."

"But?"

Peck shifts uneasily in his seat. "I hadn't heard of them.

I asked Greg to let me check them out but he was in a hurry, just showed me a business card and told me he'd already agreed to a deal with this guy. Well, there wasn't much I could do. I asked him for copies of the contract documents and he never gave them to me. But the name on the card rang a bell—Alexander Kristich. I couldn't place him at first, but then I thought—not that name exactly, but close—Sandi Krstić. There was a fuss about him three or four years ago, up in Queensland, peddling property finance on the Gold Coast. A lot of customers got burnt, ASIC was slow to investigate and when the press got too nosy he disappeared."

"You think it's the same man?"

"I don't know, maybe. Greg said you're a copper. Maybe you could check him out."

"Have you got anything specific against him?"

"No, nothing. But anyone lending money to Greg at that stage was either a hopeless businessman or a shark."

"So what should we do now?"

"Well, maybe you should talk to Peter Rizzo. If you can get me their books, bank records and copies of any loan agreements and contracts Greg may have entered into, I might be able to draw up some kind of balance sheet and forecast for you. I'll have to charge the estate for my time though."

Harry agrees and makes a note of the documents Sam Peck needs.

IT IS RAINING WHEN he turns into the short stretch of private concrete road that serves the small industrial estate on Crucifixion Creek. There are weeds growing through the cracks in the roadway and puddles forming on the uneven surface. At the corner is a forlorn yard stacked with half a dozen shipping containers, and beyond it a small ceramic tile warehouse, a spraypaint workshop, a monumental mason's yard heaped with stone slabs, and several unidentified sheds. Among them Harry sees the sign for *Greg March, Builder.* Two utes stand out the front.

Inside a man is bent over a long bench assembling cupboard units. There is a strong smell of sawdust and raw cement. In one corner of the shed an office has been partitioned off and a man is sitting inside at a table talking into a phone. Harry knocks on the open door and the man looks up, finishes his call and gets to his feet.

"Peter Rizzo? I'm Harry Belltree, Greg's brother-in-law. I'm here on behalf of Mrs. March."

They shake hands. "Terrible business. We're all in shock. How is Nicole?"

"Taking it hard."

"Of course."

"Nicole and I are Greg's executors, so I need to get a picture of the business."

"Yeah, of course. I've been trying to do the same thing." He gestures to a tall pile of papers in a tray.

"You're not on top of it?"

"Over there is my desk." Rizzo points to it. Clear surface, phone and computer neatly squared up, a shelf of numbered file boxes above. "I handle the running of the jobs. Subbies, suppliers, making sure they deliver on time, that kind of thing. Greg's desk's over there . . ." It is hard to see the desk itself because of the spillage of building plans and papers. "Greg handles . . . handled the other stuff—clients, planners, the banks, all that stuff. He let me in on some of it, but . . ." The look of bafflement on Rizzo's face tells its story.

Harry goes over to Greg's desk and pulls out a drawer at random. It is full of envelopes from the ATO, all unopened. He says, "The accountant needs to get a handle on how it all stacks up at this moment."

"Yeah, I suppose so. I've just been worrying about keeping the jobs going."

"Do you have any help? A secretary?"

"Did have. Jamila left last week—maternity leave. She was a smart girl. Maybe I could ask her to come back for a week to help me out. Greg was supposed to get another girl, but I don't think he got around to it."

"Things piling up, were they?"

"Yeah, money worries. He was talking about laying a couple of the blokes off."

"Well, if you could gather up all the financial stuff, and maybe make a summary of the jobs and where they're at, we can get the accountant started, and then we can all sit down together and decide what needs doing."

"Okay. In the meantime, can I pay the guys' wages?"

Harry thinks for a moment. It occurs to him that he's only ever worked for the government—the army or the police—and this is very different territory, a murky place of uncertain decisions and unknown consequences. "I guess so. Make a record of everything you spend, and send it daily to Sam Peck."

"Sure."

"Try to hold off paying invoices."

Rizzo gives an unhappy laugh. "From the phone calls I've been getting, Greg's been doing that for a long time."

"Any idea what he was doing out here that night? Was there an emergency of some kind?"

"Not that I know of. Been wondering about that myself. I can't think of anything, unless he was working on the books. He certainly didn't say anything to me about coming here."

On the way back Harry thinks about Nicole. Does she understand any of this? Does she know what was going on?

NINE

NOTHING HAPPENS THE NEXT day. He does a lot of running.

On the following day, at the end of her shift, Deb Velasco gives him a call. "Harry, hi. How's it going? Those two calls you asked about. They came from the CBD, through the tower in Bond Street."

"Right. Thanks."

"You asked about other calls that night? Nothing."

"Oh."

The disappointment must have sounded in his voice, because she adds, encouragingly, "But he left his phone on. We've tracked his movements. He did big circles in the western suburbs—Bankstown, Punchbowl, Lakemba, Riverwood."

"Really?"

"Yeah, for more than two hours. So the guys are asking themselves what he was looking for. Drugs? Girls? Boys? Sorry, but . . ."

Harry takes a deep breath. What does he know? What

does he really know about his brother-in-law? "I've no idea."

"Yeah, well. I didn't tell you, okay?"

"Of course. Thanks, Deb. Thanks."

He pictures her, weary, putting her gun in her locker— one padlock—glancing at his shameful double locks, wondering if she should be cutting him loose.

Jenny has found emails on Greg's computer from "Sandy." Bland confirmations of meetings. Is that Alexander Kristich, aka Sandi Krstić? Harry asks her to do a search. When Krstić vanished from the Gold Coast there were rumours he was living in Vanuatu. There is a Google photo from the Vanuatu *Daily Post* of him drinking on a palmy beach with the Australian high commissioner.

JENNY HAS THIS THING. She keeps thinking about Greg's call that fatal night. About the sounds in the background. She claims they are distinctive, that they can be tracked down. Harry is not convinced. What blurry background noises can a mobile phone pick up? This is Jenny's compensation, he thinks. And it's true that her hearing has sharpened considerably since the disaster. But don't all lobbies sound alike? After some gentle resistance he agrees to take her on a tour of the CBD tower blocks.

They concentrate on the hotels first, the Marriott, the Sofitel, the Hilton, the Intercontinental. On and on, wandering through the lobbies, Jenny frowning with concentration, then shaking her head. "Not here." Then they focus on the office towers. Jenny thinks there was an echo of some kind, a reverberation in the sounds, and thinks the surfaces must be hard—all of them are—and the space large, but most lift lobbies are relatively confined. She is excited by the tall lobby of Grosvenor Place, and spends some time testing the sounds from different positions, but finally shakes her head once again. Finally they reach the atrium of the Gipps Tower and as soon as she hears the chimes of the lifts she grips Harry's arm and whispers, "This is it. This is where he phoned from."

Harry looks around, noting the cameras, the position of the information desk. Then he goes over to the board listing the tower's tenants. His eye stops at the twenty-third floor—a lawyer, an advertising consultancy, and Bluereef Financial Services. He takes pictures on his phone of the whole list, and leads Jenny back out onto the street.

They go to Nicole's house. At the front door they meet Bronwyn, leaving to pick up the girls from school. She tells them that Nicole is very low today.

Inside they find Nicole in the living room, staring out of the window. When she turns they can see how pale and drawn she looks. In just a few days she seems to have lost a lot of weight.

"There's a rock shelf just under this floor," she says, her voice flat. "When Greg bought this site we came here and clambered down to the shelf and sat there together, Greg going on about how he was going to build our nest here, and we would never leave it, and one day when we were old, sitting on our deck together overlooking that view, we'd remember that day."

Tears are running down her cheeks, and Jenny wraps her arms around her and holds her tight as she sobs. Harry makes tea, and when Nicole has become calmer, Harry broaches the subject of paperwork.

"You know, insurance policies, bank statements, that kind of thing?"

"Greg handled all that," Nicole says despairingly. "I think it's all in the study."

"Would you like me to take a look?"

"Would you, Harry? I'd be so grateful. We didn't have any secrets."

Harry hopes not. But the stuff in the study is all domestic—bills, some share certificates, school reports, an insurance file. Greg took out a policy on his own life just six weeks ago. Did he sense his own mortality?

TEN

THE CORONER HAS RELEASED Greg's body for a funeral, which takes place on a blustery winter day, the trees in the crematorium grounds swaying and flailing in the wind. All Greg's employees have come, all men except for the heavily pregnant Jamila. Peter Rizzo tells Harry that she's been helping him with the books, and they should have something ready for Sam Peck soon, maybe tomorrow. Greg's daughters stand on each side of their mother, cheeks and noses pink in the chill, bravely shaking hands.

That night Harry is woken from a dream of sliding out of control down a steep scree slope. The phone. He sucks in a deep breath and looks at the time—2:26. "Hello."

"Harry? Hello. Peter, Peter Rizzo." The voice is barely audible above a roaring noise. "There's a fire, Harry, at the depot. I'm there now."

"I'm on my way." He tells Jenny and grabs his clothes.

He sees the glow from blocks away. Closer, there are tongues of orange flame flicking above the rooftops of the

Creek and an ominous red glow reflecting off the under-side of a large black cloud. The entrance to the industrial road is closed off by emergency vehicles and Harry sees Peter there, standing mesmerised by the sight.

"Paint," he says. "We took a big delivery of paint to finish off the Punchbowl job."

And timber, Harry thinks, and plastics, and all Greg's business records. He wonders if Peter did it.

"How did you hear?"

"Someone called triple-O, and the cops had my num-ber for emergencies. By the time I got here it was an inferno. They're trying to save the buildings on each side, but they'll be lucky I reckon." He turns to Harry with a desolate expression on his face. "It's a bloody catastrophe, mate. On top of everything else . . ."

They stand side by side watching the fire brigade struggle to control the blaze, feeling the gusts of heat on their faces.

"Harry!"

He turns and sees the reporter, Kelly Pool, pacing towards him, face manic in the eerie glow.

"Is this a crime scene? Is there a murder?"

He turns away, but she won't be shaken off. "Come on, Harry. Why are you here?"

"I'm not on duty, Kelly. I knew the owner, that's all."

"The builder who was stabbed? He was known to you lot?"

"No, he wasn't *known* to me. He was a relative. And that's not for your column."

"Come on, Harry. Something's going on, isn't it? First the murder, now this."

"If you know anything, you tell the cops. They're over there."

She comes right up close to him and says in a hoarse whisper. "We need to talk. There are other things going on."

"What other things?"

"Coincidences, Harry. Too many."

She's just desperate for a story, he decides, looking at her wild hair, her over-eager eyes. He turns to Peter. "I'm going now," he says. "We'll talk in the morning."

He heads for his car and Kelly chases after him. "I mean it, Harry," she cries. "We can help each other . . ."

He slams the door and drives away.

When he gets home the lights are on for him. Jenny is in her dressing gown at her computer, whispering into the headset. She smells rather than hears his arrival, her nose twitching. She gets to her feet and removes the earphones.

"Better not touch me," he says, aware of the chemical stench on his clothes, in his hair and deep in his throat. When he's had a shower and thrown his clothes into the machine she's made coffee and toast. The darkness is paling in the eastern sky through the kitchen window.

"Was it bad?"

"Nothing will survive that fire. Peter Rizzo was out there. He looked like he knew that was the end of the business."

"Is that what's bothering you?" She puts a hand on his arm.

"That, and a few unanswered questions."

"About Greg?"

He nods, then remembers she can't see that. It still catches him out. "Yes, about Greg."

"I discovered he had another email address," she says. "One that's not entered on his home computer. It doesn't have anything over a month old, all personal messages."

"A woman?"

"It's not clear. One person, though. They sign themselves 'J.' They're more ultimatums than love letters—*I hate being like this. I want everything to be resolved. What are you going to do?* That kind of thing."

He thinks of Jamila, eight months pregnant, and tells Jenny about her.

She ponders. "That could fit. I'll check the messages again. Oh God, poor Nicole. We won't tell her."

But they may have no choice. It could be a motive for murder. Would her family have arranged for the boy to meet Greg and kill him? Could they have firebombed the depot?

"I've also been trying to find out more about Alexander Kristich," she says. "He and Sandi Krstić, if they are the same man, seem to lead a charmed life. He got into all kinds of trouble in Queensland and Vanuatu, before that the Philippines and Malaysia. He seems to have a knack of getting in with influential people who pull strings for him—allegedly."

"A con man."

"Well, yes. With a darker side. His first wife died in a fall from the balcony of a twenty-third-floor apartment on the Gold Coast. And a man who lost his life savings in one of his scams and went on TV to complain was killed a week later in a hit and run."

"The twenty-third floor," Harry says. "That's where he is now, in the Gipps Tower."

"Oh yes . . . His lucky number."

LATER THAT MORNING HE returns to the Creek to view the place in daylight. Greg's building is just a blackened hole now between shattered brick side walls. Faint traces of steam still rise into the air and the whole site stinks of toxic smoke. Harry has to jump around large puddles from the fire hoses to approach the scene, fenced off now by police tape.

The black shell of a ute stands in the forecourt. He can see several men in yellow protective clothes moving about inside the collapsed shell, between crumpled roof sheeting and steel trusses hanging limp like spaghetti.

When one of them comes outside to get a drink of water from his truck Harry goes over and flashes his police ID. "Found anything?"

"Looks like it started in that corner over there, at the back."

"That's where the office was. Cause?"

The man shrugs. "Not yet. We're testing for an accelerant."

"Any signs of a break-in?"

"Oh mate, if there ever were signs they're gone now. But you're welcome to take a look."

He gives Harry a jacket, gloves, mask, helmet and a pair of boots, and they go into the ruin, stepping carefully over the hazards. All that's left are the husks of steel equipment, piles of charred timber, puddles of melted plastic. In the corner where the office stood, the side wall has collapsed inward. What might once have been a computer casing is visible beneath a heap of blackened bricks. Paper has all gone to smoke and ash. Harry remembers a safe in one corner, but when he hauls away a twisted steel beam and slab of brickwork, he finds the burnt-out steel box, deformed by heat or impact, the door burst open and the contents incinerated.

Harry's foot crunches on something as he leaves the office area, a shard of rippled glass. The kind that was in the window at the back, where the wall has fallen outward into a narrow yard that separated the building from the rear boundary fence. He goes over and examines the remains. Looks over the back fence at the roofs of neighbouring buildings and an odd watch-tower construction standing up against the sky.

Inside again, he shows the fireman the glass on the floor. "It came from that window—the one on the wall that fell outwards. How do you reckon these bits got over here, unless maybe someone smashed the window from the outside?" He shows the man where things had stood, explaining that the windows in the office partition facing into the workshop had clear flat glass. The man nods, making notes on a device he's carrying, and crouches to pick up samples.

Harry thanks him and leaves them to it.

As he returns to the street he sees someone on a big Harley over there watching him. The figure is motionless and clad all in black. Black helmet, black glasses, black scarf over the lower half of his face. Harry moves closer, round towards the back of the bike. The man revs the throttle and roars off as Harry takes a photo of the number plate and the symbol on the man's back, a bird's skull surrounded by a halo of orange lettering—*Crow Australia 1% MC.*

Harry's phone beeps in his pocket, a text reminding him of his follow-up appointment with the police shrink.

"SO HOW HAVE YOU been this past week, Harry?"

"Good, good. I've had some time to be with the family, you know." He's rehearsed this in his mind, the steady tone, the relaxed posture, remembering all the while that she's seen every avoidance routine in the book.

"How are they coping?"

"It's difficult, but we've got support. Nicole's mother has been a big help to her and the girls. She's very sensible, very capable. Now the funeral's past I think things will settle down."

"And do you need more time with them?"

"There are still things to sort out, but we're pretty much on top of it. No, I'd like to get back to work." A little smile, sad, resigned, but open. Not holding anything back. This must be what suspects feel like under interview; he imagines how phoney his expression would look on an ERISP video. "You don't look convinced."

"I am still concerned, Harry."

"What's bothering you?"

She smiles at his attempt to take over. "A few things. For example, when most cops go through a traumatic experience they like to go into all the particulars—number of wounds, how deep they were, how much blood, that kind of stuff. It's a cop thing. But not you. You haven't said a word about all that."

It's true, he recognises what she's saying—they all love to rehash the gory details. Their way of debriefing, perhaps, and perhaps he was like that once. Not anymore.

"I think the army got me out of doing that," he says. "We handled things differently."

"How?"

"Oh . . . we spent more time keeping fit, working out. Having to be alert all the time changes your perspective somehow."

She's not convinced. She waits for him to say more, but he keeps silent.

"You're a bit of an enigma, Harry," she says finally. "All right, if you're sure you don't need more time, I'll clear you for duty."

"Thanks."

He takes a deep breath as he walks out, feeling relieved until he switches his phone back on. A missed call from Sam Peck.

"Sam."

"Harry!" The accountant sounds rattled. "We need to talk."

"Okay, I'll come over."

But first he runs a check on the motorbike at the Creek. Registered to one Benjamin "Benji" Lavulo. Convictions for assault and drugs.

Harry parks in a lot behind the shopping strip, and steps out into the smell of frying. The heater is on full blast in Sam's office. He's got his sleeves rolled up and his forehead is glowing pink, sweat stains under his arms.

"What's up, Sam?"

"We've had a bankruptcy notice served on us, mate." He shows Harry the document.

"Who's this come from, building suppliers?"

Sam shakes his head. "We know Greg owed money to a few of them, but this is a single creditor, Bluereef Financial Services. Served by their lawyer, Nathaniel Horn."

The lawyer's name seems familiar. Then he remembers—the list of tenants on the twenty-third floor of the Gipps Tower. Harry studies the papers, and his eye snags on a figure. "This . . ." he shows Sam. "That's not possible, is it? It's huge."

"First time I've seen it. But there are copies of supporting documents, contracts signed by Bluereef and both Greg and Nicole, putting up their joint assets as guarantees against loans."

"What assets? The business, you mean?"

"I mean *everything*, Harry—the business, the premises at the Creek, their house, its contents, the shares in Nicole's name, her jewellery, the cars, everything. If this is kosher, she'll be lucky to walk away with the clothes on her back."

Harry is stunned. "Would Nicole have agreed to that?"

Sam dips his head. "Maybe Greg didn't really explain it to her. I've seen him hand her papers to sign that she didn't read. She trusted him. The only bright spot is his life insurance. They shouldn't be able to touch that."

And the dark little thought that has been lurking in the back of Harry's mind for the past week finally emerges into the light. It was suicide. What Greg was looking for, circling the western suburbs in the small hours, was someone to kill him, in exchange for his car and the cash that was all over the inside of the wreck. *He wana me do it*, that's what the dying boy said. In the end it was all that Greg could do for Nicole and the girls.

"She'd better get a lawyer, Harry," Sam says. "The trouble is, we have nothing to argue with. All Greg's records have gone. Apart from odds and ends about his current contracts that Peter Rizzo's been able to give me, we've got nothing. Tax'll be a nightmare."

They talk about the best way to handle this, who to get advice from.

"You'll have to prepare Nicole for the worst, Harry," Sam says. "This is going to get ugly, I can feel it. The terms of those loans were extortionate. Greg must have been out of his mind."

WHEN HE GETS HOME he tells Jenny, and she turns away from him, shocked, her face tilted up as if straining for some light she cannot see. "No," she says, "it can't be that bad. Even her jewellery? How could Greg let that happen?"

"I think it may be worse than that, love," and he grips her hand and tells her about the killer's last words.

He watches tears forming in her eyes. Then her mouth sets and she turns back to face him. "What can we do?"

"Not much by the sound of it. All Greg's records have gone in the fire. We should get a lawyer for Nicole, and—"

"No," she interrupts. "I mean, what can we *do* . . . to protect Nicole and the girls from these people?"

"I don't know, maybe find out what Bluereef have been

up to. They're crooks. There must be smoking guns if we knew where to look."

"Can't the police do that?"

"I can try, but . . . The Queensland police had a crack, and ASIC. Neither of them got anywhere. I've just been stood down for a week because I got too involved. They're not going to listen to me pushing for action just because he was a mug, there'd have to be some pretty concrete evidence of a crime."

Harry's memories of Greg are crumbling. He no longer has a real handle on who Greg actually was. He remembers a scene in this room, when his parents still lived in this house. Greg and Harry's father were sitting together over there at the front window, playing chess. Engrossed in the game, they barely acknowledged him as he came in. He had recently returned from overseas, Afghanistan or maybe earlier, Iraq, and was feeling suspended, not fitting in. The sight of them together pierced him, as if Greg now occupied a place that should have been his, if he hadn't gone off soldiering in two wars with which both his mother and father thoroughly disagreed.

Not that they hadn't been interested. They'd asked. But when he tried to describe it their faces had clouded over with distaste and disapproval.

ELEVEN

THE NEXT DAY HE returns to work, day shift. The second padlock has been removed from his locker and he senses the relief on the others' faces as they nod and mutter their welcome back, mates. Toby Wagstaff gives him a wink and Bob the Job himself comes to Harry's desk and shakes his hand.

He settles down. He has to make a case to the Crime Commission in favour of planting bugs and tapping phones in the houses of a number of people peripherally connected to a suspected murderer called Victor Nguyen. The idea is to trawl for incriminating material against these people on other matters, so then the police can squeeze them for evidence against the main target, Nguyen.

In between gathering and composing his submission, Harry makes searches on Bluereef, Kristich and the lawyer Nathaniel Horn. The solicitor's past clients include a star list of socialites, politicians, footballers and celebrity crooks, charged with everything from acts of indecency to drugs, fraud and murder. Kristich is much as Jenny said. Harry sends requests to Queensland for information on the deaths of Krstić's wife and of the man who went public with claims of fraud. In the middle of this he gets a call from the central switchboard saying there's a Kelly Pool on the line for him. His first impulse is to say he's not available, but then he relents and takes the call.

She is brisk and businesslike, in the manner of someone giving it one last shot. "Thanks for speaking to me, Harry. I'm not pestering you for no good reason. I believe I have information that will be of interest to you. I think you should give me twenty minutes to explain." She suggests a pub, a good choice. Not too far from headquarters but not too close.

"Ten," he says.

In the event it takes somewhat longer. For a start she keeps him waiting, and he's on the point of leaving when she bursts into the bar, coat flapping, threatening to send glasses flying from the tables. "Sorry, sorry! Bloody traffic. What are you drinking?" He holds up his glass, "Fizzy mineral water."

She comes back with the drinks and subsides onto a stool. "Well." She takes a deep breath and a gulp of the house Shiraz. "Harry, there's something going on at Crucifixion Creek. That siege, the builder's murder, the fire— a lot of coincidence, don't you think?"

Ah. She wants there to be a conspiracy. "The last two may be related, but it's hard to see what they've got to do with the siege."

"Agreed, but the gunman was a former Crow, yes?"

That hasn't been made public. "Where did you get that from?"

"I told you, I know my turf. And the Crows are definitely Creek turf. And there's something else. Do you remember that old couple who died together in a café at Balmoral Beach a week or so back?"

Harry frowns, wondering if she's a little mad. "Yeah? So?"

"They owned property—three houses—on Mortimer Street, in the Creek."

"I thought they were from the North Shore somewhere."

"Yes, that's where they lived, but they also had these investment properties. And the woman who found them lives in one of those houses, and that's how I became interested in that strange story."

Harry drinks his beer and glances at his watch. "Anything else?"

"Well, yes. Our local Councillor Potgeiter, who thinks the Shooters Party are a pack of bleeding heart lefties, wants to erect a memorial to Aboriginal reconciliation in the Civic Centre . . ."

Harry looks at her.

". . . thereby making possible the removal of the memorial in Bidjigal Park in the Creek."

"Yeah, well," Harry drains his glass. "It'll make an interesting article in your paper, I'm sure. I'll keep a lookout for it." He starts to get to his feet.

"Harry!" she almost yells. "That old couple were murdered!"

Heads turn. Harry stares at her. "What are you talking about?"

"That old couple." She leans in to him, willing him back into his seat. "A couple of months ago they were rich. Then they got tangled up with some finance company who turned them into paupers, in connivance with their son. He's very cagey about the whole thing."

"What finance company?"

"I don't know, I've just got a name, Crosstitch, but I can't track him down." She sees the expression on his face. "You've heard of him?"

"Kristich," he says, and spells it out. "Alexander Kristich. Previously Sandi Krstić from the Gold Coast. You'd better tell me the whole story."

So she does.

"You went and spoke to the son?"

"Yes. He wouldn't see me at first, then he changed his mind."

"How did he explain what had happened to his folks?"

"Dementia. But I don't believe him. Mrs. Bulwer-Knight says there was nothing wrong with them when she last saw them a month ago."

Harry has made enquiries about Kelly Pool. He's picked up the story of her run-in with the Murdoch editor. Now he wonders just how desperate she is for a second chance, a redeeming scoop. How likely she is to find it working for the *Bankstown Chronicle*.

"Then he threatened me."

"Oh?"

"I think that was the real reason he agreed to see me. He said his lawyer will go for me—and the paper—if we print anything about his parents he doesn't like."

"Did he say who his lawyer is?"

"No. So what do you know about this Kristich character?"

"He's just one of those names that comes across the desk from time to time. An elusive man, from all accounts. You can look him up."

He was aware of her searching look. "Come on, Harry. There's more, isn't there?"

"Kristich's lawyer is Nathaniel Horn. Heard of him?"

"Of course! I've seen him on TV."

"It'd be interesting to know if he's also the lawyer for the old couple's son."

"Yes."

"But the odds are he isn't. The thing is, Kelly, crimes don't come evenly spread across the city. They come in clusters, and sometimes the clusters just happen. No reason, just coincidence. If you want to start a fire somewhere, what better place than a run-down dump like the Creek? Maybe you read in the *Bankstown Chronicle* that that's where the guy who got stabbed nearby had a business."

"No, we didn't print that."

"But you take my point. Coincidences happen all the time in the real world. They don't necessarily mean anything."

Kelly glares at him. "Once is happenstance, twice is coincidence, and the third time it's enemy action."

"Who said that?"

She blushes. "Goldfinger."

He laughs and gets to his feet.

"But what are you going to do?" she says.

"Nothing. You haven't given me any grounds. What are you going to do?"

"I'm going to write a story, Harry, and it'd be great if you could help me. If you could find out that the son's lawyer is Horn, say, I'd write you up as the great detective. It would do you good."

No, it really wouldn't. That's the last thing it would do. "No, Kelly," he says. "You're not going to mention my name and you're not going to contact me again, okay?"

As he walks back to headquarters he phones Garry Roberts the pathologist. Yes, Garry did the post-mortems on the old couple and yes, he did specifically examine their brains for signs of Alzheimer degeneration.

"And?"

"Nothing," says Garry.

Harry then phones Jenny and asks if she can hack into Justin Waterford's computer, find out if he knows Kristich or Horn. She says she'll try.

When he arrives home there is a small pile of computer printouts on the kitchen table. Since neither Jenny nor her whispering electronic friend has any use for hard copies, he realises they are for him. First he pours two glasses of wine and asks Jenny about her day, and turns the roasting chicken over for her.

"I got into Waterford's computer all right," she says. "There's some copies for you over there." He sways back as she points over her shoulder with the knife in her hand, dangerously close to his face. "Oops," she says. "Was that near you? Sorry."

He picks up the papers. First some pages from websites referencing Alexander Kristich and Bluereef Financial Services. They are all from a two-day period, four months ago.

"That's all there was on Kristich," she says. "Waterford just looked him up that time, then nothing."

"Right." There are more Google searches, this time for Nathaniel Horn, all within the past week, and an exchange of emails with the lawyer's office, confirming the time of a meeting.

"Not much," Jenny says.

"It's enough. He knows them." And he tells her about his meeting with Kelly Pool.

"You didn't tell her about Greg and Kristich, did you?"

"No."

"That's the most important thing, isn't it? What did he do to Greg, and how can we now protect Nicole?"

"Yes."

"If I could get into his computer I might find a record of their transactions, and then we could have them looked at by our lawyer."

So after dinner she sits down with her little spy and gets to work. Harry sits with her for a while, reading, until he suddenly lurches upright and realises he's been asleep. She hears his grunt and tells him to go to bed, that she'll join him soon. But she doesn't, and when he wakes in the morning the bed beside him is empty, and she's still in the front room, working.

"I can't bloody do it," she says wearily. "He's got some new NGFW with IPS I've never seen before."

Harry has no idea what that means. "You've been at it all night?"

"Yes. I'll get some sleep now and try again later, but I really don't think I'm going to get anywhere. I also tried getting in through Horn's computer, but it's equally well protected."

Later, when he gets home, he can tell from her expression that she's failed. "I'm sorry," she says, despairing. "It's hopeless. I can't do it."

"What if you had his computer?"

"What?"

"I mean, physically here in front of you. Could you get into it then?"

"I . . ." She's staring right at him. "I know someone who could probably help me."

"Okay. So could you bypass the security systems in the Gipps Tower—cameras, locks?"

"What? I don't know."

"Why don't you try?"

"Harry . . . I don't want you to do that."

"Just try."

By midnight she's worked out how to do it. She can give him the master entry code for all the electronic locks in the tower, and can pause the cameras and freeze the images on the monitors in the security centre for a limited period. "Thirty minutes, Harry. No more than an hour."

"Right, I'll go and get changed."

"You're going now?" She looks terrified. "If they catch you you'll lose your job, everything. You'll go to jail. It's not worth it, Harry."

He kisses her and she clings to him and finally he has to ease out of her grip. "Don't worry."

JENNY CLOSES THE FRONT door after him and turns back into the house, feeling sick with foreboding. What if they arrest him? She has to try to block this feeling of helplessness every time he goes off to work, to face who knows what. She hates feeling so vulnerable.

She climbs the stairs, up past the bedroom floor to the attic room under the roof. Up here where a small window looks out through the branches of the plane tree, it feels like a children's tree house. This was Harry's father's sanctuary, his study, and there is still a faint lingering smell of the small cigars that he liked to smoke when he had to do some serious thinking. It comforts her to come up here. She misses them both, Mary earthy and indomitable, and Danny with that impish sense of humour that used to delight Greg and Nicole's little girls, filling their house with shrieks and giggles. And Jenny listening to them with an ache in her belly, wanting so much to have children of her own to join in.

The walls are lined with shelving carrying hundreds of books, box files, diaries and law magazines. Somewhere among them may be the answer to why he and Mary died, if Harry is right in his belief that their deaths were deliberate. In the hours he's spent searching the documents he's come up with a long list of possible lethal motives. Danny Belltree was involved in a lot of cases during his long legal career.

Jenny sits in his old office chair and runs her fingers

over his smooth cedar table top. By the time she was released from hospital after the crash, Harry had moved back into his parents' house. He brought her here, and they have been here ever since. It's a much nicer home than the ugly little flat in Bondi, but still, she doesn't know if it was a good idea. Surely the constant presence of his parents in every room fuels his obsession to explain their deaths—when in truth, as the coroner decided, there may not be an explanation to find.

When she returned from the hospital and first began to learn how to live a blind life, she started with this house. She learned from painful experience its traps and dangers for the unsighted. And she trained her memory and inner eye to reconstruct its geometry, its details. She felt the dimensions and texture of each piece of furniture, each picture on the walls, and built their images in her mind. Over there, for example, in the angle beneath the sloping surface of the roof, is a 1965 photograph of the young Danny and Mary on the Freedom Ride in Moree, protesting for the civil rights of Indigenous Australians. She looks impassioned, pretty and pale. He stands at her side, awkward. Proud. It was through them, doing research work in Danny's chambers, that Jenny first met Harry. She sometimes wonders if they chose her for him.

TWELVE

IT IS NOW ONE-FORTY, the same time that Greg died, which seems auspicious somehow. He finds a parking space in The Rocks and walks back up into the business district with the bag slung on his back. As he approaches the glass cylinder of the Gipps Tower he makes a brief call to Jenny, "Ready to go." He pulls on latex gloves and walks down the ramp of the tower's basement to a pedestrian door at the foot, where he taps in the entry code on the keypad. Half expecting nothing to happen, he tries the handle. The door opens silently and he steps inside. Halfway down a bare corridor there's a door into one of the fire escape stairwells that rise through the building and he begins his climb.

When he emerges into the lobby of the twenty-third floor there is only low-level emergency lighting. No lights show through the glass doors of the tenants' offices that he passes to get to Bluereef Financial Services—also in darkness. Again the entry code works. He holds his breath as he opens the door, bracing for an alarm that may be independent of the main tower systems, but there is no sound. He is in a small reception area—a computer on a desk and filing cabinets behind. He opens a door opposite. This looks like the principal's office—Kristich's—with a large desk and computer on one side of the room and a conference table and chairs over against the external wall—full-height glass that looks out to the shimmering lights of the CBD. There are no pictures on the wall and the furnishings look generic, as if rented and ready to be abandoned.

There is another room beyond this one, and the glow of a light through the half-open door. Harry pads silently across the carpet to see. The light comes from a lamp on a low table beside a sofa facing a TV. A private sitting room? There are some men's magazines and a couple of used glasses. A champagne bottle, Krug. One of the glasses has traces of lipstick.

He returns to the office and searches the desk drawers, finding nothing of interest. Then out to the reception area, to the filing cabinets, which are locked. It takes him a few minutes to find the keys in the receptionist's desk, and he begins a search through the files. The first drawer is full of blank forms and letterheads, the second booklets and forms relating to tax and property, the third staff files. The client files start in the fourth drawer. Each file is identified by a number rather than a name, and they are in numerical order, so that he has to open each one in order to identify the client. It takes him some time to discover one for Waterford, and then another for March. He pulls them out, and is about to relock the cabinets when, out of curiosity, he flicks through a few more files and comes upon one with the name "Belltree" scrawled on the front. He freezes, then slowly draws it out, turns the locks and replaces the keys.

He is in mild shock, his heart thumping. Now the computer. Which one should he take? He decides the one in Kristich's office is more likely to contain sensitive material, and heads back there. As he steps towards the desk he feels a tightening in his scalp. There's something—a smell . . . And as he turns, a voice from behind him.

"Who the fuck are you?"

The man is a black silhouette against the electric panorama beyond the window. Harry lays the files on the desk at his side as the figure moves to the wall and flips the lights. A short man going fleshy, pale hair thinning. Probably no more than forty, wearing a silk dressing gown. Harry recognises him as Alexander Kristich, and the pistol in his hand as a US Army Ruger 1911. Kristich is staring in fascination at the latex gloves on Harry's hands. His voice sounds a little slurred as he advances on Harry. "Hands up. Turn around." He waves the heavy pistol at Harry, who wonders if he knows how to use it, if it's loaded or cocked. He turns and lets Kristich feel his pockets and pat his chest.

Kristich backs off. "Well?" he demands. "Who are you?"

"I'm a student, Mr. Kristich." Harry slowly turns to face him, lowering his arms.

"A what?"

"A student of your methods. I want to learn from you."

Kristich splutters. "You're joking."

"I think you're an expert at what you do."

"Oh yeah?" Kristich waves him away from the desk,

and cautiously flips over the covers of the files. "Waterford . . . March. Why these two?"

"Because they ended up dead. I want to find out how you did that."

"You're a cop." But he sounds uncertain. "Or what? You after a little something for yourself?"

Harry says nothing, then Kristich's face clears and he laughs, as if he's suddenly decided that this is a hilarious situation. "You want to learn from me, do you? You want to know what my secret is? Well, I'll tell you. I'm a student too. I study human weakness, and then I facilitate it. Take those people . . ." he waves towards the files, ". . . the Waterfords. Great ambitions, yeah? They want to leave a memorial, a new exhibition room in the State Gallery named after them. Trouble is, it's going to cost twenty mill, and they only got about ten." He shrugs, falsely modest. "I told them I could increase their wealth by ten per cent a month. They weren't sure at first, but I persuaded them to give me a try. The first month they give me half a mill, and after thirty days I give them back five-fifty thou. The second month they give me a mill, and I give 'em one point one. Third month, two mill, and I give them two point two. And the fourth month they give me everything and I take it all. See?"

Harry sees. It's a classic con. "But how did you get onto them in the first place? How do you do your research?"

"Investment conference. Always good for networking one way or another, meet their son Justin in the bar. Wow, he is a gloomy guy. His folks have got it into their heads to give all his inheritance away. What can he do? So I tell him to get them to come talk to me."

"So you sorted it out, what, for a fee?"

"Ten per cent, but what Justin doesn't know is that I'll actually take fifty. He'll accept it. He's got no choice. I could take more, but who knows, he may have friends who need my services. Half is better than zilch after all."

"And the other case, March? You're taking half?"

"Oh no, I get the lot on that one. That loser should never have been in business. He was on his last legs."

"But won't you lose your investment?"

Kristich smirks and places a finger beside his nose. Then he looks suddenly bored and shuffles the files apart to reveal the third one, Belltree. "What's this?" and his flaccid features abruptly stiffen. He turns to stare at Harry. "Why this one?"

Harry's mind goes blank. He can't think of a word to say, but then it seems he doesn't have to, because Kristich's face breaks into a broad smile as he looks over Harry's shoulder. "About bloody time, Benji."

Benji is a large, heavily tattooed Pacific islander, the same Benjamin Lavulo that Harry identified at the Creek. "Yeah, sorry, Sandy. Whatsa problem? This guy thieving?"

"That's what we have to find out, Benji." Since he saw the Belltree file Kristich has become more focused. "Give him a good search, will you? I couldn't find anything—no wallet, no phone."

Benji does a thorough job, feeling under Harry's arms, his groin, his ankles. "No, not a thing."

"A bug, a wire?"

"No, don't reckon. Not even a watch."

"Do it again."

They wait while Benji examines Harry's hair, his ears, his shoes. "No."

Kristich points to an office chair and tells Harry to sit down. "So who are you?"

Harry stares back, says nothing.

"Lost for words, eh? You got that knife of yours, Benji?"

"Sure, Mr. Kristich." Benji takes a horned handle from his pocket and springs out the long blade.

"Okay, I'll take it and you cover him with this."

They exchange weapons, and Benji expertly works the slide on the pistol, cocking it.

"Now." They both close in on the seated Harry. Kristich waves the blade under his nose. "Just so you know, I like hurting people. What's your name?"

Harry stays silent, and Kristich crouches in front of him, a greedy smile on his lips. "All right." He jabs the knife at Harry's chest. Harry feels it pierce his skin and touch something solid, a rib. He flinches.

"Oh!" An excited little gasp as Kristich withdraws the knife and examines the blood on the tip. "You might as well give us a name to put on your grave, mate." He draws back his elbow for a harder stab. As his arm lunges forward Harry's right hand shoots out and grabs it, steering the blow away from his own body and hard into Benji's chest. With his left hand he grips Benji's hand and squeezes, pressing on the trigger finger. There is a stunning bang and Kristich topples backward, a large bloody hole in his front.

A long reverberating moment. Both Kristich and Benji are on the floor. Blood pumps from Kristich's wound for a count of four, then fades to a trickle. Benji is groaning, blood spilling from his lips, and he coughs and tries to sit up. Harry reaches down and punches the knife in deeper. He subsides, twitches for a moment and is still. Harry feels for a pulse in his neck. Nothing.

He gets carefully to his feet. Checks his shoes for blood and steps away, around the bloodstains on the carpet. This is a crime scene, he tells himself. What do you see? Take a deep breath, take your time.

He goes over to the desk and thinks about how he will pack the computer into his bag, along with all its bits and pieces—wires, keyboard, mouse and mat. Then he notices a dark grey box attached to the computer. External back-up hard drive. He slips that into his backpack along with the files, leaving the computer intact.

When he's ready he looks over at Kristich and murmurs, "So where did you come from?"

He goes back into the sitting room to take another look and sees that its back wall is in fact a set of sliding doors, now half-open. Through the gap he can see the end of a bed. Kristich lives here, he thinks. He goes to the opening and takes in the whole little windowless bedroom, and on the bed a naked woman, eyes closed. There is a syringe on the floor.

As he stares at her, wondering if she's alive or dead, she opens her eyes, taking a long moment to focus. "Who're you?" she mumbles.

"Sandy's friend," he says.

She opens her eyes wider and stares at him for a moment, then sighs, "Oh." She rolls over and drifts off to sleep again.

He backs out of the room and returns to the office, takes one last look around and leaves.

When he arrives home, Jenny is waiting. She recognises the smell of gunsmoke on his jacket from his annual drills on the police firing range. She doesn't panic. She wants to know what happened. He tells her, and is surprised by how calmly she takes it in, every detail. He gives her the hard drive, which she strokes with her fingers while he opens the files. The Waterford file contains surveyor's plans of the properties on Mortimer Street owned by the dead couple. Greg's file, similarly, has a plan of his unit in the Creek, together with the loan agreement he signed with Bluereef Financial. The Belltree file contains a single sheet of paper, a photocopy of a group photograph of the judicial officers of the Supreme Court of New South Wales. Justice Daniel Belltree's head is circled in red ink.

They discuss where they should hide the files, how they should clean Harry's clothes, dispose of the plastic gloves. He has a long shower, scrubbing his wrists and head thoroughly to remove any gunshot residue.

He's trying not to dwell on what happened tonight, but he feels strung tight as he dries himself, and when he gets to the bedroom he wraps his arms around Jenny and holds her to him. Her mouth, her body are like a narcotic, erasing the tension that grips his shoulders, his stomach. He is overwhelmed by a surge of desperate need for her and they tumble onto the bed. It is the first time they have made love for weeks, months even.

THIRTEEN

IN THE TRANSITION FROM sleep to waking he sees the woman on the bed. Her face is different, more alert, with huge frightened eyes. Not surprising, since he is covered in blood.

Jenny is already awake, and at her desk setting her little friend to work on the black box. Prying out its secrets. Harry makes her a cup of tea and leaves for work.

At headquarters he finds Deb all fired up.

"Harry! Get your gear quick. We're on our way. Double homicide in the city."

"For us?"

"Sure."

He feels like a robot as he picks up his things from his locker and follows her down to the basement car park.

She fills him in as he drives. "Little over an hour ago a woman came out of one of the lifts in the entrance foyer of the Gipps Tower wearing a dressing gown. She walked over to the enquiries desk, leaving a trail of bloody footprints on the marble floor. She said to the guy, 'Sandy and Benji are both dead,' then she passed out."

"Where is she now?"

"Still there, with security. They knew her, regular visitor . . ." Deb checks her notes, "Chloe Anastos, record for soliciting and drug use. Ambulance came and checked her out, then a doctor who gave her the all-clear apart from a hangover. Attending officers went up with security to the offices of her *companion*, Alexander Kristich, on the twenty-third floor and found his body inside with that of another man, who security identified as Benjamin Lavulo, also known to them as an associate of Kristich. Kristich has no record, Lavulo convictions for assault and drugs. Suspected involvement in two unsolved murder cases."

"Somebody killed them both?"

"Looks like it. Crime scene are there now."

As he drives along familiar streets, Harry sees them with a fresh eye, registering details—two women pushing a pram, graffiti on a billboard, a vacant shop unit—as if he may never see them again.

When they arrive they are directed down the ramp to the basement, and Harry recognises the door through which he entered last night. He sees the camera overhead, an implacable eye, and he feels a tightening in his chest, wondering if Jenny did really fix the system. Maybe he and Deb will see his face come up on the security footage. It is as if he is being drawn remorselessly into a trap of his own making.

The security man leads them down the ramp and points them to a reserved parking space, then takes them into the security suite. A local area detective is there with updates for them. Uniforms have sealed off the twenty-third floor for the crime-scene team who have also examined Anastos. Drug use is indicated, probably heroin, but she has refused a blood test. They go into the small office next door and a female detective gets to her feet as they come in. Anastos is sitting hunched under a blanket. Crime scene have taken her dressing gown and given her disposable slippers and tunic.

Deb introduces herself and Harry, and Anastos barely glances up. But then her eye catches on Harry's face, and she frowns and peers at him.

"Don't I know you?" Her voice is hoarse.

"Probably," he says. "Scooters at the Cross?"

She looks confused. "Oh . . ."

Deb takes charge of getting her story. She and Kristich went out for a meal at the Hilton then returned here, had a few drinks and went to bed some time between ten and twelve, she can't be more exact. She can't remember Benji arriving. She didn't hear anything. She had no idea anything was wrong until she woke up and went looking for Sandy and found them both on the floor.

"He has a bed up there in his office?" Deb demands.

He converted part of the office into a flat, Chloe explains. It's where he lives. Lived.

Deb snorts doubtfully and goes out to check with the security people. While they wait for her to return, Chloe sneaks another look at Harry, surreptitiously, peering through her blond fringe. Harry looks back at her and nods. She says, "Scooters?"

"Yeah, I reckon that's where it was."

"Unbelievable." Deb is back. "This is an office building. He made a nest for himself up there, a little apartment. Against all the regulations but everyone turned a blind eye."

"So he doesn't have another address?"

"Not that anybody knows of. And nothing about family members, next of kin."

A nest is right, Harry thinks, an eyrie, somewhere he could fly from at a moment's notice.

Deb questions Chloe Anastos about Kristich, about his business, and about his relationship with Lavulo. The exchanges are laboured, yielding little but mumbled claims of ignorance. It's an act, Harry decides. She is a smart woman who has been interviewed by the police many times before. Eventually they are interrupted by a call on the local detective's phone. He murmurs to Deb that crime scene are clearing the twenty-third floor and they can go up. They finish the interview and go back outside to the security control room, where Deb asks the staff for the camera tapes and other security records for the past twenty-four hours, and a list of tenants of the building. She and Harry take the lift up to the twenty-third floor.

As they give their names to the uniform at the door of Kristich's suite and go inside, Harry looks around, eyes searching for some sign of himself, something he overlooked. They pass through the reception area and into the inner office, where two men are standing in conversation. The pathologist, Garry Roberts, looks up and gives a cheery smile. He and the crime-scene guy step back to give them a clear view of the bodies on the floor.

Harry and Deb take it in, squat, peer at the knife and

gun, the shell casing lying to one side. Harry stares at their hands, wondering if he bruised them when he gripped. He can't see any marks.

"Okay," Deb says, puzzled, "what happened?"

Roberts answers in his clipped way, pointing. "Kristich—Lavulo. Kristich's prints on the handle of the knife in Lavulo's chest. Lavulo's prints on the gun."

"So . . ." Deb still doesn't buy it. "They what . . . killed each other?"

"That's how it looks."

"Who first?"

"Must have been pretty much simultaneous. Kristich couldn't have stabbed Lavulo with that wound in his chest, and vice-versa."

"Or someone else set it up?"

The two men don't like that idea. "Hard to see how," Roberts says. "I'll have a close look at them on the table, but there's no sign of them being restrained before the event or moved afterwards. It definitely happened right here, as you see it. No obvious signs anyone else was present." He points to some blood smears on the carpet leading to the door. "Assuming those are the girlfriend's footprints."

"When did it happen?"

"Hm, between midnight and three?"

"That's a big pistol," Deb persists. "A forty-five. Noisy. Anastos didn't hear a thing?"

"She'd taken heroin. And the gun was definitely fired in here—the bullet passed clean through Kristich's body and into that wall over there." He points to a marker across the room.

Deb, frowning, turns to Harry. "What do you think?"

He shrugs. "No sign of an argument?"

The two experts shake their heads. "Furniture undisturbed. No bruises, scratches. Nothing. It's like they were both standing here, close together, when something flared up, bang-bang, that's it."

Harry says, "The lights were off?"

The crime-scene man says, "They were on when we arrived, but Anastos may have done that. You're thinking Kristich surprised Lavulo here in the dark and mistook him for an intruder? Maybe he *was* an intruder. Yeah, that's what my money's on."

"Makes sense," Harry says neutrally.

Deb seems unconvinced. "Let's look around."

Harry hangs back, letting Deb discover things while the crime-scene unit finish up, removing the bodies and the last of the bagged items. Roberts puts his head around the door of Kristich's den to tell them he's leaving.

"Incidentally, Lavulo was a biker. He has a Crow tat on his left arm. Either of you coming to the post-mortem? About midday."

Deb says, "Will you go, Harry?"

He nods. It seems only right.

A little later they hear a commotion from the outer office. The uniformed officer at the door is arguing with a tall thin man in a dark suit.

"What's the problem?" Deb asks.

The man looks over the officer's shoulder and says, "Are you in charge?"

Harry recognises the face, deeply—perhaps prematurely—lined, the severely cut black hair. He's seen him on TV outside courtrooms, making statements on behalf of clients.

"Detective Inspector Deborah Velasco." Deb shows her ID. Harry is sure that she must recognise him, but she says, "And you are?"

"Nathaniel Horn, solicitor. My offices are on this floor. What's happened? They told me downstairs there's been a fatality."

"We're investigating that now, sir. I'll accompany you to your offices."

Horn doesn't move. "These are Alexander Kristich's rooms. He's a client of mine. What's happened?"

"Mr. Kristich is dead, sir. We're anxious to contact his next of kin. Can you help us?"

"How is he dead? I saw him yesterday evening. He was quite fit then."

"What time was that?"

"About six. I was leaving. We had a brief conversation."

"Did he tell you his plans for the evening?"

"No he did not. I do have an address for family members in Croatia, not here. Perhaps if you could tell me what happened I might be able to help you."

"We believe he died in the early hours of this morning, and we're treating his death as suspicious."

"An intruder?" For the first time Horn's face expresses something like alarm.

"Why would you say that?"

Horn's face closes down again. "What else would you mean? Now look, I am Mr. Kristich's executor, and as such I need to secure his personal papers."

He makes to move forward into the room, but Deb stands in his way. "This is a crime scene, sir. You can't come in."

"I can advise you," he says impatiently, "if anything is disturbed or missing."

"Yes, we'll need to speak to you again. In the meantime Detective Sergeant Belltree will escort you to your rooms to make sure everything is in order there."

Horn peers at Harry, then turns on his heel. As he opens his office door he looks back over his shoulder and says, "Belltree? Are you related to the judge?"

"His son."

"Really?" Horn stares at him for a long moment, registering his face. "Well . . ." he makes a theatrical sweep of his arm, "be my guest, Sergeant Belltree."

Harry has a quick look through the offices, then gets Horn to check the Croatian address of Kristich's relatives. "You didn't really expect to find anyone here, did you?" says Horn as he writes it down. Then, "It wasn't suicide was it?"

"No."

"Was it the whore? Chloe, did she kill him?"

Harry looks at him. "You think that's likely?"

"Well, that's the thing, isn't it? You never can tell."

When he returns to Kristich's suite Deb is examining a box of bullets. "Forty-fives, in a drawer in the bedroom. Does that mean the gun was Kristich's? How did it end up in Lavulo's fist?"

"Or Chloe's? Horn just asked me if she killed Kristich."

"Did he? There's traces of heroin in the bedroom and a few other stashes hidden away in various places—ecstasy and ice, I'd say. Looks to me like Kristich was dealing."

"Phone records and computer then."

"Right. And there's documents in the filing cabinets in the outer office."

They search for a while longer, then Harry suggests he take Chloe Anastos to the local station for a formal interview, and then start checking the CCTV disks. It's a relief to get out of Kristich's nest and wind down the car window and smell the fumy morning air of the city. Chloe has had a friend bring her clothes, and she is more alert. He lets her light up in the car; she sits in silence, blowing smoke out of the window. In the interview he gets her to fill in some background on her relationship with Kristich and Lavulo, then releases her.

He settles down to play the CCTV recordings, wondering what he will do if he sees himself appear. After an hour he relaxes. Jenny's intervention appears to have been faultless, with each camera showing an unvarying, eventless image between 1:46 and 2:46 that morning. He calls Deb to let her know that he hasn't been able to find any record of Lavulo entering the building and is sending the disks down to tech support for a more thorough search, then he sets off for the Glebe morgue.

Garry Roberts carries out the two post-mortems at his usual steady pace. There are no surprises, no unexplained bruises. Roberts' only comment is mild surprise at the force that Kristich must have applied to drive the knife so deep into Lavulo's chest. They will have to wait for results from the toxicology lab to find about drugs.

Harry walks out into the sunshine with a feeling of cautious relief.

FOURTEEN

KELLY POOL SLAMS ON the brakes as the radio news comes on, leading with two men found dead in a city office tower overnight. One identified as the financier Alexander Kristich, police treating the deaths as suspicious, a task force formed to investigate. She pulls into the kerb and checks the news feed on her phone. There is nothing more. She swears softly to herself. It was only two days ago that Harry gave her Kristich's name. After their meeting she did a search and came up with the link to Bluereef Financial Services and an address in the Gipps Tower. She'd been planning to go there, try for an interview, maybe trap Kristich on his way in or out. The paper wanted her at the trial of a teenage car thief in the local magistrates court, then the opening of a new wing in an Islamic primary school, and she'd left Kristich till later.

Now this. It's as if she's caught up in a firestorm, with things exploding all around her, unable to see where any of it's coming from. Tomorrow the big dailies will have profiles of the dead man, maybe dig up a few angles, but they won't know what she knows, all those tantalising connections—the couple at Balmoral Beach, the Creek, the homicide detectives sniffing around. Something big is hidden in all this, and by rights it's bloody well hers. She throws a reckless U-turn and heads into the city.

There is one police car parked up on the kerb outside the Gipps Tower, but otherwise everything seems normal. She finds a parking station and walks into the foyer of the tower, people coming and going to the lifts as if nothing unusual has happened. She checks the tenant board and takes the lift up to the twenty-third-floor lobby; she sees the name Bluereef Financial Services over to her right. Through the glass screen there's a uniformed police officer sitting just inside the door. She hesitates, and at that moment the door to one of the other suites opens and a man comes towards her. "Can I help you?"

She recognises him immediately, the black slicked hair, the hatchet face, the clipped phrasing—Nathaniel Horn, solicitor to the crims.

"Oh, um, I was hoping to see Mr. Kristich."

"I'm afraid that won't be possible. Are you a client?"

"Not exactly. I heard a news report that suggested he was dead, and I thought I should check."

"Why, may I ask?"

"I'm a reporter, Mr. Horn. Were you his solicitor?"

"I think you should leave, Ms. . . . ?"

"Only I have heard that he was mixed up in some pretty shady business deals and I wondered if that could be why he was murdered."

Horn's hand reaches out suddenly and grips her arm.

He presses his face in close. "I don't know you. What is your name? Which paper do you represent?"

"Let go of my arm or I'll call that cop."

He releases his grip. "You're out of your league, whoever you are. Get out before you get yourself into trouble."

"I can quote you on that, can I?" She turns on her heel and walks towards the Bluereef door. She takes a photo through the glass: the uniform, and behind him people removing files and putting them into evidence bags. No sign of Harry Belltree. When the cop gets to his feet she turns and heads back to the lift. As it descends she takes a deep breath, a little unsettled by Horn's venom but pleased too. There's something really big here. She needs to speak to Harry, but now is not the time. What else? Speak to Phoebe Bulwer-Knight again? Maybe she's heard something.

AS SHE PULLS INTO the kerb she sees two men—bikers wearing colours on their leathers—carrying a sideboard out of Phoebe's house to a small van. The lettering on the side of the vehicle reads *U-Remove*. Kelly goes over to them and says, "What's going on?" They glance at her through their Ray-Bans but don't reply or stop what they're doing. At the back of the van they heave the sideboard up and its corner cracks against the steel door. A piece of timber splits off and drops to the ground. Kelly goes through the open door of the house and finds two more bikers in a front room, hurriedly shoving the pieces of a fine china dinner service into a cardboard box while Phoebe looks on, kneading her hands. She recognises Kelly with a smile of confused relief but can't remember her name.

"Kelly, Kelly Pool, the reporter, Phoebe. Remember?"

"Oh, of course!"

The two men have stopped what they're doing, staring at Kelly, although the light is so dim she wonders if they can see anything through their shades.

"What's happening, Phoebe?"

"Um, these gentlemen are helping me to move."

"Really? Where are you going?"

"To stay with my sister in Lindfield, I think. I haven't seen her in twenty years. We had a falling-out but we'll have to manage now, won't we? It's very convenient where she lives, near the library." Phoebe sounds doubtful.

"But why? Why are you moving?"

"My lease has been terminated, you see. I had a letter, and then these men came with a van."

"Can I see the letter?"

Phoebe goes to her handbag and produces an envelope. The letter, dated two days ago, is from Nathaniel Horn, solicitor, on behalf of Bluereef Financial Services, owners of 8 Mortimer Street, demanding immediate evacuation of the property following non-payment of rent for a period in excess of six months.

"Phoebe, I think you should stay where you are. The owner of this company died last night and everything will be up in the air for a while. It will give you a chance to work things out properly. You should get your own solicitor to advise you. I can suggest someone local who—"

She is interrupted by one of the bikers, a huge wall of a man, who moves between them, plucking the letter from her hand and sliding it into his jacket pocket. He takes hold of Kelly's arm and bundles her out into the hallway.

When she yells for him to let go he growls, "You're trespassing, lady." He pushes her against the wall, pats her down and takes a business card from her wallet, then shoves her through the front door.

She stumbles out into the street, furious, and grabs her phone. Takes a picture of him standing there in the doorway, arms folded like a bodyguard in some ridiculous cheap movie. "Bullies!" she yells. She can see the headline, BIKER MOBSTERS: OLD LADY THROWN INTO THE GUTTER.

WHEN SHE GETS BACK to her car she sits for a moment breathing hard. She is more shaken by the encounter than she should be, and she wonders if she's getting too old for this sort of thing. She drives out of Mortimer Street and pulls over again, willing herself to calm down. But what the hell is going on? Those bikers seem to be taking over the whole of Crucifixion Creek. She needs help; thinks of Harry Belltree. It occurs to her how involved he is in this—the siege, his knowledge of Kristich, the connection to the murdered builder, the fire. Harry is involved *personally*, she thinks. She has to get him to talk.

She starts the car again and heads back to the office, where she retrieves Greg March's funeral notices, then searches company records, the phone book. Finally she grabs her bag and heads out again. There is a florist on the corner, where she buys a forty-dollar bunch of flowers before picking up her car.

The woman who answers her knock seems slightly unco-ordinated, hair awry, a flush in her cheeks. "Mrs. March?"

"Yes? Ooh . . ." Nicole stares at the flowers that Kelly thrusts at her. "They're lovely."

She's started early, Kelly thinks, then feels she's being uncharitable. Probably on sedatives.

"I'm from the *Bankstown Chronicle*, Mrs. March. Your husband worked in our area, and we wanted to express our deepest sympathies. We're all so upset at what happened."

"Oh, thank you . . ." Nicole frowns at the flowers, as if having trouble focusing. "Would you . . . ?"

"Maybe just for a minute, thank you. I don't want to intrude." Kelly steps in and closes the front door behind her. "My goodness, this is an amazing house. It's beautiful."

"Thank you. It was Greg's masterpiece."

"He built it himself?"

"Oh yes."

Kelly goes over to the top of the stairs. "And it goes down all those levels—and wow, the views!"

"Yes. Um, I'll show you if you like."

"Oh, I'd love to see. It's so original."

They go down to the main living area, Nicole clutching the flowers, a little unsteady. She puts them on a table and offers Kelly a seat.

Kelly says, "People are just so upset that this sort of

99

thing could happen, with the fire on top of everything else."

"I know." Nicole shakes her head. "I can still hardly believe it."

"I suppose the police think the two things are linked?"

"I . . . I'm not sure. I haven't spoken to them since the fire. My brother-in-law has handled all that. He's with the police."

"Really? I know some of the cops in that area. What's his name?"

"Belltree, Harry Belltree."

Kelly feels the buzz of revelation. So that's the connection. "I wonder if they think it could be to do with the bikers down there."

"Do you think so?" Nicole looks alarmed. "I hardly ever went over to Greg's depot, but I remember once I picked him up there and one of the bikers came in to see him. Greg was quite angry, and told him to go away. When I asked him about it afterwards he said they were just troublemakers. Do you know something about them?"

"There have been stories."

"You should speak to Harry. I'm sure he'd want to hear anything that might help them."

"Yes, maybe I should. Do you have his contact details?"

"I'm not sure where he's based, but I could give you his phone number." She gets her mobile phone from her handbag and gives Kelly his home and mobile numbers. "He's very nice, very approachable. I'm sure he'd like to talk to you."

"Right. I was wondering if there was a photo of Greg with the family that I might use if I can persuade my editor to do a feature?"

Nicole obliges, and Kelly jots some notes on his life and work. When she gets up to leave, Nicole says, "Of course, we had our ups and downs over the years. Being a small builder isn't easy. I remember Greg saying that he sometimes felt there was a conspiracy against him."

"Really? A conspiracy?" Damn. Too eager. Nicole's face shuts down.

"That was just his way of putting it."

Kelly thanks her and leaves.

FIFTEEN

the homicide suite at Parramatta HQ, Deb is yelling into a phone. He gets the idea that someone in authority is being uncooperative. She finally slams the phone down and glares at Harry. "Bastard lawyer Horn—he's got an injunction to prevent us accessing Kristich's computers or paperwork."

"What?" Harry pulls up a chair. "He can't do that, can he? With a homicide?"

"Well he has. He's got a magistrate to put a forty-eight-hour block on access pending a review by a higher court. Strike Force Gemini is stuffed before it's begun."

"That's very interesting, isn't it? Where are they now, the computers and paperwork?"

"We brought them back here for analysis, but our lawyers have now got them secured in a locked room that we can't get into."

"Okay, what's your theory?"

"I think . . . Lavulo and his biker mates were supplying Kristich with drugs, which he was then distributing to his business and social contacts. Lavulo came to put the squeeze on Kristich, up the price or whatever, they quarrelled and knocked each other off. Now Kristich's customers—'people of influence,' shall we say—are scared shitless that he's kept records."

Harry ponders. "Get tech support to hack into the computers?"

"Come on, Harry."

"Start preparing a case for the Crime Commission to get involved?"

"Sure, but that'll take time."

"Okay, another idea—Lavulo was a member of the Crows. That's where the drugs will have come from. We should pay them a visit."

"Raid the Crows?" Deb thinks for a moment, then begins to nod. "If we can find a link there to Kristich, then Horn's case will collapse. Let's go get the big man's OK."

"There is one thing you should know, Deb. I have a previous involvement with Kristich."

"What?"

"Well, indirectly. You know about my brother-in-law, of course. Well, I'm one of his executors, and I've had to look into his business dealings. It seems his building business was in financial trouble and he'd taken out a big loan from Kristich's company Bluereef on crippling terms. It'll probably leave my sister-in-law on the breadline, so I had a look into Kristich's background. He had a previous life as Sandi Krstić in Queensland. Sailed pretty close to the wind—I spoke to one of the cops up there who investigated him, and he was into fraud, dubious business practices. Implicated in the death of his wife, who fell from a Surfers tower block, and a man he'd ripped off who was causing trouble. Never charged. He fled to Vanuatu then reappeared down here with a change of spelling. His pattern seems to be to ingratiate himself with influential people who ease his way."

Deb frowns, staring at him. "Jeez, Harry, why didn't you tell me this before? When we were going to the Gipps Tower scene?"

"Yeah, I was surprised when you mentioned his name. I wondered if there could be another Kristich, so I didn't say anything until I was certain, but I'm telling you now. It's him all right, and I'm sure there's plenty of dirt to be dug. Maybe we should go up to Brisbane and talk to the guys there."

Deb looks thoughtful.

"Or I could withdraw from the investigation if you think I'm compromised. I've already been in enough trouble about getting involved in Greg's murder."

She thinks, then says, "I'll talk to Bob Marshall. See what he says."

"Right." He stands. "I'll get back to the Nguyen case, yes?"

She nods.

An hour later Deb comes to his desk. She looks happy. "Bob agrees about hitting the Crows. In fact he wants to be in on it personally." She grins. Detective Superintendent Bob Marshall did a number of years in SWAT teams before the TOU was formed. He makes no secret of his nostalgia for the days of more exciting policing.

"Good. Did you mention my problem?"

"Yes. He says it's okay, as long as you let us know of anything relevant in connection with your brother-in-law's dealings. He wants you on the team, Harry. So do I."

"Thanks, Deb, I appreciate it."

"There is one strange thing."

"What's that?"

"The tech guys can't find any trace of Lavulo going into the Gipps Tower."

"Really?"

"Yes. The only thing I can think is that he was able to tamper with the system. It seems he knew some of the security people on duty last night."

WHEN HE GETS HOME that evening he tells Jenny about his strange day, investigating his own crime. She listens closely, her mood swinging from horror to relief. He senses something else too, a kind of suppressed elation perhaps, that they are doing something to put things right for Greg and those he's left behind. He can't share that feeling. *I killed two men.* It's the first time he's allowed himself to articulate that thought.

He wants to talk about something else. "Any luck with the hard drive?"

"Yes. Most of the files are password protected, but I've had some successes. I'm fairly confident that I'll be able to open them all eventually. And there's one in particular . . ." Her face lights up. "It's some kind of trust fund that Kristich was managing in the name of Tubby Bell. It's worth over two million dollars. I think I can access it."

"Oh? Who's Tubby Bell?"

"I assume it was a code name he was using. And I was thinking I could divert it into another account, one that we control, for Nicole and the girls."

He stares at her, watching his beautiful damaged wife turn into a thief. It's more shocking than recognising himself as a murderer.

"He owes it to them, Harry," she insists. "I can't see Sam Peck getting anything for them, can you?"

He has to agree with that.

"Just think about it." she says. Then, "Dance with me."

He puts on one of her favourites, Sting, "When We Dance," and holds her close, thinking.

At the end of the song, still holding her, he whispers, "Kristich's lawyer's persuaded a magistrate to block our access to his computers and documents. I think there are people with influence who are worried about what we'll find. If they're successful, we could end up with the only record."

"Tell me the magistrate's name. I'll do a search for it on the hard drive."

"Yes, but Jenny, be careful. If you access anything outside of this room, transfer any moneys, whatever, you've got to be a hundred and ten per cent sure no one can trace it back to us."

"Don't worry," she says. "I understand that very well."

SIXTEEN

"SO THEY PHYSICALLY DUMPED her in the gutter, did they?"

Kelly Pool's editor, Bernie Westergard, peers at the blurry enlargement of the picture of the big biker that she took on her phone.

"Well not literally, no. It's a figure of speech."

"Not in a court of law it's not, Kelly."

"Come on, Bernie, they were forcibly evicting a confused old lady with a day's notice to quit. She's lived there for forty years, for God's sake."

"You have studied the notice to quit, I take it? Passed it through to legal?"

"No, but—"

"This is no good. You don't really know what was going on. You've gone off half-cocked here." He shoves her article and the photo back at her across his desk. "Come on, Kelly, you're an experienced reporter. This is what I'd expect from an intern."

She gathers up her work and walks stiffly away, fuming. But by the time she gets to her own desk her anger has died and doubt has seeped in to take its place.

Perhaps he's right. Perhaps she's regressed. There *is* a story there, but perhaps she's just not capable of pinning it down anymore. If she ever was. Christ! She thumps her fist on the desk in frustration. Yes, Bernie was absolutely right, it was a hopeless, sloppy, amateurish piece of work.

She packs up her things and heads off home.

Home is a ground-floor two-bedroom flat that she shares with a schoolteacher, Wendy. The other occupants in the block probably think that they're a couple, but they're not, just two middle-aged professional women who live together without too many dramas. Wendy moved in temporarily five years ago after a divorce, and stayed. She has a grown-up son who occasionally looks in. Now she is sitting at the kitchen table with a glass of white wine and a pile of school essays that she is in the process of marking.

"Hi," she says, scanning Kelly's face. "Shitty day?"

"I was manhandled by two thugs and humiliated by my editor. Otherwise fine. You?"

"The usual, staving off chaos. Why did Bernie humiliate you?" Just like Wendy to focus on the work drama and not the thugs.

"Don't want to talk about it." Kelly gets the bottle out of the fridge and pours herself a big one. She sits down with a sigh and kicks off her shoes. It's comforting to watch someone else working. Then, when the last essay is marked, she tells Wendy about her run-in with Bernie.

"Hm." Wendy thinks about it in her methodical way. "Maybe he was right, but you were right too, weren't you?

I could hear it in your voice. You know something stinks, and you want to go after it."

Wendy sometimes—no, often—has this very annoying school-teacherly way of pointing out the bleeding obvious and its inevitable consequences. It makes Kelly feel like she's back in year ten. "I think," Kelly says, refilling their glasses, "that I'll steer well clear of stinks for a while. There's a very exciting unveiling of a new set of traffic lights tomorrow that I can't wait to lavish my purple prose on."

"No you won't. I've been watching you this past week. You've got something big brewing, haven't you? This was just a little setback. You'll bounce back."

"Jeez, Wendy, sometimes you're a real pain, you know that?"

"Yes, but an honest pain. I'm usually right, aren't I?"

And Kelly subsides and starts to tell her about the big thing.

"Wow," Wendy says finally. "My kids would say that was awesome. And that was the guy in the Gipps Tower last night?"

"Yes, it's like it's erupting all around me and I'm the only one to really be able to put it all together. Except that I can't, not yet."

"You need to talk to the detective again, don't you?"

"Yeah, but he told me not to, and he'll be in the thick of this new enquiry."

"All the more reason to try."

"I can't ring him at work again, he'll go ballistic."

"What about home? Is he in the book?"

"Doubt it. But I do have his home number."

"Well go on then, try it."

Kelly does. A pleasant female voice invites her to leave a message, and after a hesitation she says, "Hello? I'd like to leave a message for Harry, if I've got the right number. It's Kelly Pool, Harry. Sorry to have to contact you again, but it's important I speak to you." She gives her number and hangs up.

IN THE DARKENED ROOM, the song comes to an end. Harry and Jenny become still, holding each other, and Harry thinks of the fairytale that haunted him as a child, the two babes lost, dying together in the wood, their bodies covered with leaves by robins. The mood is broken by the ringing of the phone, then the voice of Kelly Pool.

When the message finishes Jenny asks who she is, and Harry explains. "I don't know whether she's a loose cannon, or someone who could help us."

"How?"

"If you find something on the hard drive that they don't release, she might be one way we could get it out."

Jenny thinks about that. "Depends on whether we could rely on her to protect her sources." Then, "Invite her over."

"What, here?"

"I want to meet her."

So Harry returns the call. He hears the rising tone of relief and excitement in Kelly's voice as he tells her the Surry Hills address. "But Kelly, no one else can know about this. No one, you understand?"

"Um, yes, yes of course, Harry."

But Harry catches the slight hesitation. There is a background noise. Is someone with her? He starts to ask, but she hangs up.

Forty minutes later there is a knock on the door. Harry takes Kelly's coat and introduces her to Jenny. He watches the realisation grow in Kelly's expression as it does with everyone meeting Jenny for the first time. "Jenny lost her sight three years ago in the same car crash that killed my parents," he explains.

"Oh that's terrible, I remember that so well. I'd forgotten there was a third person in the accident though."

"If that's what it was," Harry says, then cuts her off as she begins to form a question. "Sit down, Kelly. What did you want to talk to me about?"

She takes out a recorder and he says, "No recordings. You can take notes, but no mention of our names."

"Right." She takes a deep breath. "Well, it's about Kristich, obviously, but more than that. I've brought you a copy of an exposé of Sandi Krstić. A reporter with an affiliate of ours on the Gold Coast wrote this but it was never published. There may be something in there that you haven't got from your sources. At any rate, you know that he was a white-collar crook with connections to the rich and powerful, and I think that recently he has been involved in events in Crucifixion Creek. Too many weird things have been happening—the Waterfords' suicide, the murder of the builder and fire at his depot, Councillor Potgeiter's motion—and they . . ."

"Hang on," Jenny says. "Councillor who?"

"Sorry." Kelly explains about the council resolution.

"It's just that if you knew Potgeiter, the last man on earth to have an interest in Aboriginal history, you'd see how crazy it is, him proposing to erect a monument in the new civic centre."

"Yes, so?"

"So I think he wants to free up Bidjigal Park for the council to sell. I think the common link in all of these things is properties in the Creek. Earlier today I was down there and I found the old lady who discovered the Balmoral Beach couple, and who was living in one of their Mortimer Street houses, being evicted by Crow gang members—thrown out onto the street after living there for decades. I think that Kristich was working to clear people out of the Creek. Probably acting as an agent for someone else, one of his rich mates, probably a property developer. Someone who has plans for the place."

"You sure they were Crows?" Harry asks.

"Oh yes, covered in badges and tatts. Bloody thugs, they physically threw me out. In fact, I wouldn't be surprised if the Crows are part of it. I mean, even that siege, Harry. That was an ex-Crow wasn't it?"

"But how would that be related to what you're talking about?"

"I don't know. The woman who was murdered there owned that house. Maybe he'd been sent in to make her sell up. Sounds far-fetched, doesn't it? I can't find any connection between Kristich and the Crows, or between him and the builder, but something dirty was going on down there and Kristich was in the thick of it. I can smell it."

Harry sits back, glancing at Jenny. He can read nothing from her expression. "So what are you going to do now?"

Kelly sighs. "Nothing. Not unless I can find something more. I wrote a piece for the paper about the Crows evicting the old lady and my editor threw it out. Said there was no evidence to back up the accusations I was making, and he was right. But I wondered if you've got anything on Kristich's death, something that might relate to what I'm saying? A link to a property developer maybe?"

Harry shakes his head. "No, nothing like that."

"Oh. Oh well . . ."

"Tell me, Kelly," Harry says, "if someone gave you something, someone who had to remain anonymous, could you protect their identity?"

"Yes, yes of course."

"I mean, *would* you protect their identity, no matter what they threw at you?"

"Yes. I'd go to jail, anything. I would never reveal it."

Again Harry looks at Jenny, who turns her face towards them suddenly and says, "Kelly, would you do me a favour? Would you go next door to the kitchen and make us all a pot of tea while Harry and I talk about this? You'll find everything you need in the cupboard above the sink. There's a bottle of wine in the fridge if you want that."

"Okay . . ." Kelly looks at them both and gets to her feet. "Sure."

When she's gone, closing the door behind her, Jenny says, "I like her. I think she really cares about all this."

"Not just because she's desperate?"

"She wants the story all right, but that may not be a bad thing. I think we should help her."

"Okay. But first a test." He gets to his feet and goes through to the kitchen, where Kelly is waiting for the kettle to boil. She has taken the bottle of wine out of the fridge but hasn't poured it. He picks it up and gets three glasses. "Forget about the tea. Come through."

They return to Jenny and Harry pours the wine. "Does anyone else know you're here, Kelly?" he asks.

She hesitates a moment. "Yes. I share my flat with a friend, a schoolteacher. When I got home this evening I told her about what a frustrating day I'd had, and it was she who suggested I ring you. She was there when you called back, and I told her where I was going."

"Well, thanks for telling us; I don't think we can go on without being honest with each other."

"Right. Does that mean I've blown it?"

"Not necessarily. But when you get home, tell her I wasn't able to help you and I've made you promise never to contact me again. You'll need to convince her that's true, okay?"

"All right."

"I don't know if you appreciate how vulnerable you'll be if you publish a story about Kristich and Crucifixion Creek. If the police think you have an inside source they will throw the kitchen sink at you. Track your phone, bug your flat, investigate your contacts . . . And that's just the good guys."

"Yes, okay."

"What I can tell you is known to a number of other officers, but they'll know that you've contacted me in the past, and so I'll come under suspicion. So: from now on there must be nothing to link us. It will probably be a good idea if you try to get interviews with other people in homicide and local area command. Spread the risk."

"Right, I can do that."

"Did you come down Crown Street?"

"Yes."

"There are lots of cameras there. I'll show you a route back to avoid them. What? You think I'm being paranoid? Believe me, you've got to become paranoid too. Now, regarding a link between Kristich and the Crows, I can tell you that the second person killed in Kristich's offices was a man named Benji Lavulo, a member of the Crows."

"Brilliant! How do you spell that?"

"His name has not been released. Probably won't be for another day or two."

"Why not?"

"No comment. The second thing I can tell you is that Kristich had a lawyer by the name of Nathaniel Horn."

"I met him. I went to the Gipps Tower and bumped into him on the twenty-third floor."

"You went up there?"

"Yes, just for a look. I didn't get anything from Horn except a faceful of menace. He was very hostile."

"Well, it's probably good that you've had a brush with him. He's persuaded a court to block police access to Kristich's papers and computers."

"So there's stuff in them that he doesn't want made public."

"Presumably."

"Anything else?"

"There may well be some kind of police action against the Crows within the next day or two. I'll try to give you a warning so you can cover it. You shouldn't publish anything beforehand, but aim to have it out as soon afterwards as you can."

"That's great!" Kelly is excited, writing quickly in her notebook. "How about the builder? You knew him, didn't you? Was he connected to Kristich in some way?"

"No comment." Harry reaches into his bag and hands her a mobile phone. "Never contact me using your or my phones again. Use this one if you have to. There's a number in its address book where you can get me."

"Okay."

"As soon as you breathe a word of what you now know, Kelly, you're in the firing line. Remember that."

She says goodbye to Jenny, who wishes her luck. Harry describes the camera-free route out of Surry Hills and at the front door he stops her, speaking softly so that his wife won't hear. "Kelly, I want you to think about Jenny and how vulnerable she is. If anything happens to her because you screw up, you'll answer to me."

She holds his gaze and says, "You can trust me, Harry."

SEVENTEEN

AT TWO THE FOLLOWING afternoon they all gather in the operations room—the Strike Force Gemini detectives from homicide and local command, inspectors from the gangs and drugs squads, and three representatives of the Tactical Operations Unit, including Deb's partner, Damian Berardi. Deb introduces them as they wait for things to start, and he takes Harry's hand in a hard grip. "Hi, Harry," he growls. "Good to meet you at last. Deb's told me all about you."

"All good I hope, Damian. She hasn't told me a thing about you." They grin at each other as if these platitudes hide some common knowledge.

Bob Marshall opens the proceedings, emphasising speed, control and secrecy. He spells out the aims of the operation, to find evidence of criminal activities including drug use and possession of illegal firearms and other weapons, but most importantly to seize documentary evidence of illegal operations, clients and collaborators in the form of notebooks, files, computers, phones and other electronic devices. All such documentary evidence will be handed over immediately to a special task unit which will have its own vehicle and will, with tech support, begin recording and analysing such materials as soon as they become available. Everyone found within the premises will be cautioned and taken to the local station for processing and held for interview.

He hands over to the senior TOU officer, who describes the target, the fortified clubhouse of the Crow motorcycle gang at the south end of Mortimer Street. On the wall are enlargements of maps, street plans and aerial photographs taken that morning by a helicopter of the Aviation Support Branch. There are potential difficulties in the approach along Mortimer Street to the main doors of the compound; the street is narrow and most of the houses are now believed to be occupied by Crow members and their families. There's an alternative approach from the other side of the clubhouse, through the premises of a shipping container yard separated from the compound by a high wall topped by razor wire. A second warrant has been obtained for entry to the yard for that purpose.

Deb Velasco, as operational head of Strike Force Gemini, then outlines the plan, identifying the members of each group and their tasks. When she finishes they break down into their teams to work out their individual roles. Harry is to head the group tasked with searching for the documentary evidence. They itemise the equipment they will need and plan how they will work their way through the building. There are no internal plans of the clubhouse and its ancillary buildings and only a hazy notion of what they may find inside. They talk about safes and electronic equipment and possible hiding places.

And then they wait. The raid begins at 8:00 p.m., when they hope they'll find the most bikers inside. They break up to get their gear together, to have a meal and a rest, and to phone home. Harry uses another unsourced mobile to send a text to Kelly, "20:00."

HARRY AND HIS TEAM are in an unmarked white van, the fourth vehicle in a convoy of five for the initial assault. In the lead is the TOU's black Lenco carrying Berardi and his ninja mates. They drive at speed down Mortimer Street without obstruction and come to a halt in front of the heavy steel gates. Behind them the fifth vehicle stops to form a barricade across the street entrance. Uniformed police pour out of it and deploy along the street to prevent people coming out of the houses. The arrest teams in the second and third vans wait as the loudspeaker in the Lenco announces the raid and demands that the gates be opened.

Without a pause for a reply, the back of the truck opens and armed men in black jump out, among them a pair carrying a thermal lance. They run to the gate and get to work on the hinges, the plasma beam slicing through the steel like ice cream until they jump back and wave at the truck to rev up and charge the gates. The impact sends the gates crashing back into the yard behind and the assault and arrest teams race in. There is the noise of an explosion from inside the compound.

To Harry, standing waiting behind his van, the scene has an unreal quality. There has been no sign of life from the compound or from the houses along the street. He looks up at the deserted lookout tower above the clubhouse and thinks of Afghanistan, tenses for the zip of incoming fire but there is nothing, only the barking of a dog. He leads his team towards the gates.

As they step over the flattened steel they are met by a smell of dust and burning. They are on one side of a yard about twenty metres square, in which stand several Harley-Davidsons and some brightly coloured children's play equipment. The high wall on the far side of the square has a hole blown in it and the second assault team is climbing in from the container lot. Debris from the explosion has knocked over a couple of the bikes and buckled a swing.

The door of the clubhouse stands open and Harry walks in, then stops as he takes in a bizarre tableau. Four men—like cartoon bikers with their beards, ponytails and tattoos—are sitting around a table calmly playing cards, seemingly oblivious to the black uniforms and bristling weapons that surround them. There is a pool table over to one side, and on the wall beyond it a huge shield bearing the Crow colours above a red banner inscribed with black lettering: WE CRUSH OUR ENEMIES.

Deb is yelling at the card players, attempting to get them to identify themselves. When they ignore her she has them hauled to their feet and their wallets searched. They are the club president Roman Bebchuk, the vice-president Frank Capp, the sergeant-at-arms Hakim Haddad and a fourth biker, Thomas O'Brian. Harry recognises O'Brian. Their eyes meet briefly before the man turns his head.

Beyond them Harry sees a door into a back room, which he discovers to be a small office, and he leads his team in there to begin gathering up a collection of battered paperbacks, a DVD set of *Sons of Anarchy*, a computer and a number of note and account books. While they work, Harry examines a collection of business cards in a plastic tub. Among them he finds a card for *Chieftain Smash Repairs*. He makes a note of the address in Mascot and bags the cards. There is a safe in the corner of the room, a relatively new strongly armoured steel box with a digital lock. It probably weighs over three hundred kilograms, and when the card players refuse to disclose the combination the thermal lance comes out again. When the door is off they find club badges, DVDs, a large wad of Australian currency and a number of large plastic bags filled with a white crystalline substance.

Harry calls Deb in and her face lights up with relief. They have found little else to justify the raid, but this should be enough.

THE FOUR MEN ARE taken to the local police station for interview. All four nominate Nathaniel Horn as their lawyer and refuse to speak until he arrives, which takes some time. While they wait, Bob Marshall calls a strategy meeting. The inspector from the gangs squad goes over what is known of the Crows. There isn't much to tell. They are a single-clubhouse gang which split off eight years ago from one of the bigger clubs in the city's west to establish their own territory based around Crucifixion Creek. Until now they have kept a low profile. Bebchuk, the president, has a history of drugs and violence and spent some years with an outlaw club in California. Harry tells them that he knew O'Brian, the fourth card player, in the army in Afghanistan. They served in the same special forces company.

"His nickname was Rowdy," Harry explains, "because he was a man of few words. We won't get anything out of him."

They debate whether Harry should conduct the interview with O'Brian, but in the end Marshall vetoes the idea. "Let's see how it goes," he says. "We'll hold Harry back in case we need to go about it a different way."

Harry wonders what that might be.

Deb and the gangs inspector will lead the interview teams, with Harry, Bob Marshall and a number of others observing on the big screen in the theatrette on the next floor. There is a subdued air of disappointment among the observers as they take their seats to await the first interview. More was expected from the raid. But Marshall lightens the mood with stories of past raids, the gaffes and cock-ups and bloody-minded obstructionism, which get them all laughing.

"Ah, here comes the vulture," Marshall says at last, and they straighten in their seats, watching the black-suited figure of Nathaniel Horn entering the interview room. For a brief moment the lawyer glances up at the camera, and Harry feels a frisson go through the watchers.

There follow two hours of tedious silences, "no comment's and inarticulate grunts. Gradually however a defence position becomes clear—Benji Lavulo is to be blamed for everything. Benji was the club treasurer and, so it is claimed, the only one who knew the safe combination. The gangs inspector's incredulity at this suggestion is met with blank innocence. Benji was a bit of a loner, apparently. Secretive. They have no idea what he might have been doing in the office of Alexander Kristich, a man of whom they have never heard.

While this is going on, a note is passed to Superintendent Marshall from technical support. The white crystals are indeed methamphetamine, and a single set of fingerprints has been identified on the plastic bag as matching those of Benji Lavulo. Marshall vents a loud obscenity and sinks lower in his seat.

In the early hours of the morning the four men are charged with several offences that probably won't stand up and released on police bail. A despondent Strike Force Gemini and its support team disperse into the night.

MEANWHILE, NOT FAR AWAY, the only person who is pleased by the evening's events is sitting in her living room finishing a bottle of wine. Having snapped a few pictures of the Mortimer Street raid with the paper's telephoto lens camera, Kelly dashed to the office and finished her new article inspired by Harry's revelations in time to meet the deadline set by Bernie Westergard for the next day's edition. Bernie was waiting in his office with a sour expression on his face when she rushed in and slapped the piece down in front of him. He frowned and shook his head at the title, "Biker gang link to CBD murders," but read on, ominously silent as he turned the pages and examined the pictures.

Finally he said, "You've shown this to the lawyers?"

"All but the bit about the police raid. I was the only reporter there, Bernie. That's a scoop. It all is."

"Are you going to tell me your source?"

"No. I can't. That was a strict condition of them speaking to me."

"But they would be in a position to know all this stuff about Lavulo and the Kristich files?"

"Oh yes."

"So, a member of the police." He looked at her, considering. "They'll go for you, Kelly, you and the paper. There'll be pressure. You ready for that?"

"Absolutely."

"Hm. Of course, they may be pleased to have it out in the open. But they'll still go for us."

And that's when Kelly knew he was going to print it.

So now she sits alone in her living room savouring the moment, trying to be temperate in her enjoyment of a feeling she hasn't had for a very long time. She aims for a campaign that will build momentum, sweeping her irresistibly upward. First she must establish her credibility. Tomorrow is only the beginning.

EIGHTEEN

THEY ARE QUIET THE next morning, filing into the office, yawning from the adrenaline hangover. On the way in Harry buys a copy of the *Bankstown Chronicle*. Kelly's story is the lead on page one, complete with a dramatic picture of the TOU forcing their way into the Crow compound. The article reveals the name of the second dead man in the Gipps Tower and his association with the Crows, and links this to the police raid and to other disturbances in the Creek. It doesn't mention the suppression of Kristich's files. Harry wonders why not. He dumps the paper before he reaches work.

Mid-morning Deb emerges from Superintendent Marshall's office and says, "Something's up. The boss got called upstairs suddenly."

Marshall returns half an hour later, clutching a newspaper that Harry recognises. His face is set in a puzzled scowl. He calls Deb and Harry in to his office.

"Seen this?" He hands them the paper.

Deb says, "Kelly Pool . . . Isn't that the reporter that spoke to you, Harry?"

"At the Stefan Ganis siege, sir. That's her beat. She recognised me, wanted to ask questions. Persistent too. She's tried to contact me a couple of times since, here and at home. What's she got?"

Marshall frowns at him before replying. "She knows that the other victim with Kristich was a Crow. Knows his name. How?"

"Security at the Gipps Tower identified Lavulo," Deb says. "Could be them."

Marshall thinks about that. He obviously likes the idea. "All right. Let's just make sure no one in this building is leaking. The lawyers think we'll get a ruling on the Kristich material today. They're hopeful. How about the Crow records?"

"Coming through bit by bit. So far the most interesting thing is copies of old invoices for dietary health supplements. A Chinese company based in Vanuatu, suspected in the past of selling pseudoephedrine and benzyl chloride."

"Which powerfully suggests a Crow meth kitchen somewhere," Marshall nods. "Good. But unless we can prove that anyone apart from Lavulo was involved we may have trouble making a case. So, Harry, how well did you know O'Brian?"

"Pretty well. Six months together in Kandahar province in 2002. He was a very good soldier."

"Will he talk to you?"

"He might, but I don't think he'll sell out his mates."

"Okay, but you could suggest that information about what Lavulo was doing in Kristich's office might take some of the heat off him and his mates. Anything else he can tell you about what the Crows are up to could be helpful." He taps the newspaper. "It says here they've been evicting people from houses in the area. What's that about? And what was the connection with the Ganis siege down the road from their clubhouse?"

Harry nods. "Right."

"The guys are monitoring all their phones. They'll give you his number."

When Harry gets back to his desk he gets O'Brian's number and makes the call. He hardly recognises the voice that answers, distant, suspicious of the unknown caller ID. "Rowdy, hello. This is Harry Belltree."

"Oh yeah?" He doesn't sound surprised.

"Can you talk?"

"What about?"

"I'd like to meet you."

"Not a good idea."

"See the *Bankstown Chronicle* this morning? I might be able to help take the heat off you blokes."

"Why would you do that?"

"Just a chat, Rowdy. No pressure."

There is a long pause. "Where?"

"Wherever you feel comfortable. Your choice of place and time."

"I'll get back to you."

The line goes dead.

"Any luck?" Deb has been listening.

"I don't know. He said he'll get back to me."

She nods. "That Kelly Pool, bit bloody cheeky phoning you at home, Harry."

"I thought so."

"What'd she want from you?"

"I don't know, I cut her off. Maybe she was looking for someone to confirm the Lavulo tip."

"Hm."

"That business about a Chinese company in Vanuatu. Kristich spent time in Vanuatu when he left Queensland. Maybe we should find out who his contacts were over there."

"Yeah, good idea. Why don't you do that?"

Ten minutes later Harry's phone rings. O'Brian will meet him in an hour in the first-floor café of David Jones at Elizabeth Street in the city.

"Funny choice," Deb says.

"Probably the last place his biker friends would go."

AND IT IS CERTAINLY that, the café full of lady shoppers from the suburbs laden with DJ department store bags. Rowdy is already there, glowering, at a table in the far corner. As Harry shakes hands and sits down, a waiter appears and reels off a list of the special teas. They order black coffee.

"My boss reckoned you chose this place because none of your mates would come here."

"So they put you up to this, did they?" He studies Harry's face, as if trying to restore some lost memory.

"Yeah."

Rowdy nods and Harry says,

"Anyway, good to see you again. How have you been?"

"Not bad. You?"

Harry shrugs. "Bit of a hard time adjusting when I got back. Settled down eventually."

Rowdy nods. "So you joined the big blue gang and I joined the Crows. Comrades in arms, Harry, just like the army. Hard and loyal. So don't expect me to dob them in."

"That's what I told my boss."

"What does he want you to do?"

Rowdy has changed. There is a flat tone in his voice, like that of a man grimly determined not to show that he doesn't much care anymore.

"He wants to know what Lavulo was doing in Kristich's office the night they killed each other."

"Is that what happened?"

"Forensics says there's no other explanation."

"So what's your theory?"

"Kristich had a stash of crystal meth in his office safe. They'll try to match it to the stuff they found in yours. Is that right? Was Lavulo supplying Kristich? Did they fall out over a sale?"

O'Brian's face hardens. "I don't know anything about meth."

"Yeah, I didn't think it was your scene." He shrugs. "People change."

"Not me, not about that."

This hints at a point of friction within the gang, and if Rowdy were a suspect in the interview room Harry would press harder. He decides to let it go for now.

The waiter arrives with their coffees. "Sure I can't tempt you boys to one of our special cakes?"

Rowdy says, "Fuck off." He glowers at Harry. "Anything else your boss wants to know?"

"What's all this in the paper about you guys kicking old ladies out of their homes?"

"That's crap. She was moving. They were doing her a favour, helping her load her stuff into the removals van."

"Okay."

"Anything else?"

"That's about it." Harry sips at the coffee. "There is something I'd like to ask, not for my boss. For me."

"What's that?"

"A while ago, my mum and dad were killed in a car smash, and my wife was blinded."

"Oh." O'Brian frowns. "That's bad."

"Yeah. It's become a bit of an obsession with me. An unhealthy obsession, according to the people I work for. The thing is, the coroner recorded an open verdict—the skid marks were unusual and the investigators couldn't tell if it was an accident or if the car was deliberately run off the road. They were in a silver BMW, but there were traces of white paint on one wing. And a patrol car reported seeing a white tow truck further down the highway at around the time it happened, but it's never been traced."

Harry pulls out a copy of the photo of the tow truck he found in the siege house. He shows it to O'Brian. "Like I said, I've got a bit obsessive, especially about tow trucks. I found this picture on the wall of the house where that siege was a few weeks back, near your clubhouse. I assume it belonged to Stefan Ganis, the guy who died there. He was ex-Crow. Can you tell me anything about this?

This is personal, Rowdy. I won't pass it on if you don't want me to."

O'Brian fingers the picture, silent. Finally he says, "When I first joined we had a different president, guy called Tony Gemmell. He was the one who led the break-away from our old club and set the Crows up in the Creek. Great character, ex-army, Vietnam. Great guy. But he was getting on. He'd taken a battering over the years and his hips and knees were playing up. Got so he couldn't really handle the bike—fell over a couple of times, looked bad. We were getting new recruits, guys who hadn't been with us when the Crows were founded. One of them was Roman Bebchuk. He thought Tony was a joke, and persuaded a circle of guys around him that we needed a new president. Things got a bit heated, and in the end Tony decided to quit. When he left, Bebchuk was elected president and his blokes took over. Including Stefan Ganis. He was always a bit of a problem—erratic, a bit crazy. Eventually, about a year ago, he stepped badly out of line and Bebchuk was forced to kick him out. He hung around the fringes of the club for a while causing trouble, until eventually, I don't know what happened, he got into that blue with his woman and got himself killed."

All this comes out in a rapid low monotone. After his previous terseness Harry wonders if it contains some-thing Rowdy particularly wants him to understand.

"And yes, he had a tow truck. That one. I recognise the logo, *13 Auto Smash*. He was in business with his cousin, but they closed the yard years ago. I don't know what happened to the truck."

"What happened to the cousin?"

Rowdy shakes his head. "No idea."

"Know his name?"

Another shake.

"Well, when was it they closed the yard?"

Rowdy thinks, stroking his beard. "Around the time there was the bust-up with Tony Gemmell. That was three years ago, winter, like now. That's all I can tell you." He checks his watch. "Meter."

Harry nods. "Thanks, Rowdy." He waves for the bill and the waiter approaches cautiously. Harry pays and they rise to leave.

At the door O'Brian turns to him and says, "Watch out for Bebchuk, mate. Hard is one thing, but Bebchuk is mean."

They make their way down to the ground floor and walk through the cosmetics counters towards the street doors. A woman's voice calls out, "Rowdy? Is that you? What ya doin here?" Rowdy mutters a curse and Harry walks quickly away.

On his way back he detours through Mascot. Among the light industrial sheds and warehouses and car hire depots near the airport he finds the smash repair place on the business card. It appears deserted, an empty concrete yard protected by a chain link fence, and a shed that looks unoccupied. He gets out to take a closer look and a large Alsatian lopes out from behind the shed and snarls at him. He continues to his office and reports to Deb on his meeting with O'Brian.

"It was pretty much what I expected; he wouldn't say anything against his mates and claimed he knew nothing about drugs and had no idea what Lavulo was doing in Kristich's office. The only thing I picked up was a hint that there are divisions within the Crows, between Bebchuk's inner circle and the rest like O'Brian."

"Your mate's trying to distance himself in case we find out more about the drugs," Deb says.

HE LEAVES WORK EARLY and heads home feeling dispirited.

Jenny is at her computer surrounded by papers scattered all over the desk and the floor around her. "I've got in a tangle," she says, flustered. "It's all so complicated and I've messed up the hard copies I was making for you. I've no idea where they all are now." As she gets up she scuffs them with her feet, sending them fluttering.

"It doesn't matter. We can sort it out later." He reaches for her and draws her close. "I was thinking, why don't we just sell up and get out of Sydney."

"What? Are you joking? Where would we go?"

"I don't know—Switzerland maybe. That place we read about with the eye clinic. Somewhere with clean mountain air and real winters, with snow crunching under our feet."

She laughs. "What brought this on?"

He tells her about his meeting with Rowdy O'Brian. "I think he's burnt out. Am I like that?"

"No." She strokes his arm. "Anyway, we can't go anywhere until we've sorted all this out. Nicole needs us."

"I know."

"She's not doing well. She's had a row with Mum. Well, you know what Mum can be like."

He does. She's getting more impatient as she grows older.

"Nicole's coming round with the girls in twenty minutes. I'm sorry. I had to ask her over. She needs to talk."

"Sure. I'll get changed."

By the time he's ready they're here. He listens to them through the bedroom door, the girls' happy cries dying away as Nicole starts to rant. She stops abruptly, forcing a smile as he emerges. He says hello, hugging them in turn, then says, "Hey girls, we need stuff from Thomas Dux. Want to give me a hand?"

"Yes!"

Jenny whispers her thanks. She gives them a list of the groceries they need, and they collect bags and take off down the lane and up to Crown Street. The girls love exploring this area, the glimpses into cafés, bars, odd interiors. They are stopped by an old man whose eyes light up at the sight of the two girls. He wants them to try something that he holds out in a grubby paper bag. They move on and come to the grocer. Both girls grab baskets and run down the aisles, soaking up the smells, grabbing bread, bunches of vegetables, fruit. They fill up the bags and return to the street, paying a visit to a butcher. Harry buys wine and, laden, they turn back for home. On the way they come to a small playground, deserted. The girls drop their bags and run for the swings.

He watches them, egging each other on to reach higher. They're too old for this, he thinks. It's like they need to go back to a less complicated time for a little while. When they reach home they grow silent again, hearing their mother through the closed kitchen door, raging, weeping.

Harry searches for something loud and distracting and shoves an old DVD into the player. It is a Disney animation, a favourite of theirs four or five years ago. Harry watches with them, stabbed by the thought that the last time they played this Jenny saw it too.

After a while the kitchen door opens and Jenny calls to him softly. He gets up and joins them, closing the door. Nicole has been weeping, her eyes red, and she is gulping a large glass of wine. Jenny sounds hesitant as she begins.

"Nicole has been talking about their finances, darling. There seems—"

Nicole cuts in, her voice angry. "Sam Peck is bloody useless, Harry. He doesn't give me any idea what's going on. All he says is not to spend any money! That's ridiculous. When I told him I had to pay the girls' school fees he said I shouldn't." She glares. "Their fucking school fees, Harry! Of course I've got to pay."

"It's not Sam's fault," Harry says gently. "The fire destroyed most of Greg's records and he's got a terrible job trying to work things out."

"But the bank will still have their records, won't they? They can still tell us how things stand, surely? Sam's so bloody secretive. I wonder if he's trying to rob me."

"No, no. I've been keeping in close touch with him."

"He asked me if I had any money of my own that I could use, but I have almost nothing. The electricity bill just came in and the rates and he tells me I can't write any cheques or use the credit card. Then he suggested I sell some jewellery for God's sake—my jewellery!"

"Look, we can help out until things get cleared up."

"I don't want money from you!"

"Just a temporary loan. How much are the school fees?"

She tells him and he wonders if he misheard. He had no idea they would be so much. He sees the surprise on Jenny's face, then she recovers. "We can cover that, can't we, Harry?"

"Yes, sure." He has to think about it. "Tomorrow lunchtime, we'll set up a new account for you with our bank, Nicole, and I'll transfer some funds to see you through this sticky patch."

"Oh . . ." Nicole sags and the tears begin to flow again. "Thank you," she sobs. "I just didn't know what to do. I'm lost without him."

"Now come on," Jenny urges her. "Help me make dinner for us all. What did you get, Harry?"

LATER HE TAKES THEM home and when he returns Jenny is sitting at her computer. He feels a strange pang of jealousy, watches her intimacy with the machine, then she turns towards him and removes her headset and smiles, and he just feels tired.

"Are they all right?"

"I guess so. I didn't have the heart to tell her the house will have to go."

"What about that account I found? I think she's entitled to it."

"I don't know, Jenny. We don't know who the money belongs to, do we?"

"Bells. The name came up again in the files I managed to get into today, and other names, all nicknames—Rooster, Crystal, Pol, Chippy. Could be anybody. I think they must all be crooks. Don't you? Why else disguise their real names?"

He is silent for a while, then says, "I've been thinking about that name, Bells. Suppose it stands for Belltree?"

"What? How could it be?"

"My dad. Could it be him?"

Her mouth drops open. "But . . . why would your father have an account with Kristich?"

"Perhaps he was bent too. How can I tell?"

"Oh, Harry." She goes to him. "How can you think that?"

"How well did I know him, really?"

She shakes her head. "I think your work is getting to you."

"Yeah, well, we thought Greg was straight, didn't we?"

"He was just desperate. Come on, let's go to bed, you're exhausted."

"We should sort through your printouts."

"They'll keep."

That night he dreams he is trapped in a room with a cast of strange characters—Rooster, Crystal, Pol, Chippy. He has a gun, and they are waiting for Bells to join them. His arrival is imminent, almost palpable, and Harry protests, "Why do I have to do it?"

NINETEEN

THE NEXT MORNING HARRY picks up the papers at Central Station before catching the train out to Parramatta. Another Kelly Pool scoop fills the front page of the *Bankstown Chronicle*, ATTEMPT TO SUPPRESS KRISTICH FILES. Harry smiles to himself, she's spinning it out. The story continues on pages two and three, with pictures of Kristich at social functions alongside celebrities and politicians. On page four there is an account of the recent crime scenes in and around Crucifixion Creek, with a map and more photographs. Finally, the paper's editorial follows up, raising questions about Kristich's activities and his connections with the Crows. It's almost as if the *Chronicle* has decided to become a single-issue paper. The other dailies have followed in its wake, printing versions of Kelly's revelations of yesterday.

When he gets to the eighth floor he finds everyone reading the *Chronicle*. There are muttered expletives, "How the hell did they know that?" Deb is on the phone. She gets to her feet and calls him over. "Your girlfriend's hit the jackpot today, Harry. The boss wants to see us."

Marshall is sitting at his desk, wearing his uniform and an angry frown. He takes one of his antacid pills before he speaks.

"I'm going to Jack D'Arcy's funeral in an hour. The commissioner will be there, and she'll be wanting answers. Where did this come from? Not from the coroner's office, not from the ambos. This time there's no fucking doubt, is there? It's come from here, from Strike Force Gemini, from us!" His fist comes down on the copy of the *Bankstown Chronicle* lying on his desk. "So who's the ratbag pig's arse leak?"

Deb takes a deep breath. The whole floor must have heard his roar through the thin partitions. "I've no idea, sir."

"Well, you'd better find out, Inspector! It's your bloody strike force."

"Could it have come from the legal office, sir?"

Marshall growls, baring his teeth. "Find out. I don't want vague speculation, I want answers."

"I suppose," Deb says cautiously, "it could work in our favour, if it puts pressure on them to release Kristich's computer. That's what we really need for a breakthrough."

"Are you telling me, *Inspector*, that your bloody team deliberately leaked this information to the press in order to cruel the lawyers?"

"No, sir, of course not."

"Well . . ." Marshall's mood seems to take an abrupt swing. "In your shoes I might have done it, years ago. But these days it's not on, Deb. It's just not on. The bloody lawyers have got us all by the throat. They'll crucify whoever did this, if they catch them. And the commissioner's a careful woman."

"Well, we'll do our best."

"Yes, yes." He says it without much conviction. "Course you will."

When they get outside Harry remarks that she handled it well.

She stops, pulling him aside out of sight of the others. "Are you the ratbag pig's arse, Harry? Are you Kelly Pool's little helper?"

"Don't you trust me?"

"I don't know, Harry. She seemed very friendly."

"Tap her phone, then. Bug her home, her office."

Deb stares at him for a moment, then says, "It's already done," and marches away.

AT LUNCHTIME HARRY TAKES a car into the city and meets Nicole to take her to the bank where she opens a new account, into which he transfers an initial deposit.

When they get back to the car he says, "That'll tide you over for now. I'll make arrangements to transfer more shortly. You should talk to the school. I'm sure they'll help you work something out. They won't want people saying they acted harshly."

"Yes, I'll do that. The trouble is, with all this in the papers now about the bikers and the Creek, I'm afraid people will think Greg was mixed up with them somehow, what with the fire and everything. I still don't understand what he was doing out there in the middle of the night."

"He was just working late at the depot. It was the end of the tax year and his books were in a mess."

"I suppose so."

"Have you thought about going back to work, Nicole? Get out of the house, meet new people, start a new life?"

"Oh . . . I don't know. It feels too soon."

"Yeah, sure. Sorry."

"Don't be." She puts a hand on his arm. "I do appreciate all you're doing for me, Harry. Jenny's very lucky. You're a good man. I've always known that. And I know how difficult the last few years have been for you. It must be so hard, living with someone and unable to see things together, or share a meaningful look."

It's an awkward moment. He starts the car and drives her home, then returns to headquarters. On the way he switches on the news. The New South Wales opposition has attacked the state attorney-general and the police minister over their handling of the Kristich affair, alleging a cover-up. When he gets back to the office he finds people tidying their desks and putting on their ties. Strike Force Gemini is to be visited by some important people.

It's four in the afternoon before the team is assembled in the briefing room and Detective Superintendent Marshall escorts the visitors in. He introduces the commissioner and the police minister, Derryn Oldfield. The minister steps forward. The audience sits stony-faced, bracing for a politician's platitudes and waffle, but when he begins to speak Harry senses a shift of mood. Oldfield is direct, without any of the bluster of parliament.

"If you were listening to the radio earlier today you'll know that the attorney-general and I have come under attack over the Kristich murder enquiry, and I wanted to come here today to say that you have my complete support. I understand that you are working to resolve a difficult case under trying conditions of press speculation and legal obstruction, but I have confidence that you will not be deflected from your duty to bring all the facts out into the light of public scrutiny, no matter how embarrassing they may be for some people. And to that end, I am very happy to inform you that we have just received word that the Supreme Court has now cleared your access to all of the material seized under authorised warrants, including Alexander Kristich's computer."

There is a stir of interest, then someone begins clapping and others join in. Oldfield continues, about the importance his government attaches to the war on organised crime, outlaw motorcycle gangs and public corruption.

As he speaks, Harry watches him closely, troubled by some memory. He has seen his face many times before on TV and in the press, but he tries to recall a more recent sighting, and then it comes to him, the image of Sandi Krstić in Vanuatu with the Australian high commissioner. Could that have been Derryn Oldfield, now a member of the New South Wales upper house and minister of police? Harry joins in the applause as Oldfield finishes his speech and the commissioner steps forward with a brief, brisk demand for progress.

The meeting breaks up, but before the VIPs leave Marshall brings Oldfield over to meet Deb as head of Strike Force Gemini. When they've exchanged a few words he also introduces Harry, standing next to her.

"Belltree?" Oldfield says. "Interesting name. Any relation to the judge?"

"Yes, sir. He was my father."

"Really? Well, well. I didn't know he had a son. You
have big shoes to fill."

"Yes. You knew him?"

"By reputation of course, and we did meet a few
times." He turns to Marshall and says, "I'm afraid I must
be getting back to Macquarie Street, Bob. Good to meet
you, Harry, and you too Deb. Let me know if there's anything I can do to help with the good work," and he gives
them a big smile and walks away.

Several hours later they are packing up for the night
when two people arrive from technical support. Deb
welcomes them and everyone clusters around.

"So what have you got for us?" she asks.

They glance at each other, then the senior one, Yeang,
says, "Nothing."

"Oh. Well, how long is it going to take?"

"No, I mean there's nothing. Kristich's hard drive is
empty."

"Empty?" Deb stares at him, incredulous. "How can
it be? You mean someone's deleted the files?"

"No, if they were just deleted we could retrieve them,
but the drive has been wiped."

"You'll have to explain that, mate."

"Well, someone's used a drive-wipe utility on it that
overwrites the data with ones and zeros, so it's hard to
read. The utility can make as many passes over the data
as you want, although it takes time, and each pass makes
the data harder and harder to retrieve. The Department

of Defence specifies three passes for most material, but you can do more."

"And this one?"

"It's had a lot more. It's impossible to retrieve anything."

There are groans of disbelief.

Deb says, "When was this done?"

"Couldn't say."

"I mean, before or after we took possession of it?"

"We can't tell. I'm sorry."

The boss is in a meeting at police headquarters in the city. Deb says she has to speak to him urgently and eventually he comes to the phone. She explains what's happened, then hands over to Yeang who says it all again.

Harry murmurs to Deb, "How did he take it?" and she shrugs.

"Disbelief. I mean, how is this possible, Harry? What's going on?"

WHEN HE GETS HOME he searches out the photograph of Kristich in Vanuatu. The caption doesn't name the high commissioner, but he looks very similar to Oldfield. He tells Jenny about it, and she says it shouldn't be hard to check. While she does it, she says, "I think there are pictures among that stuff I printed off yesterday. Though I couldn't see, of course." She smiles towards where she supposes he is, although she's slightly off-target, and he thinks of Nicole's remarks in the car earlier. Her manner was intimate, almost flirtatious. Or had he imagined that?

He picks up the stack of printouts and begins to leaf through them. If Kristich had a file of photographs on his computer Jenny hasn't found it yet. But there is one picture that seems to be part of an email Christmas greeting. The message reads, "We three kings . . . Merry Christmas guys." The sender is "Chocky" and the photograph is of three men seated in the stern of a yacht, grinning, wearing dark glasses, stripped to the waist, raising champagne flutes at the camera. On the left is Kristich, in the centre the high commissioner figure from the Vanuatu picture, and on the right someone Harry doesn't recognise.

"Yes," Jenny says. "Derryn Oldfield was the Australian high commissioner to Vanuatu between 2004 and 2006. He was elected to the Legislative Council in the 2007 election."

"How about Chocky? Have you come across that before?"

"Oh yes, another nickname I suppose."

"Yes. I think he's one of these three guys." He describes the picture.

Jenny sighs. "I wish I could see it. I may have missed so many things."

"Don't worry, we'll do it together."

They work through the material that Jenny has been able to retrieve so far from the hard drive, Harry making notes, trying to find connections. After a while she says, "I've been trying to work out these nicknames. It would be so much easier if we knew who they were."

"Yes."

"Pol, for instance. Could that mean a policeman, or a

politician? Maybe Rooster is a rugby league player or fan. I've found another like that—NRL, National Rugby League? And Crystal? Is that a reference to crystal meth? A drug dealer? Bebchuk?"

"Could be. What about Kristich himself?"

"Oh, that's obvious from the correspondence. He signs himself '47.' "

"Why 47?" Harry ponders. "Kristich, Alexander Kristich, AK—AK47! It's cryptic, like a crossword puzzle. Maybe they're all like that. Maybe we should list the people we know he knew, and try to match them to a clue. What about his two victims—Greg and the old couple."

"What was their name?"

"Waterford."

"Well, how about Waterford Crystal? And 'Chippy,' that could be Greg. He was a carpenter."

They play it like a game together, coming up with outrageous puns and obscure references.

"What about Oldfield?" Harry asks, and Jenny stares up at the ceiling for a moment, then says, "Tubular Bells! You remember? Mike Oldfield?"

"Bells." Is that possible? Oldfield, not Dad. "You could be right. Are there other references to Bells apart from the offshore bank account?"

"I think there were a couple of emails . . ." She asks her computer to find them. "Yes, the latest last month, the thirteenth, from Kristich to Bells. *Thanks for coming round last night, mate. Got that sorted. All good, 47.*"

So Bells is still around. Definitely not his father. Harry relaxes, relieved and ashamed. "In that case," he says, "I think you should go ahead and take that money for Nicole. Are you sure you can do it without it being traced back to you?"

"Yes." She reaches out to find his hand. "I'm sure it's the right thing to do, Harry. If we find out otherwise, I can always put it back."

They go on. Rooster might conceivably mean chook, as in Bebchuk. Pol still stumps them.

"Now I need to go back through the references to see if they make sense with those people," Jenny says.

Harry hears the ring of a mobile, not his usual one, but the one whose number he gave to Kelly Pool. He gets it out of his jacket pocket and answers. "Hello, Kelly."

"Harry, have you seen my stuff?"

"Oh yes, everyone has. You've been stirring things up a bit. What's coming tomorrow?"

"More about Kristich's former career in Queensland. I've been getting all kinds of messages from members of the public, people who knew Kristich, were burnt by him. Trouble is, it's hard to verify them. Do you have anything for me?"

"I have a photograph that might interest you. I don't know, it may be quite innocent. Kristich on a yacht, drinking champagne with two other guys. I think one of them may be Derryn Oldfield, our police minister. The other one I don't know."

"A yacht? That's interesting. Any idea of the date?"

"I'm guessing it was when Kristich was in Vanuatu. Oldfield was the Australian high commissioner there."

"Shit, I didn't know that."

"There was a caption with the picture. It said, 'We three kings.'"

"Oh, lovely. Maybe I can identify the third man. Harry, after what went on in parliament today, a picture of Kristich with Oldfield would be explosive."

He wonders if this isn't going too fast, getting out of hand. He doesn't mention the wiped computer drive.

"How can I get hold of it, Harry? Can you email it to me?"

"No. They're bugging you, Kelly, like I said they would. You're not calling from home, are you?"

"No, I'm in the mall, getting something to eat."

"Okay . . ." He thinks. "There's a litter bin at one end of the concourse in Central Station." He describes the location. "Go there in forty minutes and you'll find a brown envelope in the bin. Give me a call afterwards to let me know you got it."

"Right. Thanks, 007."

He changes quickly into his joggers and sets off. As he runs down the hill towards Central, hood up, he wonders if he's got it all wrong. It may just be coincidence and wishful thinking. So what if Kristich and Oldfield met in Vanuatu? Of course they would, expats together. Is he just giving Kelly material to ruin a good man's reputation? But then he thinks of Tubby Bell and his offshore account. It's got to be him. Hasn't it?

TWENTY

THERE IS A QUEUE at the newspaper stall the next morning, everyone buying the *Bankstown Chronicle*, and Harry is lucky to get a copy. The yacht photograph is spread across the front page. Kelly has identified the third man as Maram Mansur, a property developer with interests in both Sydney and the Gold Coast. A picture of his luxury yacht *Rashida* is featured on page two, along with an apartment block in Surfers Paradise built by his company Ozdevco Properties, the building from which Kristich's wife had her fatal fall. Closer to home, Kelly reveals that a quantity of methamphetamine was seized in the recent raid on the Crow clubhouse, similar in type to drugs found at Kristich's office.

Bob the Job is in a foul mood. He shakes the rolled-up paper at them like a weapon. "We don't need a strike force or a murder squad in this state, we just need Kelly fuckin' Pool. She knows it all! Where is she getting it from? Aren't we tracking her?"

"Yes, boss," Deb says. "We know she paid a visit to Central Station last evening, then drove straight back to the newspaper office. We think she must have met some-one there who gave her this stuff."

"You think? Don't you know?"

"The guys lost contact with her in the crowd for a few minutes."

"Jeez, they're as useless as tits on a bull. The commis-sioner spat a turd when I told her about the hard drive last night. Reckons it could cost us all our jobs."

"What do you want us to do?"

"Wait. The commissioner's reviewing the situation. Till then we wait."

Deb is very pale when they leave his office.

Harry says, "It's not your fault, Deb. There's nothing we could have done."

"That's not good enough, is it? He's right, we're bloody pathetic." She grabs her coat. "Come on."

"Where are we going?"

"To interview your girlfriend."

She sits silent in the passenger seat, coiled tight, while he drives. Collateral damage, he thinks.

THE OFFICES OF THE *Bankstown Chronicle* are almost de-serted when they arrive. The receptionist explains that Mr. Westergard and Ms. Pool had a late night on the paper last night and won't be in till noon. "Everybody's been ringing in, wanting to speak to them. It's just amazing."

"Well we're the police," Deb snaps. "So you ring him up and tell him that if he and Ms. Pool don't get their arses down here quick smart we'll go and drag them out of bed and they can spend an amazing night in the clink."

The girl jumps to it, and after a few minutes comes back with the information that Westergard and Pool will be with them in fifteen minutes and would they like to come to the meeting room and have a cup of coffee while they wait.

She leads them through the office area to a small meeting room. On the way Deb asks if the desk in the middle of the room surrounded by a storm of journalistic flotsam is Kelly Pool's. The girl nods. "Yes, the cleaners know to leave her area alone." The phone at the front desk starts ringing and she hurries away. Deb waits till she's gone, then goes over to Kelly's desk and pokes around for a moment. She takes something from her pocket, strips off a wrapping and reaches her hand beneath the desk. Then she goes over to a cubicle marked "Editor" and does the same thing to his desk before returning to Harry who has been standing watching her.

It's more like half an hour before they arrive, Deb becoming twitchier with every passing minute. Her grim mood contrasts with that of the two journalists, who look buoyant and eager to start a new day.

"Sophie looked after you? Wonderful." Bernie Westergard beams at them. "How can we help?"

Kelly is settling herself in a flurry, searching through a large shoulder bag. She produces a recorder and notepad. She avoids looking at Harry.

Deb introduces herself and Harry, her manner stiff and formal. "We are detectives assigned to Strike Force

Gemini, which is investigating the deaths of Alexander Kristich and Benjamin Lavulo at the Gipps Tower last Thursday night. It's clear from your recent newspaper reports that you have information relating to this matter and we would like to know what it is."

"I see." Westergard looks vaguely puzzled. "Well, I think we've published just about all we know about the two deaths, haven't we, Kelly? I'm sure you know far more about it than we do, Inspector."

"You're saying that you do not intend to publish any further information about those deaths?"

"Oh, I couldn't promise that. We're getting information coming in all the time from concerned members of the public. Who knows what may crop up?"

His geniality is getting to Deb, Harry sees, but the little silver recording machine is restraining her. He wonders how long it will be before she explodes. "Look," he says, "we're running a murder investigation. Do you have any information that may be relevant to our enquiries?"

"Well, how can I tell?" Bernie beams. "I don't know where your enquiries are taking you."

"Well, let's start with Crucifixion Creek. I think you once indicated to me that you were convinced something was going on there, Ms. Pool? Is that right?"

"Yes. I tried to get you interested and you didn't want to know. You referred me to your media unit."

"So tell us now."

"Well, I think it's a lot bigger than the Crows. I think—"

But Bernie raises his hand. "Just a moment, Kelly. I can assure you that we have no firm evidence of any criminal matters that we could pass on to you. We have suspicions, but we're in a different position to you. We don't need proof of wrongdoing to raise issues of public concern. We ask questions, that's all."

"Bullshit!" Deb bursts out. "You stated as a fact that methamphetamine was found in the raid on the Crow clubhouse. That wasn't a question, it was a fact, and one that wasn't in the public domain. By releasing that information you undermined our enquiries. You did it again by releasing information about Kristich's computer."

"Ah yes," Bernie sighs, but still with that twinkle in his eye, "I fear that the court is annoyed with us about that. The matter was sub judice. We may have to pay—"

"I'll make you pay big time if you don't tell me how you came by that information."

"Oh now, Inspector, please. There's no question of us revealing our sources, you know that."

"I can make a case that you have materially obstructed a homicide investigation. I can have you both arrested."

Bernie sits back with the sort of benign smile worn in religious paintings by Christian martyrs being flayed by barbarians. "You may do your worst, Inspector. The people will decide on the justice of the matter."

Harry tries again. "We're seeking your cooperation, Mr. Westergard. You have seriously pissed off the whole of the New South Wales police force and exposed yourself to possible prosecution. A bit of cooperation would be timely for both of us."

Bernie adopts a more serious expression. "Look, as far as the computer business is concerned, let's just say that we have legal friends who are always on the look-out for

Nathaniel Horn's spoiling tactics. As for the meth, well, what else do outlaw motorcycle gangs do? And there were the rumours, right, Kelly?"

"Yes. People living in Mortimer Street complained of strange smells coming from the clubhouse. Then the raid. We put two and two together."

"And what about your next revelations? Is there anything you'd like to share with us?"

"Well, we have an abiding interest in corruption. It is the poison that eats away at our democracy from the inside."

"From your next editorial?" Harry says.

Bernie chuckles. "We believe there may be some kind of property scam going on in our neck of the woods, centred on the Creek. One of our elected representatives, Councillor Potgeiter, has been doing some odd things lately. We're hoping to prod him into showing his hand."

Potgeiter, Harry thinks, *Pot, Pol Pot, Pol*—could that be it?

"Nothing to do with Kristich, then?"

"Oh, I didn't say that. We think he may have been involved in whatever's going on. But we don't envisage any more murders, if that's what's bothering you."

WHEN THEY ARE GONE, Kelly settles down to work on her fourth day of revelations. For her it is the most important episode, but also the riskiest and most speculative. It is The Great Creek Conspiracy, the bee in her bonnet that has been buzzing around ever since the siege and her first conversation with Phoebe Bulwer-Knight. The picture of the "three kings" clinched it for her, and yet it is proof of nothing, and she knows how dangerous bees in bonnets can be. All she can really do is raise questions. Why was Kristich acquiring properties in the Creek? Why are properties in the Creek being firebombed and evacuated? Could it be connected to the proposed new south-west underground rail line? Everyone knows it will create a property bonanza wherever the stations are located, but the announcement on the route has been delayed again and again. The Kristich files might provide answers, but they are still in legal limbo. So she has no proof of anything, only speculation, and a cast of characters, which the three kings photograph has confirmed: the financial shark (Kristich), the state government minister (Oldfield) and the property developer (Mansur), backed up by a chorus of venal supporters, the local council (Potgeiter), the enforcers (Crows), and, just possibly, the bent cops (Strike Force Gemini).

She spends the day trying to find something tangible. A tip-off from a member of the public sends her down to Rose Bay where Mansur's yacht *Rashida* is moored. She hires a small boat and goes out to it, but a crew member who appears to speak little English tells her that no one else is on board. She goes on to Ozdevco Properties' registered offices, but is refused entry. It's the same everywhere she tries. Everyone, from Oldfield to Potgeiter, is unable or unwilling to speak to her.

In the end she makes what she can of the material she has, backed up by plans from the Department of Infrastructure and Planning and other public documents. She shows it to Bernie Westergard, who is uneasy. But there is a momentum now that they cannot afford to lose. New advertisers have been pouring in and they are doubling the size of the paper. He fiddles with this and that, changing the headline then changing it back again, and finally agrees to let it go.

It is almost midnight when Kelly leaves the office. She is exhausted and calls a cab, which drops her in the street outside her building. There is a light on in the Greek couple's window on the second floor, but her own flat is in darkness. She puts her key in the door and calls out "Hello" as she steps inside. There is no reply, and she feels for the light switch. She sighs, glad to be back, looking forward to bed, and drops her bag, pulls off her coat and steps into the living room. And stops. Everything—the TV, the table, the paintings, the sofa and chairs— everything is smashed and ripped and trashed and heaped in a ruined pile.

"Jesus," she whispers. "What happened?"

She turns towards the kitchenette and dining space and it's the same thing, smashed crockery and appliances plastered with tomato sauce and milk and muesli and all the other contents of the cupboards and the fridge, which lies gutted on its side.

"Wendy!" she cries. "Wendy!"

She runs to Wendy's room, having trouble forcing the door open against the debris inside, and there she sees her flatmate's bleeding legs extending from beneath the broken bed frame.

She stumbles back to her bag and pulls out a phone and rings triple-O, calling for an ambulance and police, then runs back to Wendy and tries to lift the bed off her. It's impossible, an impossible weight, but she finally manages to heave it upright against the wall, and turns back to look, and gives a loud wail as she sees what they've done to her friend.

TWENTY-ONE

FROM A GLIMPSE OF window at the far end of the corridor she realises that it is light outside. In here it is a timeless bright electric dazzle. Through the glass screen she can see the swaddled figure of Wendy, still as a corpse on the intensive care bed. She has been stabilised, the damage recorded, the coma monitored. They beat her savagely, she has been told, probably with baseball bats. There are many shattered bones and skull fractures. The doctors are concerned about swelling and permanent damage to the brain.

The police officers who called at the hospital were routinely sympathetic and comforting until she told them about Strike Force Gemini, the Crows and her work. Then they became cautious and stepped away to make phone calls. "They were after *me*," Kelly tells them. "They made a stupid mistake."

She gets to her feet, weary and aching from sitting there, and goes out to find a coffee. At the shop they have the morning papers, the *Bankstown Chronicle* among them. She picks it up, feeling sick with shame at the sight of her lead article. How glib, how easy to write clever words. How remote and pathetic they are compared to the violent reality of the world they describe. It's her fault that Wendy is in here, close to death. She imagines once again her terror, and throws the paper into the bin.

Towards noon Bernie calls to find out where she is. He is shocked to hear what has happened and says he'll come to the hospital, but she says no, Wendy's parents will be here soon and then she'll leave and try to get some sleep. Bernie is concerned, but she can hear something else in his voice too, a note of triumph. "Have you been following the reports, Kelly?" he asks. She says no.

"Well, I have to say the first reactions to the paper this morning were disappointing. People were a bit dubious, starting to say we'd gone out on a limb, and then Oldfield stands up in the house to answer questions on his conduct as police minister, and he has to come clean that the Kristich records aren't going to be released to the police after all. The hard drive is 'digitally compromised'— that was the phrase he used. Big uproar, people shouting across the floor that he's the one digitally compromised and he has to resign. Then he says he'll be taking legal advice on recent scurrilous reports in the press, but in the meantime he's spoken with the premier and agreed to stand down as police minister."

Bernie has forgotten about sounding concerned, and is getting excited. "I tell you, Kelly, this is a big win for us. And now they've really done it. Attacking you in your own home! I'll make sure the media all know about it. You'll get the evening news, no worries."

"Jesus Bernie, Wendy's in a fucking *coma*. I don't want to talk to bloody Channel 9 news."

"Oh. Yeah, okay, I'll speak to them myself, shall I? Sorry, Kelly. It must be very upsetting for you. You got anyone there with you? A friend?"

"I just want some time to think about this, Bernie."

"Sure, sure. And your flat was ruined, was it? You'll need somewhere to stay. The paper will pay, Kelly. Anywhere, the Hilton, the Sheraton, wherever you like."

"Thanks."

"You sound very tired. Go and get some rest."

He hangs up and she heads for the lobby. As she approaches the doors she sees Harry Belltree coming through.

"Kelly!" He takes hold of her arm and moves them out of the way of the throng passing in and out. "You're okay?"

It touches her that he seems really concerned. "I am, but my flatmate's nearly dead."

"I've only just heard. She going to be all right?"

"They don't know."

"Hell. I looked in on your flat on the way. Looks like a Crow special."

"What, not your lot? Your Inspector Velasco seemed ready to smash a few chairs yesterday."

"No, Kelly. No, no."

Was there a trace of doubt in his frown? "Anyway," she says, "I'm done."

"Can I give you a lift?"

"You don't want to be seen with me, Harry. You'll be compromised. And I just want to be alone."

WHEN HE GETS BACK to the office he finds that another team meeting has been called. Deb is in conference with Marshall, and when they emerge she looks sombre, Marshall grim and dyspeptic. "Gentlemen," he begins, then corrects himself quickly, "*Ladies* and gentlemen, I am instructed to stand down Strike Force Gemini."

There is a murmur of surprise and unease. He ploughs on.

"Inspector Velasco will draw up a final report for the coroner concerning the deaths of Kristich and Lavulo, concluding that they killed each other with no other persons involved. A full investigation of Kristich's financial dealings will be carried out by the fraud squad. The gangs squad will take over all matters relating to the Crow motorcycle gang. Any matters of possible corruption relating to the activities of Kristich and the Crows will be referred to the Independent Commission Against Corruption. You will complete all reports and other paperwork and return to your former duties. That is all."

He wheels about and marches off, and a grumble of discussion breaks out across the room. Deb gestures to Harry.

"You can help me write the coroner's report," she says, stiff with anger and hurt pride.

"I guess he's just doing what he's told," he says.

"It's a bloody mess. It's my first time to lead a strike force and it falls apart in my hands."

"Not your fault. You just have to roll with the punches."

"Don't give me your bloody platitudes, Harry," she

snaps. "You're not going to come out of this unscathed either. Come and see me in an hour with your notes and records."

They work through the report for an hour, then Harry says, "You know about the attack on Kelly Pool's flat last night?"

"I heard."

"I went to the hospital this morning."

"Good of you."

"Her flatmate was beaten half to death."

"Yes, that's terrible, but there must have been quite a few people wanted to do that to Kelly." She snorts a laugh. "Me included. I was going on about her last night to Damian, and he offered to go out there and do it himself."

Harry stares at her, shocked. "And did he?"

"What? No, of course not. It was a nice thought, though, that he'd kill someone for me. It's his sensitive side. You're touchy about her, aren't you, Harry?"

He just shakes his head, looking down at the pages in front of him without focusing.

"Who's handling it?" Deb asks.

"Local area command."

She shrugs.

"It's unfinished business, Deb. We should be dealing with it."

"Of course we should, we should be dealing with all of this. But we're not."

Harry says, "There are a few loose ends that we should tie up in order to finish this report."

"Like?"

"I want to interview the minister. Oldfield."

"What?"

"I think it's vital that we find out if he's had any recent dealings with Kristich."

Deb looks at him, trying to read his mind. "What are you fishing for?"

"If Kristich was supplying drugs to people powerful enough to prevent us accessing his records, Oldfield may be one of them. Kelly's photograph of the three kings gives us the excuse. We have an obligation to the coroner to clear this up."

"Oldfield won't see us."

"Remember his last words? 'Let me know if there's anything I can do to help with the good work.' I think we can put it to him that we're doing it for him, to make sure his name doesn't have to appear on our report to the coroner. Which I'm sure he wouldn't want."

"Waste of time." Deb taps her pen on the desk, thinking. "But okay, I'll try him."

She picks up the phone and eventually is put through to a staffer at Parliament House who tells her that Mr. Oldfield has gone from the building and has left instructions that he is not to be contacted except in an emergency.

"I think the minister would feel that it is very much in his interests to speak to me. Why don't you call him now and give him my contact number?"

She draws squares and spirals on her pad as she waits. When her phone rings she speaks deferentially, very polite, anxious to do the right thing as she lays it out for him. Eventually she makes a note on the pad and hangs up. "He's at home. He'll see us."

HOME IS ON POINT Piper. Not far, they discover, from Maram Mansur's huge mansion overlooking the inner harbour and the city skyline. The Oldfield house is a more modest affair but still highly desirable, a stylish modern home on one of the most expensive stretches of real estate in the country. Large areas of glass survey those prime city views, and Harry wonders how a public servant could afford this.

"Couldn't this have waited? You know what sort of a day I've had," Oldfield says as he shows them in. He leads them to a large table that looks as if it belongs in a boardroom more than a dining room. The whole space has a spare, efficient, workplace feeling that reminds Harry of Kristich's nest in the Gipps Tower. He wonders if there is a Mrs. Oldfield; there's no sign of a feminine touch.

"Of course," Deb says. "We do apologise, but we're under a lot of pressure now to wrap up our enquiries and complete our report to the coroner concerning the Kristich and Lavulo deaths. We just want to be quite certain that we don't need to mention your name in the report, Minister."

"My name? Good heavens no, certainly not. Why on earth should you?" He looks amazed. His manner now is aloof, patrician. Far from the team player he projected in the strike-force briefing.

"It's the photograph in the *Bankstown Chronicle*," Deb says apologetically, "On the yacht."

"Oh!" Oldfield's face clears. "I see. Well, that was taken years ago, in Vanuatu. I was high commissioner between '04 and '06, and of course I had to socialise with Australian businessmen out there from time to time, people like Kristich."

"What was his business out there?" Harry asks, and Oldfield looks slightly put out.

"I really can't recall. Import-export? I'm not sure."

"And did you maintain contact with Kristich when you both returned to Australia?" Deb continues.

"No. I may have attended functions where he was present, I don't know."

"Did you ever visit his offices in the Gipps Tower?"

"No, certainly not."

Harry clears his throat. "So . . ." he looks puzzled, pointedly underlining something in his notebook, ". . . you say you didn't visit Mr. Kristich in the Gipps Tower recently?"

"What?"

"The Gipps Tower." He smiles apologetically at Oldfield. "Perhaps it slipped your mind."

Oldfield stares at Harry for a moment. "I see. Anything else?"

"No, I don't think so."

"A visit to the Gipps Tower?"

"Yup."

Oldfield sighs, as if suddenly overcome with fatigue. "Politicians need two essential qualities, Sergeant. It is nice if they have more, but these two are essential—ambition and paranoia. Ambition to drive you forward," he smiles without humour. "And paranoia to cover your back. Political life is littered with obstacles and traps that derail people who don't have those two qualities. Sandy Kristich was one of those traps. I'd heard vague rumours about him since he returned from Vanuatu, but I hadn't bumped into him. Then he contacted me out of the blue last month and asked me to call in to his office to discuss a proposal. He was always a persuasive character, and against my better judgment I agreed."

Another sigh, Oldfield pointedly consults his watch. Deb prompts, "A proposal?"

"Yes, well, after a couple of drinks, jolly reminiscences of the Vanuatu days etcetera, he got around to what he wanted, which was to engage me as a confidential advisor. To find out the thinking of the working party on the preferred route for the south-west underground rail project, he said, and to identify ways to, ah, gain input into that decision. I gathered that he saw himself as an intermediary between myself and a third party he didn't name. I made it clear to him of course that I wasn't prepared to bend the rules, and that if I ever was to enter into such an agreement with anyone, I would have to disclose it to the parliamentary register. He didn't like that idea, and that's where our conversation came to an end. In effect, I felt that he was proposing to bribe me to subvert the planning process, something I neither could nor would contemplate. But he never framed it in such a way that I could make a formal complaint to the police or anyone else. So that's it." Oldfield fixes Harry with his patrician gaze. "May I ask how you learned of the meeting?"

"Sorry."

"Well, I was quite wrong to lie to you, but it was the paranoia kicking in. To be associated in any way with Alexander Kristich at this moment would be political suicide. I hope you'll accept my sincere apologies."

Harry turns to Deb, who is looking at him with an odd expression. "Anything else, ma'am?"

She clears her throat, examines her notes and says tightly. "No, I don't think so. We'll leave it at that. Thank you for your co-operation, sir."

She waits until they are in the car before she explodes. "Where the hell did that come from, Harry? Why didn't I know about his meeting Kristich?"

"It was just a punt, Deb. I reckoned he was lying to us and I thought I'd call him on it. I just got lucky. But if he lied about that I'll bet he's covering up other things too."

Deb takes a deep breath, snaps her lighter and drags deeply on a cigarette. "Okay," she says at last. "And if Kristich took notes of their meeting, the wiping of his computer was very convenient for Mr. Oldfield." The cigarette has calmed her. "Now what?"

"That's the problem, isn't it?"

"I'll report this to Bob, but without further evidence I can't see it going anywhere. There must be people all over town scuttling around erasing emails, diary references, file notes on meetings with Kristich. Soon he'll be the man who never was."

TWENTY-TWO

OVER DINNER JENNY TELLS him about her progress. "It's like . . ." she struggles for an analogy, "reconstructing sheets from a shredded document, or disentangling a ball of dozens of cables." But neither quite captures it. She has been concentrating on a cache of notes made, presumably by Kristich, over the previous twelve months, recording cryptic transactions of various kinds with other nicknamed players, along the lines, "18k to Rooster," "told Pol to contact Chocky sap," "Chippy panic, spoke to Tubby."

More of these nicknames have cropped up. A lover of word games and crossword puzzles, she has entertained herself trying to decipher them, and has printed off a list of her guesses for Harry:

47	=	Kristich
Crystal	=	Waterford
Bells	=	Oldfield
Chippy	=	Greg
Rooster	=	Bebchuk

```
Chocky   =   Mansur
Pol      =   ?
NRL      =   ?
Tuba     =   ?
```

She waits while he studies it.

"Okay . . ." He tells her about seeing Oldfield today with Deb, and of his reluctant admission that he had met Kristich, which suggests that he is Bells. "And I had an idea about Pol. I wondered if he could be the local councillor that Kelly Pool keeps going on about—Potgeiter, Pot as in Pol Pot."

"Yes, that could work." She whispers an instruction to her computer.

"How do you get Mansur for Chocky?"

"Maram Mansur, M&M, chocolate drops."

He laughs. "Right. The last one's new, Tuba."

"Yes. It crops up a few times. He sounds like an intermediary of some kind."

Harry thinks, then says, "The lawyer, Horn—Tuba."

"Okay, yes. That just leaves the football player, NRL."

She has been mapping the connections between the different names. She brings up the diagram of nodes and links the computer has created to illustrate this, a picture she can only imagine. It shows some of them—Rooster, Pol, Bells, Chocky and Tuba—having strong interactions with Kristich and with each other, while others—Chippy, Crystal and NRL—are more peripheral.

"I've found some pictures, but you'll have to tell me what they are—here."

This is the most frustrating thing, that she can't see these. All the computer can tell her is that this is image number X and this is number Y. It can't describe them. It is a limitation of the program she will have to see about fixing.

He tells her there are photographs of people, buildings, documents. They look like a kind of visual diary of events, but to interpret them they will have to correlate the pictures, which only Harry can see, to the text documents that only Jenny can navigate. They sit side by side at her table and begin to go through them.

"This one looks interesting," Harry says. "It's four blokes standing drinking at a bar . . . There's Kristich, and Oldfield. I don't know who the other two are."

He gives her the reference number of the document and she gets to work on her computer. "6.4:13/1" she says at last.

"What's that, a date?"

"I suppose so. And there's another document titled 6.4:13/2."

She gives him its computer number and he flicks through the images. "Got it. A hotel bill for six nights beginning 6 April this year at the Le Meridien Hotel, Jakarta, Indonesia, in the name of Mr. Joost Potgeiter, paid for with Alexander Kristich's credit card. Do we know what Potgeiter looks like?"

"Yes, I've got all their pictures."

She brings them up and he says, "That's him. The other two men in the bar are Potgeiter and Mansur. This is brilliant, Jenny."

He hugs her and they both laugh, and then the front door bell rings.

"Probably Nicole," he says. He gets to his feet and goes out to see.

Jenny hears the door open, then Harry's voice. "Sir?"

Her heart stops. Have they come to arrest him? Then she hears a voice she recognises. Bob Marshall.

"Sorry to drop by without warning, Harry. I've been in meetings in Goulburn Street, and not having seen Jenny for so long . . . Is it a bad time?"

Jenny gets over her surprise, remembering how Marshall visited her in hospital after the crash. He's known for it, his personal contact with the families of injured officers.

"No, not at all. Come in, sir. Let me take your coat."

"Bob, please. Can't be saying 'sir' in your own home for God's sake."

Panic seizes Jenny. She quickly exits the file and tries to gather up the papers on the table and shove them in the drawer. A couple drop to the floor, and she's bending down to find them when she hears Harry again.

"It's Bob Marshall, Jenny."

"Oh!" She rises to her feet and turns to him, smiling. "Bob, what a lovely surprise!"

She feels him gently take hold of her hands and kiss her on the cheek. He makes his apologies again and offers her the box of chocolates he's brought with him as she leads him away from her desk. Harry says, "Let me get you a drink, Bob."

"Well, I have got the luxury of a driver waiting out

there, and after the day I've had a drop of scotch would go down a treat."

Jenny leads Bob to the seats in the bay window on the far side of the room from the computer. He goes on, "I was sitting in this meeting, Jenny, listening to these people droning on about best-practice this and benchmark that, and my mind wandered off and it came to me that it must be three years since your terrible accident. And now you've had another tragedy with your brother-in-law. How's the family coping? Your sister's husband, is that right?"

As they talk Harry returns with the glasses. Jenny takes hers, and Bob proposes a toast to happier days. Then he says, "But tell me, Jenny, if it's not an intrusive question, I saw you sitting over there at the computer and . . . well, I know you used to be an expert in that field but you surely can't use it now, can you?"

So she tells him about the accessibility programs that allow her to interact with the machine and he shakes his head in amazement. "What, you can use emails, all that?"

"Enough so I can do a bit of work from home."

"Big law firm, wasn't it? Research?"

"Yes."

"Well, well." She hears Bob get up, his heavy footsteps going over to her desk. Harry has taken hold of her hand, squeezing it.

"You've dropped some papers . . . What's this? Kristich?"

Harry is going over to him. She says, "I'm always nagging Harry to give me things to work on; I need the practice. Of course I can't get into e@gle.i or use any in-house information, only what's on the web. But you'd be amazed what's out there."

"So you've got your own IT tech, Harry. Lucky man." He ambles back to sit with them again. "This reminds me of the old days, when Betty was alive. We used to have the blokes and their wives round, put our feet up, have a good yarn. Before your time, Harry. You never met Betty, did you? Great woman. Tower of strength to me. Maybe I've got lazy since she went. I should do it again— have you all over for Sunday lunch, you two and Toby Wagstaff and his missus. And Deb and Damian—he's a good bloke. What do you think?"

"Great."

"Hm." Bob swallows the last of his drink and gets to his feet. "Well, I'd best be off. Good to see you again, Jenny. You're looking really well."

When he's gone she says, "What was it he saw?"

"Just a page from the Bluereef website. Nothing incriminating." He lets out a deep breath. "What was all that about though?"

"I think he's lonely," Jenny says. "Going back to an empty house after a bad day. Does he have kids?"

"Two sons. Both overseas I think. They look exactly like him—he keeps a photo on his desk, him and Betty and the two boys."

"I think it was kind of him to call. Gave me a fright, though. I couldn't remember what I had lying on the desk." Then she smiles to herself. "You know what the women say about Bob, the wives at police functions."

"What?"

"That he's got this presence, and what a spunk he must have been when he was young."

She feels Harry's arm around her waist. "Enough drama," he says. "Let's go to bed."

HE WAKES FROM A deep sleep, the sound of a bell ringing in his ears and the trace of a dreaded smell in his throat, the one that makes him throw up at barbecues, the smell of the roadside bomb, of burning flesh. He gets up and sees the glow of an outdoor light, the one triggered by someone coming to the front door. He pulls on a tracksuit and goes downstairs, where the smell seems stronger. The light gleams through the glass panel in the front door. He opens the front door and gags. Something big and black and burnt is lying on the doorstep. Holding his breath, his eyes adjusting to the glare, he makes out the shape of a head, of shoulders, legs. He takes a deep breath and immediately gags again at the overpowering smell and turns away to throw up into the banksia beneath the front window.

It's human. Naked, skin streaked and blackened with blood and scorch marks. He runs back into the house and calls triple-O, shouting upstairs to warn Jenny.

He returns to the body and squats beside it. Tries to find a sign of life. He reaches in to where the throat might be and when he presses the flesh it comes away in his fingers. On what might be the upper left arm the whole limb is black charred meat, right down to the pale line of a bone.

The ambos arrive, closely followed by the cops. By the light of their flashlights he gets a better idea of the anatomy.

"Holy Jesus," the ambo breathes. "They've taken a blowtorch to him—an oxyacetylene torch. Must be. They've written something on his back."

Harry peers at it and sees three huge letters carved deep into the torso by the flame, *D O G*.

"Is he dead?"

"Oh my word yes."

"Let me see his face."

They gently turn the skull. The features of the right side are clearer. One of the cops says, "You know him?"

It is Rowdy O'Brian.

HE WATCHES THE ROUTINE unfold with a nightmare clarity. The two general duties officers are soon joined by others who attempt to secure the scene, but since the only access to the front door is down the narrow laneway this is difficult. Through the front window he sees Toby Wagstaff, duty inspector from homicide, arrive in the street at the end of the lane, but he has to wait for the crime scene team to give him clearance before he can come in to talk to Harry. Eventually they are seated together in the sitting room, Jenny in the kitchen making coffee.

"So Harry, here you are again. Up to your neck in shit." He regards Harry, concerned.

"Looks like it."

"Do you feel up to talking to me?"

"Yes, of course."

"You're a marvel, you know that? You'll be the death of the old man." Wagstaff chuckles and runs a hand through his curls as if to flatten them, but they bounce back up. "So you know the victim."

"Thomas O'Brian, nickname Rowdy. We were in the army together in Afghanistan in '04. I hadn't seen him since then, but I recognised him among the people we pulled in at the raid on the Crows."

"So he's one of them, a biker."

"Yes. We couldn't get anything out of him in interview and Bob Marshall suggested I try to see him privately, see what I could find out. So I contacted him and he agreed to meet me at the David Jones café in Elizabeth Street. I reported all this to Deb."

"Was he any help?"

"Not much, not prepared to dob in his mates. But he told me that the club had been split by the take-over of the current president, Roman Bebchuk, who he warned me was a vicious bastard. He's the one who did this."

"How would he have found out that O'Brian met you?"

"Rowdy chose the David Jones café because it was the least likely place any of the gang would visit, but on our way out a woman recognised him, called out his name. I shot off. I don't know who she was, but she might have seen me."

"Hm. Kind of obvious though, isn't it? Leaving him on your doorstep with 'dog' carved into his back?"

"Brutally obvious."

"A warning?"

"Maybe."

"Pretty personal, anyway. And your wife . . ." He looks towards the kitchen.

"Yes, that's what really gets me. She is extremely vulnerable."

"Okay, we'll pick up Bebchuk. Anyone else?"

"His inner circle is his vice-president and the sergeant-at-arms. Their details are all on file. There may be others they use for dirty work. I'm guessing it would have taken at least three of them to do this, to torture him, transport him over here and get away fast."

"Yes, well, we'll see what CCTV tells us. Where do you think it was done?"

Harry thinks. "They're not stupid. We didn't find much when we raided the clubhouse, and they'll know that's the first place we'll look. I'm guessing somewhere else, but I've no idea where."

"Let's hope the post-mortem comes up with something."

"Then there's the attack on Kelly Pool's flat last night."

"Who?"

"The *Bankstown Chronicle* reporter, the one who's been running the Kristich story. Her flatmate was badly beaten up, probably mistaken for Pool."

"Yes, of course. You think this is linked?"

"Certain of it. Same people. This is war, a war of intimidation. They're warning everyone else to stay in line and keep their mouths shut."

"How do you mean, everyone else? Who are we talking about?"

"The people who know what Kristich was mixed up in."

"Which we don't know because his hard drive was wiped, yes." His eyes stray over to Jenny's computer. The desk is now clear of papers, the screen blank.

"Still," Wagstaff goes on, looking doubtful, "this is pretty blatant. The press are out there now. They'll make a big thing of it."

"Maybe," Harry says. "Bikers killing bikers? Who's going to care?"

WHEN THEY'RE ALL FINALLY gone, at least for the present, Harry sits alone in the darkness. He drinks another glass of whisky to try to wash the burnt taste from his throat.

"Harry? Are you there?"

"Yeah, love, over here."

She comes and sits beside him and holds his hands. "Are you all right?"

"Not really."

"Tell me. Were you close? In the army?"

"Oh . . . There was a house . . ." He sees it again in his mind's eye, the faded rags over the windows, the smell of goats. "He got me out of a tight spot. But it wasn't just one thing, it was everything, the fundamental thing—stick with your mates, cover each other's backs—that stays with you forever. And I didn't do that. I exposed him to harm. This happened because I asked him to talk to me. I wrote his death sentence." He swills down the last of the scotch. "And what a death."

"No. You couldn't foresee that. You weren't responsible."

But Harry knows she's wrong.

TWENTY-THREE

A NIGHT IN A luxury hotel room has not made Kelly feel any better. She packs her bag, puts the empty wine bottle in the bin and checks out. She gets a cab back to the hospital, where Wendy is still in a coma. While she's there Kelly gets a call from Bernie.

"Where are you, Kelly?"

"The hospital."

"Oh, yes, right. Any change?"

"No."

"No news is good news, I suppose."

She mentally puts a blue pencil through the cliché.

"Seen the paper?"

"No."

"We've made a big thing of the attack on your place and Wendy. Threats against the freedom of the press. Violence to stifle debate, all that. Demanding action."

"Ah." She finds his enthusiasm depressing.

"Yes, well. And I had a call from that developer. Maram Mansur. Very smooth gentleman. He is amused by your suggestion of his foresight and would be delighted if it were true, but it's the first he's heard of the rail corridor coming to Crucifixion Creek. However, he is very annoyed about our slur on his business practices and is instructing his lawyers to take action."

"Oh."

"And something that came in too late for the papers—a dead Crow biker was dumped in a laneway in Surry Hills last night. Want to take a look?"

She's about to say no, then asks for the name of the lane, and recognises Harry's address. "Okay," she says. "I'll go and see."

When she gets there she finds the lane cordoned off. Now that it's daylight, a team of people is working in the lane, doing a fingertip search on hands and knees. She reaches into her bag for the phone Harry gave her, but as she lifts it out she realises it was this one she used to call the emergency services from her flat when she discovered Wendy. She freezes, then turns and walks away. When she gets up to Crown Street she takes the SIM card out of the phone and grinds it under her heel, then throws the phone into a rubbish bin. She tries to calm her breathing. She's never been like this before, so rattled and panicky. Is it a symptom of age? Is this all just getting too hard for her to deal with?

She jumps as her other phone rings. It is Catherine Meiklejohn, the editor of the *Times*. A woman she has never met but long admired.

"Kelly? I wanted to congratulate you on your fantastic work on the Kristich murders. Wonderful reporting.

An inspiration to us all. But I was deeply shocked to hear about the attack on your flatmate. I take it you were the intended victim?"

"Yes," she says, and tries to force some confidence back into her voice. "Yes, I don't think there's any doubt about that."

"Shocking. Now listen, you are obviously in a very vulnerable position, and I don't know what kind of back-up the *Bankstown Chronicle* can offer you, but if you were with us you would have a team of people working with you on this and keeping you safe, as well as helping you cover all the angles." There is the briefest of pauses. "What I'm offering you, Kelly, is a job with us, as one of our senior crime reporters. We'll start with a big feature on you and how you broke the story. Will you come in and talk to me about it?"

"Um, thank you. I'm really flattered. But . . . I have been working closely with my editor, Bernie Wester-gard . . ."

"Sure. I know Bernie, and he's a realist. Well, it's up to you, Kelly. It's your career. But you might only get one bite at this."

"Right. Can you give me a couple of hours to think about it?"

"Of course. Let me know by midday, okay?"

"Yes, and thank you again."

She kills the call and takes a huge breath. Has she just blown it? Surely Catherine could hear the weakness in her voice, her indecision? Yet the offer stands. She doesn't know whether to scream and dance a jig or run home and bury her head under a pillow. Except she hasn't got a pillow to go home to. And Catherine was right—she needs help. Back-up, resources, people full of energy to bounce ideas off.

She stands in the middle of the footpath and straightens her spine and sets her jaw. She tells herself she is as tough as she needs to be, and as persistent. She created this story through her own efforts, and she'll continue it the same way.

There is a café across the street, and she goes over and orders a toasted sandwich and coffee. Tries to get her brain to think clearly. She wonders what she'd say to Bernie. The *Chronicle* has been her refuge for so many years now. She owes it a lot, but it's time to come out of the shelter.

Her phone again, Bernie—as if he's listening to her thoughts. "Kelly? The ministers of planning and transport have just issued a joint statement. They deny that there are any plans to run the underground rail line anywhere near the Creek. They hope that this will put a stop to misleading and mischievous rumours emanating from certain minor organs of the press."

"They actually used those words?"

"Same as. Doesn't look good, Kelly. Does your source have anything new for us? We need a new angle."

"I'm working on it." She rings off. No, this does not look good. And the timing—what will Catherine Meiklejohn make of it? Is her big idea just an illusion? What evidence did she have for it, really? She imagines the whole thing, her whole campaign, collapsing in an embarrassing heap, all coincidence and false conclusions amounting to nothing more than the desperate imagination of a failed reporter. What does she have to give the *Times* now? Can she offer anything without Harry?

She goes over to the counter and tells them that her mobile isn't working and she needs to make an important phone call. She offers the girl five dollars, takes the café phone and dials Harry's special mobile number.

"Yes?" His voice is barely a whisper.

"Harry, can we talk?"

"What phone are you on?"

"This is a landline from the café I'm in. I had to destroy the other mobile. I think I compromised it using it to call triple-O when I found my flatmate."

All this comes out in a rush, then she waits, listening to the silence at the other end. Finally he says, "Can't talk now. Don't call this number again," and hangs up.

She mutters a pathetic little curse, at herself, at Harry, at fate, then replaces the handset.

Bereft of ideas, she walks down the hill to Central, where she buys a ticket out to the northern suburbs. The train is almost empty and she stares out of the window as it rumbles across the Harbour Bridge. The sky has turned dark and raindrops begin to stream across the window. Kelly wonders if she should ring Meiklejohn back and say she can't do it.

At Lindfield she gets off and walks back along the Pacific Highway through the town towards the public library. There she explains that she's trying to make contact with someone who's recently moved into the area, and describes her.

"Oh, Phoebe! Yes of course. She comes here a lot."

"Do you have her address?"

"Well we do, but—oh, you can ask her yourself. Here she is."

Kelly turns and sees the old lady coming through the doors, wrestling with an umbrella. She seems frailer now than before, a little more unsteady on her feet. When Kelly greets her she looks bemused, and Kelly has to remind her.

"The last time we met was in Mortimer Street, when you were moving out. I was wondering how you are, how things are going with your sister."

"Oh . . . yes. And you came all the way out here to ask me that?"

"Well, not only that. Let's sit down."

They make their way to a table in a quiet corner.

"I come here a lot," Phoebe confides. "To get out of Delia's way. We're going through a period of readjustment. It didn't take us long to fall back into our old ways—she bossing me around and me answering back. I've had to stand up to her, but it's so exhausting. I do miss my own home."

"Oh dear. Do you keep in touch with any of the other people in Mortimer Street?"

"Well, there aren't any of them left, apart from the bikers. That dreadful man who was so rude to you—Roman, they call him. The others all left over the years. I like to think of Mortimer Street when it was a friendly place with young families, children playing in the street."

"Ah," Kelly is disappointed. "So there isn't anybody else I could talk to about what's been going on in the Creek?"

But Phoebe is gazing into the distance, lost in her

memories. "I thought I must be going gaga, seeing the children again. I mean, I knew they were all grown up now. Little faces at the windows, peering through the blinds like ghosts."

"What?"

"I thought it must be the Italian children, Rico and Bella, but that couldn't be right, because they came back when they were grown up, to see their parents before they passed away."

Kelly pulls the strap of her bag over her shoulder and prepares to make a move.

"One of them waved to me, but then the motorbikes came down the street and they vanished."

"You saw children in the houses—recently?"

"Oh yes, several times. At least I thought I did." There is something rather unnerving about Phoebe's dreamy words. "Someone else to talk to, did you say? Well, there's Mrs. Fenning, of course—Donna. She's still there. I forgot about her."

By now Kelly hardly knows what to believe. Mrs. Fenning probably died twenty years ago.

"Where does she live, Phoebe?"

"Donna? Oh, at number eleven, on the other side of the street, a little further down. Cacti."

"Sorry?"

"She has a cactus garden in the front of the house. All rocks and gravel and, ah, cacti. Quite clever I suppose, but not my idea of a garden. I do miss my plants."

Kelly does vaguely remember seeing cacti in the street. "And she's still there?"

"Well, as far as I know."

TWENTY-FOUR

HARRY CALLS IN AT work but they tell him politely to go away. After trying without success to get information on progress, he decides he'll have to wait until Toby Wagstaff comes back on duty to get some answers. There is a message from the psychologist, which he ignores.

As he drives back out of the basement car park the rain turns heavy, lashing the windscreen and running in a rippling sheet down the concrete ramp. His phone chimes and he sees a message from the accountant Sam Peck asking him to ring.

"Hey, Harry, how are you? I've got Peter Rizzo here with me now, and we're wondering if you can spare a moment sometime soon to talk about options."

"How about now?"

"Perfect."

Harry heads in that direction, taking a detour past the offices of the *Bankstown Chronicle* to drop off a package.

They are sitting side by side at the table in Sam's office, flanked by piles of documents. Harry gets the impression they've been at it for some time, sleeves rolled up, ties loosened, empty coffee mugs and a half-eaten bun with pink icing pushed to one side. Sam welcomes him, Peter hanging back a little awkwardly until it's his turn to step forward and shake hands.

"Let's sit," Sam says, indicating chairs around his desk. "Coffee, Harry?"

"No thanks, Sam. What's up?"

"Okay. Peter and I have been having a few discussions about how we can handle the building business."

"Doesn't that belong to Bluereef now?"

"Well," Sam holds up his hands, a sly smile on his face, "that's the point at issue. As you know, we had a letter from Bluereef's lawyer, Horn, immediately after Greg's death, giving notice that Greg had defaulted on his loan and that Bluereef would act to take possession of his assets as set out in their agreement. This was challenged by Nicole's lawyer, requesting further documentary evidence, but since then Kristich has died, and Bluereef, of which we understand he was the sole proprietor, has been incommunicado. So . . ." more hand gestures, cunning winks, "this may provide us with an opportunity to take care of a few problems."

"Oh yes?"

"Yes. Problem number one," a finger goes up, "what do we do about Greg's clients, with their half-constructed buildings? Problem number two," a second finger, "what do we do about Greg's workforce, who need to be paid? Problem number three," third finger, "what do we do with the building company assets—trucks, premises, equipment—which all need money for maintenance, fuel, taxes, etcetera, etcetera? These are all major headaches for us, and in particular for Nicole, who simply doesn't need any of these problems, agreed?"

"Okay. So what do you suggest?"

"Well," a sideways nod to Peter, "Peter has come up with a plan that, after due consideration, I believe might suit Greg's estate and Nicole's interests very well indeed. In short, Peter is proposing to form his own company to which Greg's executors will sell the assets and liabilities of Greg March Builder Limited."

"Can we do that, if Bluereef has already given notice that they believe the company belongs to them?"

"Well, it depends how it's done. Let's say Peter approaches client A, and explains that Greg March Builder is no longer able to continue with the project. The client will then be faced with months of delays, arguments with subcontractors and additional costs. However, if the client will write to Greg March Builder and terminate their contract because of various breaches, he can then appoint Rizzo Construction who will continue the project without interruption, with the same personnel, and at minimal additional cost. How can Bluereef object to that?"

Harry shrugs.

"Then let's say Rizzo Construction approaches Greg's executors and offers to buy the assets of Greg March Builder for a sum which the parties agree, and the executors place that sum in a special account which can be preserved intact until the question of legal ownership of the assets is resolved. Who can object to that?"

"I see." And Harry does see—the carefully contained eagerness of the two men, their air of collusion, their confidence that without working capital Harry and Nicole will have no choice. "And this sum will be comparatively modest, I imagine?"

A serious, businesslike look comes over Sam's face. "We've been going carefully over the figures, Harry. The premises are a tangle of burnt-out debris, the trucks are ancient, the equipment worthless to anyone else, and there are unpaid bills; so yes, their value is modest. Nominal, in fact."

"And the additional costs that Peter agrees with the clients, to continue their projects?"

"That's entirely for him to negotiate."

"In other words, Peter is getting Greg's business for nothing."

"Not for nothing, Harry. For a reasonable negotiated sum which can be justified with detailed financial assessments. But that's not the point. Peter is agreeing to take these problems off our hands, at his risk. If Bluereef later object, they'll have to argue it out with him."

All this time they've been talking about Peter as if he isn't there. Now Harry turns to him. "Are you confident about this, Peter? You'll have to raise a bit of money, won't you?"

"I've done the sums, Harry, and I've spoken to the bank. I'm confident, yes." And he does sound confident, self-possessed, almost a different man. Harry wonders what sort of a deal he's done with Sam.

"Okay. What's the next step?"

Sam says, "I suggest that we get Peter to draw up a formal offer, with details of what's involved, and then the executors, assisted by myself, can assess it, and then negotiate or approve it as they see fit."

They agree on this. The change in the other two men is so striking that Harry can't shake the idea that he and Nicole are being screwed. But perhaps that is ungenerous. He certainly has no better idea how to deal with the situation.

TWENTY-FIVE

KELLY PICKS UP HER car from outside her home. She doesn't go into the flat, unable to face it. Instead she drives to the Creek. She parks on the main road at the end of Mortimer Street and runs through the rain down to number eleven, where the cacti are getting a soaking. She huddles close to the door and rings the bell. Across the street she sees a man standing outside Phoebe's house, watching her.

She steps back and puts a smile on her face as the door opens. "Mrs. Fenning?"

"Yes?"

It's a relief to see a plump middle-aged woman with nice clothes and hair, who looks alert and friendly. "Hello, my name is Kelly Pool. I've just come from speaking to Phoebe Bulwer-Knight, who used to live across the street."

"Yes, I know Phoebe. How can I help you?"

"I'm with the *Bankstown Chronicle*, Mrs. Fenning, and I'm researching an article on life in Mortimer Street, and I wondered if I could have a few minutes of your time?"

"Well, you're getting soaked out there. You'd better come in."

"Thank you. Oh dear, I'll probably drip on your carpet."

"Don't worry about it. Take your coat off and come through."

She hangs Kelly's coat on a hook behind the door and leads the way into a pleasant room, lighter than Phoebe's and comfortably furnished.

"Please sit down. I've been reading your articles, Kelly. *Very* exciting. I seem to be living in a crime hotspot."

There is a sceptical look on her face as she says this, and Kelly wonders if she's going to be accused of talking down real estate values.

"Well, I'd be glad to hear your impressions of living here, Mrs. Fenning."

"Donna, call me Donna. Well, we like it. It's a street with a lot of character. I know people might be put off living with a biker clubhouse at the end, but really, that's the last place you'd expect trouble, isn't it?"

"There was the police raid."

"Oh yes, that was exciting, but it was an overreaction, wasn't it? At least as far as we can tell. I mean they didn't actually arrest anyone, did they? We get on fine with the bikers. So did Phoebe."

"So your husband isn't one?"

"A biker? Oh no. He works at the hospital. That was one of the attractions of living here, within walking distance."

"And now you must be the last non-biker residents in the street, aren't you?"

"I suppose we are. We've only been here a year, so we're not one of the long-term residents like Phoebe. They all grew old and moved away, and their houses were bought up by Crows members. Very communal, really."

"Do you have any children?"

Donna looks surprised by the question, and Kelly adds quickly, "I just wondered if there are any children left in the street."

"Well, yes. We don't have any, but a couple of the Crow families do. I mean, they're just ordinary people really, with ordinary jobs and ordinary families."

They talk on for a while. Donna is pleasantly straightforward, and when she says, "Are you sure you're not going a bit overboard with your great Creek conspiracy?" Kelly finds it hard to argue.

She returns to her car, feeling dispirited, and drives to the *Chronicle* offices. It's a quarter to twelve when she gets there, and she still hasn't phoned Catherine Meiklejohn.

The offices are quiet. Bernie is away somewhere, but there is a package waiting on her desk for her. She opens it and finds a mobile phone inside. When she switches it on she finds one number in its memory. She hesitates for a moment, thinking, then leaves the office again and goes out to the car park behind the building. She dials the number and hears a familiar voice.

"Hi Kelly."

"Harry! You still want to talk to me?"

"I'm not sure, Kelly. Where are you going with this?"

"To be honest I don't know. Everyone's saying my idea

about the south-west underground rail is wrong. Maybe it is."

"Yes, maybe. I know nothing about that. But that doesn't mean something isn't going on. I'm going to send you another photo. Tell me if you recognise the people."

Kelly waits for the picture to come through, a cluster of men in a bar. She gives a little gasp of excitement. "Harry, that's Derryn Oldfield, isn't it? With Maram Mansur again. And the one next to them is Councillor Potgeiter."

"You're sure?"

"Absolutely."

"It was taken in a hotel bar in Jakarta, last April."

"And that's . . . Kristich, is it? On the other side?"

"He paid Potgeiter's expenses for the trip—airfare and hotel."

"Brilliant."

"I can get you a copy of the hotel bill."

"Yes, I'll need that."

"I don't know what it means, Kelly. Maybe there's a perfectly innocent explanation."

"Okay, I'll be careful. I'll do some checks. Thanks."

"Don't try to contact me any other way, Kelly. And watch your back."

The line goes dead. She stands for a moment, biting her lip, then phones Catherine Meiklejohn, who invites her to come to the *Times* office the following morning. As she hangs up Bernie comes into the office, puffing from the stairs, struggling out of his wet coat, grumbling to himself. She waits until he's settled at his desk, then goes over to him and tells him about the offer.

He nods. "Not surprising, Kelly. You're a good reporter. Bit wild in your theories sometimes, but they'll
knock you into shape."

She reaches across his desk and gives him a big hug.
She doesn't mention the new photograph.

TWENTY-SIX

HARRY GOES IN TO headquarters early to catch Toby Wagstaff at the end of his shift. The inspector is tired, wanting to get home, and with nothing good to report. "They were all out of town, Harry, in Bathurst. The whole gang. They rode out there on their bikes the night before, stayed at a hotel they'd booked, and didn't get back till yesterday afternoon. We were monitoring their phones, and the local boys and the hotel staff check it out."

"Bebchuk? You're sure?"

"Yeah. He's a distinctive figure, big man, beard. He was there."

Harry shakes his head. "They're fooling you, Toby. They did it. Bebchuk did it."

Wagstaff sighs. "Or someone else wants them in the frame. They say O'Brian was supposed to go on the ride, but never showed up. The thing is, whoever killed him made a pretty good job of fingering the Crows. His upper left arm was badly burnt, remember? That's where he had a tatt of the club colours. They burned it off. Pretty obvious pointer, yeah? Might as well stick a note on him, 'The Crows did it.'"

"What about the post-mortem?"

"Cause of death was cardiac arrest, probably while they were barbecuing him. He'd been tortured, fingers, toes broken before that."

"But when did this happen?"

"They're still working on that. Roberts reckons it could have been up to forty-eight hours before he was dumped."

"Before they all headed off to Bathurst."

"He's not sure. We've got CCTV footage of the car that brought him to your place—green Holden reported stolen twenty-four hours earlier, found torched yesterday out at Hurstville. The cameras show two, maybe three, occupants."

"That should narrow it down."

"Piss off, Harry."

HE HANGS AROUND, UNABLE to settle. When he sees Deb he complains that Wagstaff is making a mess of it, but she doesn't want to know. "Keep out of it, Harry. You're a witness, that's all."

There's an email on his computer from the psychologist suggesting he make an appointment. He deletes it. Finally he does a search on the smash repair business in Mascot. It is owned by Marco Ganis, cousin of Stefan Ganis who died in the siege. He owns a tow truck, first registered two years, colour red.

THE RAIN HAS NEWLY stopped, the pavements are still slick, trees dripping, a heavy black cloud cover in the night sky. Harry parks a kilometre away and walks quickly down deserted streets. He pulls a black ski mask over his head as he approaches the compound, which sits on a corner. On the footpath facing away from the streetlight, a gnarled paperbark tree hangs half over the chain link fence, and Harry quickly climbs it and drops into the yard. The dog stirs, then appears from the shadows behind the shed, sniffing, peering. Harry calls softly, "Here boy." It gives a deep growl and comes bounding across the concrete, then stops abruptly as the steak—half a kilo of rump—lands with a fat plop. It sniffs, licks, then grabs it and begins to chew. Harry stays motionless against the fence as the meat goes down in greedy gulps. When it's finished, the dog peers over at Harry and growls again. It begins to lope towards him, then pauses, sags onto its haunches and falls flat.

The dark mass of the tow truck fills the shed. Harry examines the bodywork carefully with his torch, the gleam of fire-engine red, then begins to scrape away at the paint, collecting the flakes into a plastic pouch. It isn't long before he finds white beneath the red. Then he hears a sound. He switches off the torch.

"Caesar? Where are you boy?"

The voice comes from the far side of the truck. Harry circles around and sees a figure reaching for the wall. As the light clicks on he darts across and grips the man's throat, showing him the gun in his other hand. The man makes a gargling sound as Harry forces him across to a metal chair at a bench, makes him sit and ties his hands behind him to the chair.

Harry searches him and opens a wallet, examining the man's licence. "You're Marco Ganis."

"Look," the man croaks. "I don't keep any money here."

Harry moves round in front of him so that the man can see him for the first time. He sees the fear in his eyes as he takes in the mask, the gun. "I don't want money. I want to know about your truck."

"Where's Caesar?" Ganis gulps. "You killed him?"

"Maybe. Maybe I'll kill you if you don't tell me about your truck. You rebirthed it two years ago, right?"

"Go fuck yourself."

Harry hits him across the face with the gun. Ganis squeals with shock, then sobs and moans for a while, spitting blood from his mouth. Harry waits till he quietens, then says again, "You rebirthed it two years ago, right?"

The man nods his head.

"Before that it belonged to you and your cousin Stefan, who's now dead."

"Who are you?" Ganis mutters. "Oh Christ, I think that was a tooth."

"Three years ago, on the twenty-sixth of June, you drove it up north to Thunderbolt's Way where you ran a silver BMW saloon off the road."

"No." Ganis shakes his head, then gives a little shriek as Harry raises the gun again. "No! I've no idea what you're talking about. I swear!"

Harry considers him for a long moment, then walks away, out of the shed to the forecourt, where he takes hold of the dog's rear legs and drags it back inside and dumps it in front of Ganis. "Now I'm going to show you what I do to people who tell me lies." He cocks the pistol and points it down at the dog's head.

"No! Not Caesar! Don't kill Caesar!"

"Up to you."

"I wasn't one of them! I was never a Crow."

"But Stefan was."

Ganis nods.

"Who was with Stefan?"

Ganis gives an awkward little squirming shake of his head.

Harry says, "If you don't tell me, or if you tell me lies, I'll kill the dog and then you. But if you tell me everything, truthfully, you and Caesar will live. Understand?"

"Stefan went with another Crow."

"Name?"

"I don't know."

Harry presses the muzzle to Caesar's skull. "Last chance, Marco."

"Roman. That was his name, Roman. Stefan couldn't stop talking about it. They ran the car off the road and then Roman went down the hill with a baseball bat to make sure they were dead. But we had to get rid of the truck, he said. So I drove it down to this bloke I know in Melbourne, and he kept it there for a year, then we brought it back with a new ID."

Harry lowers the gun. "If you keep quiet about tonight

there will be no consequences for you, Marco. Caesar will wake up in an hour. If you've told me the truth you won't see me again."

"It is the truth, I swear."

"Why did Stefan fall out with the Crows?"

"It was the drugs, chief. They made him crazy."

Harry leaves him there, tied to the chair, and climbs back out of the yard. He concentrates on remaining unseen all the way back to the car, but when he is finally seated behind the wheel he allows himself to think of Roman Bebchuk climbing down the hill with a baseball bat in his hand, to make sure they were dead.

TWENTY-SEVEN

THE SLEEK GLASS CUBE overlooking Pyrmont Bay makes a startling contrast with the scruffy little dump that she's worked in for the past twenty-odd years. As she rises up in a glass elevator to the top floor she looks out over broad acres of floor space filled with rank upon rank of the latest IT equipment served by a bustling community of vigorous young staff. She wonders if she'll be up to it.

Catherine Meiklejohn is reassuringly warm and down to earth. She glances over Kelly's CV and says with a smile, "Yes, I think I'm familiar with all this. Now I want to focus on your future." She describes the make-up of their crime desk, their resources, their strengths and weaknesses.

"We see you complementing the team perfectly, Kelly. Your boots on the ground familiarity with this city, with the western suburbs, with how it works, will be invaluable to us. But I need to ask," she leans forward, watching Kelly closely. "In light of the attack on your flat, are you quite certain that you want to continue with this work?"

"Yes, absolutely."

"Good." Then Catherine makes an offer of a package that Kelly tries hard not to goggle at—in total, with the perks, at least twice, maybe two and a half times what she's currently getting. "And we will provide you with temporary safe accommodation until we're sure you're out of danger. But I would like a swift decision, Kelly, and, if the answer is yes, as early a start date as possible."

Kelly says "Yes," and "Tomorrow."

She leaves, thankful that Catherine hasn't raised the awkward matter of her Crucifixion Creek conspiracy theory beginning to look shaky.

But it does come up the following day, after she's gone through HRM and been given a security pass and allocated a desk, when Catherine invites her up to her office again to talk about her work. She takes a folder with her of copies of her articles and supporting material.

"Kelly, before you get down to work with anyone else, there's a matter of confidentiality that we need to clear up. It's apparent from your recent articles that you have sources of information that you don't disclose. Is that right?"

"Yes."

"What can you tell me about them?"

"Well, they've insisted that I keep their identity to myself."

"All right. Can I ask, is it one source, or multiple sources?"

"Predominantly one, although I've been getting many new contacts since the first article from people who are obviously knowledgable and concerned about what's going on."

"But this primary source, are you absolutely satisfied that they would have access to this sort of confidential information?"

"Yes."

"Have you met them in person?"

"Yes."

"And you are certain they can be trusted?"

"Yes, I am."

"All right. Let's give them a name for convenience— how about 'Kelpie'? Okay?"

"Yes, all right."

"So, for example, Kelpie gave you that 'three kings' photograph, did they?"

"Yes."

"And what about the business of the south-west underground rail route?"

"No, he—they—didn't give me that. That was my own interpretation of events."

"It's been getting a bit of a knocking the last few days. Are you still confident about it?"

"To be perfectly honest, I'm not sure. But I am convinced that the three kings were involved in a criminal conspiracy of some kind, along with other people. Kelpie believes this too."

"Hm." Catherine looks, not disbelieving exactly, but needing to be convinced. "Has he given you anything else?"

Kelly takes a large print of Harry's latest photograph

from her folder and gives it to her. "Kelpie gave me this. It was taken in the bar of the Le Meridien hotel in Jakarta last April. That's Kristich, Mansur and Oldfield, and the fourth man is called Potgeiter, a local councillor whose ward includes Crucifixion Creek. Oldfield declared his trip to the parliamentary record as being for liaison with Indonesian police officials, while Kristich paid for Potgeiter's airfare and hotel accommodation. Potgeiter told his council that he was taking a holiday in Tasmania."

"What were they up to?"

"I don't know. That's one of the things I'd like to find out."

"You want to go to Jakarta?"

"Um . . ." She hasn't thought this through.

"Alternatively, we have resources on the ground there. Maybe you could talk to them and see what they can find out."

"Yes, great."

"What about this Potgeiter? Isn't he a bit out of his league?"

"That's what makes me think it must be something local to the Creek. I've heard rumours in the past that he uses influence with council inspectors and other staff to go easy with his friends when they sail a bit close to the wind."

"But surely this is something bigger?"

"Yes. I'd like to find out more of his background. He emigrated from South Africa about ten years ago."

"Okay." Catherine examines the photograph again. "I think we should hold this back until we know more about the context. On its own it means nothing."

Kelly is disappointed. She hoped that the momentum would increase with the *Times* behind her, not slow down.

"You disagree? Your first photo, the three kings, set the hares running. They all went into a panic, but it won't happen again. They're prepared now. We need the story behind the photograph to get the impact."

She's right, Kelly concedes, as she makes her way back to her desk. She was lucky before; now she has to do the solid groundwork. She feels like an amateur coming into this great machine, having to prove herself all over again. She thanks God she's got Harry.

TWENTY-EIGHT

IT IS A CHILLY winter morning and the pool looks almost as dark and forbidding as the sky. There is only one swimmer, ploughing his solitary watery furrow up and back, up and back. Harry, pulling his coat around him against the wind, watches him from the stand. After almost an hour the swimmer hauls himself out and wraps himself in his towel. He pads off to the changing room without a glance at the lone watcher in the stand.

Harry is waiting for him as he emerges from the entrance, a stocky man with powerful shoulders and a battered face. He has a noticeable limp. When Harry steps into his path, Tony Gemmell glances at him without surprise and says, "You look like a cop."

"The name's Harry."

"Not interested."

Gemmell goes to push past and Harry says, "I was in the army with Rowdy O'Brian."

"So?"

"It was my doorstep they dumped his body on."

Gemmell peers at him more closely. "And why was that?"

"We'd met a couple of days before. Somebody saw us together."

"So it's your fault he died."

"Maybe, or maybe someone just wanted rid of him. He told me about you and how things had changed for the worse since you left the Crows. He had a great respect for you, Tony."

"What do you want?"

"I want to nail whoever did it."

"Don't ask me." He keeps walking and Harry lets him pass.

"They broke all his fingers and toes, then they used an oxy-acetylene torch on him. Burned the club tatts off his arm and carved D-O-G on his back."

Gemmell stops and slowly turns back. "What are the cops doing about it?"

"Not making much headway so far. Prime suspects were Bebchuk and his mob, but they have alibis, so now they're thinking it might be another gang."

"Bullshit. What was their alibi?"

"They all rode out to a hotel in Bathurst for the weekend."

"Who says so?"

"The hotel staff. Local cops saw their bikes outside all weekend, and their phone data places them there."

"Nah, it's a set-up. Cameras?"

"The hotel doesn't have any. So they say."

Gemmell shakes his head. "There's no way they would

have gone on a ride last weekend except to set up an alibi."

"How can you be sure?"

"Because this weekend is the Presidents' Ride, and they wouldn't have gone out two weekends running."

"What's the Presidents' Ride?"

"Each year three of the west Sydney outlaw motorcycle clubs have a meet at the Swagman Hotel in Penrith. It's a longstanding tradition, and anyone who breaks it would be in big trouble."

"I see."

"Bebchuk did Rowdy all right. It's as clear as day. Bebchuk, Capp and Haddad, those three."

They stand in silence for a moment, then Gemmell says, "What did you expect from me?"

"I wondered if you might be able to tell me how I could get Bebchuk on his own, outside of the compound."

Gemmell shakes his head. "No chance. Bebchuk's made plenty of enemies. They don't go out much, and always in strength."

"Ah."

"You are a cop, right?"

Harry nods. "But not on this case. This is strictly personal."

Another pause, the two men sizing each other up as the wind whips a spattering of rain around them. Then Gemmell says, "So let me tell you about the Presidents' Ride."

TWENTY-NINE

AROUND LUNCHTIME, NICOLE CALLS in unexpectedly on Jenny. Their mother has taken the girls to the movies and Nicole, in town for some shopping, thought she'd drop in to see her sister. As she comes in Jenny smells her perfume and imagines her make-up, something Nicole was always good at. For Jenny, make-up is another one of those awkward problems now. Mostly she has to rely on Harry to tell her whether she's done a decent job.

"Isn't Harry here?" Nicole asks. "I thought you said it was his day off today."

"He had to go out. I'm not sure when he'll be back."

"Oh." Nicole sounds disappointed.

They go into the kitchen where Jenny's got out the bread and cheese she was going to have for lunch. "There's plenty for both of us."

Actually, Nicole is more interested in wine, and helps herself from a bottle in the fridge. "The truth is, Mum's driving me crazy," she says. "She's turning the place upside down and I can't find anything. She just takes over. Well, you know what she's like."

From their mother she goes on to all the other problems she's having. "God, Jen, I just didn't realise when Greg was alive how much I depended on him. The money of course, he did everything. Paid the bills, balanced the books. I'm hopeless, he never told me how it all worked. And then things keep going wrong. Have you ever tried changing a globe in one of those recessed ceiling lights? It's impossible. Mum says call an electrician, but we can't afford to do that every time a globe goes. And then one of the hinges in the cupboard doors has come off, and I can't get the lawnmower to start. I'm just useless, that's how I feel."

Jenny tries to comfort her. "Of course Harry will help with that sort of thing." She knows this side of her younger sister, how it will blow over. She hears the clink of the bottle and the glug of Nicole refilling her glass. "Better watch if you're driving," she says.

"Oh, I got a bus into town and a cab out here. I was rather hoping Harry might give me a lift home. Honestly, you don't know how lucky you are having a good man like that."

There is a wistful tone in Nicole's voice that sets off an alarm in Jenny's mind. There was a pattern—well, it happened twice, before they were both married—where Nicole would take a sudden fancy to her sister's latest boyfriend. Nicole was the pretty, vivacious one, Jenny more serious and cautious, and these two boys found Nicole's flirtatiousness irresistible. It just happened, Nicole would say, as if she'd had nothing at all to do with it. She had sexy eyes, one of them later told Jenny, who knew what he meant. She had watched the way her sister used her eyes, her wide-eyed gaze. It worries her that she can no longer see the way Nicole looks at Harry.

No, she stops herself. Of course Nicole would never do that to her. How could she think it? It's just a symptom of her own insecurity that she can imagine such a thing. All the same, she's relieved that Harry doesn't come home for lunch, and that eventually Nicole calls a cab to take her to Central to get a train home.

WHEN HARRY GETS HOME that evening he finds Jenny watching television, which is to say that she is sitting facing the set, listening to *Singin' in the Rain* and watching Gene Kelly and Debbie Reynolds dancing in her head.

He kisses her on the cheek and tells her to go on, but it's a DVD and she says she'll finish it later. They sit down for the meal she's prepared and she tells him about a new player she's found, called Curly. It seems that Curly has been providing some form of service for Kristich for several years, receiving irregular payments of a few hundred dollars at a time, cash in hand, no GST.

"Drugs?"

"Maybe. Could be."

"Curly . . ." Harry tries to think of someone with distinctive hair, or else completely bald. "How about Chloe Anastos, his girlfriend? She has big hair."

"Ah yes, I suppose it could be her." She hesitates, then says, "What is it, darling? What's wrong?"

"What? Nothing."

"There is, I can hear it, feel it. You're worried about something, or bottling something up."

He laughs, "Doctor Inspector Jenny," but it sounds off-key.

She doesn't smile, looking grave. "I've been thinking that you were right."

"About what?"

"About us going away. I would like to go to France. We could rent a house somewhere in the south, just us, and we can go to the market in the town square in the morning and smell the cheeses and the fruit, and make love in the afternoon or any time we feel like it."

Oh, he thinks, that's it. "I'm sorry, Jen. I haven't been feeling—"

"It isn't just that. Here we're trapped in the past, and it's destroying us. We can't put it right, Harry. We can't put the bits together again. It'll burn us up, kill us if we don't escape."

She's right of course, and he doesn't know how to answer her. He knows he couldn't escape so easily. In his dreams Bebchuk would always be climbing down that hill with his baseball bat, or holding a torch to Rowdy's back. "Maybe . . . maybe in a little while. September perhaps, or October, when the tourists have gone, we could take a trip." But he knows that isn't what she means.

THIRTY

IT ISN'T LONG BEFORE Kelly is feeling overwhelmed by her new environment—the new names she has to learn, the acronyms, the procedures, the equipment, the office habits, where to get a decent cup of coffee. She is helped by Hannah, a young journalism graduate from UTS, who has been assigned to her. Kelly hardly knows where to ask her to begin, but they sit down together and draw up a list of possible tasks.

Following her talk with Catherine, Kelly's priority is to gather background on the Jakarta photograph, and she asks Hannah to get details of the paper's contacts in Indonesia. "And while you're at it, make that Vanuatu too," she adds.

Meanwhile Kelly has a list of people who have been contacting her with offers of information on Kristich, Oldfield, Potgeiter and especially Mansur. They are angry residents, outraged ratepayers, cranks, serial letter-writers and people with too much time on their hands, and she has to sift the gold from the dross. It seems Mansur's company Ozdevco has been involved in a number of development projects that have upset local residents, conservationists and community groups. If the complainants are to be believed, its methods in getting projects approved have ranged from the mysterious to the brutal. Several of these projects have been within Councillor Potgeiter's ward, and it appears that Kristich has acted as Ozdevco's agent in a number of them. The complaints against Oldfield, on the other hand, tend to be on law and order issues. People seem to think he was soft on criminals and resisted attempts to strengthen anti-biker legislation.

When Hannah comes back with the contact details she asked for, Kelly gives her the letters and emails and asks her to make brief summaries and a priority list for further contact. She then picks up the phone and gets straight through to Anton, their stringer in Jakarta. She introduces herself and they discuss what she's after. While they're talking, Kelly gets Hannah to send him the photograph in the Le Meridien bar. When he's got it in front of him she describes the people it shows.

Anton listens carefully, then says, "There is one other man there I recognise, do you see on the left? Almost out of the picture, in profile, turned towards the bar lady."

"Oh yes."

"His name is Gunardi, and he is a member of the Polri, the national police."

"Well, that makes sense. Oldfield said that his trip to Indonesia was to liaise with your police."

"Yes, but as a government minister Mr. Oldfield would surely meet with senior officers, police generals. Gunardi is only of middle rank, a kompol, a police commissioner."

"Perhaps he was assigned to look after the visitors outside of the official meetings?"

"Maybe, but this Gunardi has a reputation, Kelly. That's why I recognise him."

"What kind of reputation?"

"Shady. Nothing bad enough to get him into trouble, so far. Rumours of bribes, leaning on crooks for protection. Okay, let me follow it up. Is it mainly Oldfield you are interested in?"

"I suppose so. I'd like to know if they met up there just that one time or if they went elsewhere together. Potgeiter is the odd one out."

"The ugly little man on the right?"

"That's him. He's a small-time local councillor, and Kristich paid for his airfare and hotel bill at Le Meridien for six nights. I'd like to know why."

"I'll see what I can do."

She goes through a similar process with their contact in Vanuatu, sending him the three kings photo and asking him to find out what he can about Kristich, Oldfield and Mansur during their period there.

She is beginning to feel more confident, energised by the sense of common industry. She phones her insurance company to get an assessment made of the damage to her flat, something she should have done days ago. She also phones the hospital to check on Wendy, and is relieved by the news that she has come out of her coma and is out of danger. She goes over there during the lunchbreak, and though her friend is still pitifully weak, and the doctor warns of a long road ahead, Kelly maintains her new feeling of optimism and purpose.

When she returns she sits down with Hannah and they work through the whistleblowers and complainants. "This one's a bit different," Hannah says, referring to a record of a phone call taken at the *Chronicle* reception when Kelly was out. "All he would say was that he used to work at the Department of Immigration, Multi-cultural and Indigenous Affairs."

"Is that what it's called?"

"Not anymore. They called it that between 2001 and 2006. Out of date, maybe?"

"Well, give it a try."

"He also said he would only speak to you."

"Okay." Kelly takes the note, a Sydney phone number. There is an answering machine and she leaves a message, then gets onto the next person on Hannah's list.

By late afternoon she has spoken to sixteen unhappy people who have been overshadowed, built out, bullied and threatened by Ozdevco, and a further desperate three who were almost ruined by taking loans on extortionate terms from Kristich. She's feeling wrung out when Anton rings from Jakarta.

"I've made a start, Kelly. I've established that they all stayed at Le Meridien for those six days, and that they had several meals together there. The concierge says they were picked up each day in a minibus with a local driver, and accompanied by another Indonesian, probably Gunardi. I'm afraid I don't know where they went."

"Okay. Is it possible to find out more, do you think?"

"Do you want me to approach Gunardi?"

"What do you think?"

"I would assume that he was either escorting them on police orders, or they were paying him well. Either way he won't talk to me."

"Yes, and it would tip them off. What else?"

"I could try to find the driver, find out where they went?"

"That would be good."

"It would mean bribing him. You okay with that?"

Kelly has no idea what the paper's policy might be. "I'll check and call you back. Many thanks, Anton."

She rings Catherine.

"No bribes, absolutely not. However, Anton might hire him for a day, at a generous rate."

"Thanks." Kelly rings Anton back and tells him.

She is about to leave to keep her appointment with the insurance assessor when her phone rings again, the number of the former immigration staffer.

"You left a message on my phone." The voice sounds hesitant, as if on the point of hanging up.

"Yes. I'm sorry it's taken so long to get back to you. Was there something you wanted to pass on to me?"

"Not on the phone. In person."

"I see. I don't usually do that unless I have some indication . . ."

There is a silence on the line. Then, "Oldfield overrode his department's advice that Potgeiter's visa application ought to be rejected."

"I see. All right, where would you like to meet?"

"The Domain, Mrs. Macquarie's Chair. In an hour."

"I can't do that. Make it two hours."

"Okay." Reluctant.

"Give me your mobile number," Kelly says, but the line is dead.

She hurries home just in time for her appointment, filled again with a sense of violation and despair at the chaos, but also now with anger. The assessor raises a pained eyebrow as they pick through the debris, and makes notes. "Have you got sales dockets for any of this?" he asks. Kelly shakes her head. "So . . ." he shows her a list, "these items of furniture and equipment?"

She agrees, and they talk figures. She really has no idea what things cost now. He's patient. "Any jewellery taken? Cash?"

She says not. He seems surprised that she doesn't want to claim for more.

As soon as he's gone she heads back into the city to keep her other appointment. She finds a parking spot for her car on the loop road around the Domain and walks through the trees to the convict-carved bench in the sandstone outcrop. There's a dark figure sitting in the shadows. This was a bad idea, meeting in such a place after dusk. There appears to be no one else around. She hesitates and almost turns back, but then decides to draw on her new sense of purpose and go on. She stops about ten metres away. "Hello?"

"Ms. Pool?"

"That's me."

He gets off the bench and comes towards her. "Sorry, this is a bit spooky, isn't it?"

"Yes, it is a bit."

"Most appropriate," and he gives a high-pitched laugh,

almost a giggle. He lurches towards her, sticking out his hand. "Not quite sure of the etiquette."

She shakes it, realising that he's even more nervous than she is. "What can you tell me?"

"I was encouraged to contact you when you mentioned Joost Potgeiter in connection with Derryn Oldfield. Ten years ago I was working in the office that vets applications for permanent residency in Australia. I got an instruction from the departmental head to approve Potgeiter's application, although we had previously recommended refusal. When I queried it, I was told that further information had come to hand. Well, normally that would have been that, but this time I persisted, and my supervisor told me, off the record, that a senior diplomat had used influence. His name was Oldfield."

Kelly can see that the man has become agitated, rocking from foot to foot, gripping and ungripping his hands. "I see. Why did you persist in this case?"

"Well, because of what we had learned about him. The reason for refusing the visa . . . I was abused too as a boy."

"He had abused a child?"

"A maid in a cheap hotel in Johannesburg found him in bed with two little Indian boys, aged six and eight. She reported him to the authorities but he'd registered under a false name and there was some confusion. By the time the police had positively identified him he'd left the country and come here."

"What did you do?"

"I went to see the departmental head. I told him it wasn't right, and that I would make a formal complaint if something wasn't done. He told me I didn't know all the facts, that there had been a mix-up over identity and the maid had withdrawn her statement. He also said that if I made a formal complaint to the appeals tribunal and they found against me, it would probably end my career in the service. So I did nothing." He's scratching the back of his hand, agitated. "I became sick. I had a breakdown, and I took a separation package a year later."

And you're still a mess, Kelly thinks. "Is there any documentary evidence you can give me about this?"

"No. And I won't go on the record. I simply can't go through it all again. Will you act?"

"It's difficult. I don't really know who you are. If I take this to my editor she'll need more."

"Then it's up to you to get it. I've done what I can." He spins away and hurries off into the darkness. Kelly remains for a moment, thinking of Phoebe's words, *Little faces at the windows, like ghosts.*

She shakes her head. After the business with the underground rail route she is more cautious. This may be just another red herring. But later that sense of optimism returns. Wendy is out of danger and at the weekend Kelly will arrange for the rubbish to be removed from their place and she will start again. Maybe things will work out.

THIRTY-ONE

ON FRIDAY ANTON RINGS from Jakarta.

"I found the driver," he says. "Nice chap, short of money, wife sick. The first two days he took them out to Bogor, sixty kilometres inland from here. They call Bogor Rain City, because it's always raining, even in the dry season. It's very crowded, the second highest population density in the world, and bad slums. That's where they went."

"To the slums?"

"Yes, on the north side of the city. The driver stayed on the highway outside, and Gunardi took them in on foot. Each time they were gone for several hours. He doesn't know what they were doing. They had cameras.

"On the other days he took them to townships on the edge of Jakarta—Bekasi and Depok—more slums, very crowded, poor people coming to the city from the countryside.

"So, slums, all slums. Are they working for a charity maybe? Or Australian foreign aid?"

"First I've heard of it, Anton. Could the driver tell you anything else?"

"Not much. Commissioner Gunardi made him nervous. One day the Australians were counting out money on the back seat. Gunardi took them to nice restaurants for their lunches. That's about it. They only used the driver during the day. If they went out in the evenings they would get taxis. According to the concierge they went out one night to Taman Lawang, red light district, famous for ladyboys, and another night to Star Luck Disco. It's kind of notorious, ladyboys again, and other things."

"I get the picture."

"Just your usual Australian tourists, Kelly." He laughs. "Do you want me to go on with this?"

"What more can you do?"

"I don't know. I could talk some more to the driver, see if he remembers any conversations about the slums. It would mean more money. He's worried about Gunardi, as I said. Five hundred dollars might get him to remember more."

"Okay. Do your best."

Kelly puts the phone down and sits for a while, doodling on her pad, then looks across at Hannah, head down, checking a list. "Fancy a reporter's assignment, Hannah?"

"Totally."

"Why don't you ring Counsellor Potgeiter and ask him for an interview today. Say you're writing an article on cutting planning red tape, and you believe he has some interesting ideas."

"Okay. Am I interested in his ideas?"

"Absolutely fascinated. Just don't mention my name."

Kelly listens as Hannah makes the call. She has a lovely telephone voice, very feminine and flattering. She rings off and grins at Kelly.

"Twelve-thirty. I think he wants to take me to lunch."

"Perfect."

POTGEITER ADVANCES ON THEM across the bright green carpet of the town hall foyer. He has a pugnacious thrust to his jaw and an unpleasant curl on his lips, impersonating a smile. Kelly hangs back, brandishing the largest camera she could find in the office. Potgeiter barely spares her a glance as he takes Hannah's arm and steers her towards the lifts.

As the lift doors close he looks pointedly at his watch and says, "Tight schedule of course. But if this is going to take more than ten minutes we could continue in the coffee shop next door over a sandwich." He says this to Hannah, who smiles and says, "Lovely." He beams at her, then flicks a glance at Kelly, who mumbles about having to get back to the office. That cheers him up, and Kelly reflects ruefully that it wasn't that hard to turn herself into a frumpy inarticulate lump.

When they get inside his office she gets him to pose in the oversized leather chair at his desk, pretending to answer the phone and writing in his diary. With a fountain pen, the wanker. Then she takes a chair over to the side and fiddles with the camera controls.

"Councillor Potgeiter," Hannah begins. "Thank you so

much for agreeing to see me." She switches on her recording device.

"Not at all. Always happy to talk to the press. How did you come to think of interviewing me?"

"I understand you raised some very interesting points in the recent council debates on DCP 86 and the Local Environmental Plan. I'd really like to get at the philosophy that obviously underpins your arguments. Could you tell me about that?"

Potgeiter puffs out his cheeks. "Philosophy, eh? Well, it's quite simple really. We live in a capitalist country, and it's up to public organisations like ours to facilitate the workings of a free market economy and not get in its way." He beams and continues to develop the argument.

Eventually Hannah breaks in. "And I believe you've undertaken study tours recently to investigate how other local authorities manage these issues."

"Study tours?"

"Yes, for instance last April, to Tasmania."

"Ah, yes, yes, of course."

"Was it useful?"

"Oh, yes, up to a point."

"How about Indonesia?"

Potgeiter's jaw drops open, and from the sidelines Kelly's camera clicks rapidly as she captures the bovine expression. Potgeiter turns on her and spits, "Do you mind?" Then to Hannah, "Why on earth do you say Indonesia?"

"I just thought that the problems of responding to market forces in a populous third world country like Indonesia would highlight a number of town planning issues."

"Well . . . maybe, but it's a bit distant from the problems of western Sydney." He laughs, coughs, takes a handkerchief out of his pocket and wipes his mouth.

"Have you ever been there, to Indonesia?"

"What? No, never. But look, as I was saying . . ."

Now Kelly speaks. "So you deny being in Jakarta last April when you said you were in Tasmania?"

He turns to her, face turning deep scarlet, eyes bulging, as if seeing her for the first time.

"We're just giving you a chance to retract your earlier statements," Kelly says calmly.

He is rising from his chair, spluttering. Finally he finds the words. "Get out, the pair of you!" he splutters. "Get out this minute!"

As he comes around the desk, fists bunched, Hannah grabs her recorder and notebook, Kelly her camera, and they both run for the door.

BACK IN THE OFFICE they get to work on the article. Kelly has several wonderful photographs of Potgeiter goggling monstrously at the camera. They are almost ready to run it past Catherine when another call comes in from Anton.

"I spoke to the driver again, Kelly. It seems that the Australians have been here before on trips to the slums. He spoke to some of his friends, other drivers, and a couple of them remember a group of four Australians going through much the same routine in previous years, with Gunardi as their guide. They claim to have interesting stories to tell, but I'm sceptical, frankly. I think they know there's money in it."

"So we can't be sure any of it is true?"

"Hard to know. They say they came in April, at the end of the rainy season, last year and the year before. Maybe you could see if that fits with anything else."

"Right. Thank you, Anton."

She checks her watch, time to see Catherine. They gather their material together and head for the glass lift.

The editor listens in silence as she reads the article, studies the photographs and listens to an excerpt from Hannah's recording of Potgeiter.

Finally she says, "So what do they go over there for?"

Kelly cues up another recording, this time of the immigration officer yesterday in the Domain.

Catherine looks at her. "Sex tourism? Children?"

"Could be. I know it's a stretch to assume they're all paedophiles because Potgeiter was, but, well, what else are they doing?"

"You haven't hinted at that."

"No, there are several things I've held back, including the fact that their guide was a serving police commissioner. We need to do more work."

"I'll say."

"But Potgeiter lied, and got into a fury when he realised we knew. I want to use the photograph of the group in the bar now, to see what that throws up."

Catherine thinks, then nods. "Okay, we'll do it." She

points to one of the photos of Potgeiter and smiles. "And use that one."

When she gets back to her desk, Kelly tries Harry on the secure mobile. There is no reply and she risks sending a text: *I think I know what it's all about. Potgeiter is the key. Call me.*

THIRTY-TWO

HARRY SITS IN THE passenger seat of Tony Gemmell's elderly Corolla. They listen on Harry's police radio to the
progress of the three motorcycle gangs converging on
Penrith. Tony is wearing a heavy leather jacket with the
Crow colours on the back, and his broad upper body half-
fills the car.

For some reason the Crows are taking the Great Western Highway rather than the motorway, and a patrol car
has observed them passing through Mount Druitt.
Another police patrol reports them reaching the centre
of Penrith and turning off onto the secondary road where
the Swagman Hotel sits overlooking the Nepean River,
with views from its upper veranda towards the Emu Plains
Correctional Centre away to the west.

Through the windscreen Harry and Tony watch their
headlights approaching. Most of the other bikers have already arrived, and the hotel forecourt is crowded with
ranks of bikes, men shaking hands and embracing each
other in elaborate bear hugs. A cheer goes up as the lead
Crows turn into the hotel.

Tony and Harry get out of the car. The night air reverberates with hoarse shouts and the roar of bikes. They cross the road and skirt around a knot of bearded men removing helmets and sorting out their gear. Then there is a space and ahead of them they see the Crows.

"Bebchuk," Tony points to the big man, "Capp and Haddad."

Harry nods.

"Bebchuk!" Tony says again, but this time it is an aggressive bellow that casts a sudden pall of silence on the people nearby. Bebchuk and the other two turn.

"Bebchuk you cunt, I hear you murdered O'Brian. Is it true?"

Bebchuk stares at him, folds his arms. "That's what I should have done to you," he shouts back, then nods at the other two.

A metal baseball bat appears in Capp's hand, a shotgun in Haddad's. Capp raises the bat to his shoulder and runs at Tony, who ducks smartly away and punches him in the ribs, grabs his bat and begins beating his head and shoulders with it. Behind them Harry watches Haddad raise the shotgun and aim. People scatter as Harry draws his pistol and shoots him once, twice in the chest and stomach. As he hits the ground the shotgun booms into the air.

Now the forecourt erupts in panic, people scrambling away, pushing each other, stumbling through the lines of bikes which tilt and topple and crash to the ground.

Harry raises his pistol again, holding it steady in two hands, just like the firing range. Lining it up on Bebchuk who has leapt onto his bike, kicking it into life, wrestling the high handlebars. Harry squeezes the trigger, the bang almost drowned by the thunder of Bebchuk's engine. The bike wobbles, rights itself and roars away through scattering bodies. Harry runs after it, watching its red light diminishing down the road, then runs back to Haddad and Capp's bikes, one of which still has the key in the ignition. He grabs the helmet on the seat and jumps on. Starts it and races away.

It's years since he rode a bike and it wasn't a Harley. It is sheer momentum that keeps him on the saddle through the bends. When he reaches the highway he thinks he sees the red taillight up ahead, continuing south rather than east along the route they arrived on. A minute later he realises why, as he comes to the M1 on-ramp. He can't see Bebchuk, but he guesses he's heading back to Sydney on the motorway, and he makes the turn. Sure enough, after a couple of kilometres he sees the bike up ahead. It is travelling within the speed limit but erratically, veering across lanes and causing other traffic to brake and swerve.

They reach Silverwater, Bebchuk slowing. Harry can't tell if he's aware he has a tail. At the next intersection, Bebchuk lurches off onto the exit ramp at the last minute. They are heading back to home turf, Harry thinks, to the Creek. He wonders whether to get there first, but decides to stay back in case Bebchuk has something else in mind. There have been no patrol cars, no signs of police activity. Maybe they're waiting up ahead.

But they are not, and Mortimer Street is deserted when Harry finally turns the bike into it. At the far end of the street he sees Bebchuk's headlight reflected on the compound gates, Bebchuk a dark figure hunched against the steel wall. Then the gate swings open and he disappears inside, leaving his bike outside. Harry parks the stolen Harley and follows, drawing his gun.

Across the yard the door to the clubhouse is open, a light on. Harry runs silently to the door jamb and peers in. Beyond the pool table he sees the closed door to the little office. No sign of Bebchuk. He steps in. The kitchen at the other end of the room is lit. As he pauses in the doorway he sees drops of blood on the floor. Inside, beyond the cooker, the big fridge has been pulled away from the wall. Behind it is a doorway flush with the wall. He hears a metallic sound, clicking, sliding, takes a breath and glances through the door. Bebchuk is sprawled on the floor, wrestling with the magazine of a military automatic assault rifle. Behind him is an armoury of weapons chained in a rack.

He raises his head and sees Harry. There is blood all over his left shoulder and he is having trouble handling the gun, but now he roars and lifts it and fires a burst, deafening in the small room as Harry instinctively drops, rolls and fires.

Bebchuk's head is down, the rifle lying on the floor beside his limp hand, and Harry jumps across and kicks it away, then crouches at Bebchuk's side. "Hey," Harry slaps his face. "Hey, Bebchuk."

An eye opens, rolls at him. "Hello, Belltree," Bebchuk croaks, and Harry blinks.

"You know me?"

"Oh, I know . . . all about you."

"You killed my parents. Why?"

Bebchuk grunts and blood spills between his lips.

Harry shakes him. "Why? Why did you do it? Who did you do it for?"

A cough, then Bebchuk burps a gobbet of blood over Harry's front. Harry shakes him again, hard, and he mumbles something.

"What?" He leans closer to the dying man and hears a whisper.

"Wanna know who tipped us off about their route?"

"Go on."

Bebchuk's mouth parts in a bloody grin. "March . . . Greg March." He gives another little cough and Harry pulls back as a great bubble of blood bursts from his mouth. His head flops back and his body sags.

Harry rocks back on his heels, staring at the dead man. Then he shakes his head as if waking from a nightmare. He goes through Bebchuk's pockets, takes his wallet, keys, phone, then turns and hurries out. In the club room he takes an old waterproof from a peg on the wall and pulls it over his bloodstained clothes, then runs out across the yard to the gate, all the time expecting to hear the sound of police sirens. He mounts the Harley again and drives to the end of the street. All seems quiet. He takes Bebchuk's phone out of his pocket and rings triple-O, reporting a murder in the Crow clubhouse, then throws the phone into the gutter and sets off again. He rides as far as Campsie, where he leaves the bike near the station, but instead of catching a train he heads north, jogging through quiet suburban backstreets until, after half an hour, he reaches Liverpool Road. He peels off his bloody leather gloves and stuffs them in his pockets, catches a bus into Chippendale and walks home.

It is like the replay of an old movie. Once again Jenny smells the gun, the blood. He peels off all his clothes in the little utility room and shoves everything into the washing machine on a long cycle. When he closes the shower door he stands under the hot jet, watching the blood circling into the drain at his feet, willing his muscles to relax, one by one.

When he finally emerges, Jenny is waiting with a large scotch. Only then, after the first thankful gulp, does she ask him.

"I killed the man who killed Mum and Dad and Rowdy and blinded you," he says, and tells her about Bebchuk.

"Then it's over," she says, and wraps her arms around him.

He holds her tight, rocking back and forward, then finally says, "No. He didn't tell me why they did it, or who for. But he did tell me one thing, about Greg."

When he tells her she cries out and shakes her head.

He holds her tighter as she sobs.

"I'll never believe that," she says. "Bebchuk was lying to punish you."

THIRTY-THREE

HE IS LATE GETTING in to work the next day, feeling sluggish, reluctant to rejoin the world. When he arrives on the eighth floor he finds the place deserted. One of the admin staff tells him that an emergency briefing has been called on the sixth floor, and he goes down there and slips into the back of the room, like a reluctant student late for a lecture.

Toby Wagstaff is addressing the assembled officers. Behind him an image of the forecourt of the Swagman Hotel is projected onto a screen.

"... however it seems to have taken the staff of the hotel something like ten minutes to call triple-O, and a further three minutes for the first patrol car to arrive, by which time they had all dispersed. Witnesses in Penrith report large numbers of motorcycles heading south towards the motorway.

"On the screen you can see the scene on the forecourt as secured by the arriving GD officers. The bodies of two men are on the ground. The one nearest the camera has been identified as Francis Hadley Capp, vice-president of the Crows. He appears to have been beaten with that baseball bat lying by his side, causing extensive head injuries. He is currently in intensive care. Beyond him lies Hakim Kassim Haddad, sergeant-at-arms of the Crows, killed by two shots to the upper body. His right hand is holding a pump-action shotgun which has been discharged. On the ground in the lower left of the picture are three nine-millimetre NATO cartridge cases, and in the upper left, not clearly visible in this picture, are some bloodstains."

Wagstaff pauses to turn a page of his notes and take a sip of water. Looking around the room Harry can see Deb at the front with several other homicide cops, including Bob Marshall. He recognises others from the gangs squad.

"Now the other crime scene . . ."

Wagstaff presses a button and the image switches to a large plan. Harry recognises the angular cubist heart-shape of Crucifixion Creek, pierced by the vertical shaft of Mortimer Street pointing to the square block of the Crow compound at its core.

"At 20:57, thirty-one minutes after the triple-O call from the Swagman Hotel, a second call was received saying that a murder had been committed at the Crow clubhouse in Mortimer Street, here."

He clicks again and a larger scale plan of the clubhouse comes up.

"Many of you were involved in the Strike Force Gemini raid on the clubhouse on the ninth of this month, and will be familiar with the layout of the building and yard. When a patrol car arrived at the Mortimer Street entrance at 21:01, they found the front gate open, and a single Harley-Davidson bike lying on the ground nearby. The officers went into the courtyard, and saw the doorway to the clubhouse standing open, here. They noticed several spots of blood on the concrete and followed them into the clubhouse main room; from there to the kitchen in the north-east corner."

He points.

"Inside they found the refrigerator pulled into the room to reveal an open panel in the wall behind. Now you will see that this wall is in fact the external party wall forming the limit of the Crow site, and the room which they found beyond the opening is inside the neighbouring building. This room . . ." *click*, "contains an arsenal of weapons, including military style assault weapons, as well as a substantial quantity of ammunition, as you can see in this photo taken from the opening into the room. This opening was never discovered in the Strike Force Gemini search of the building, which explains why no firearms were found in that raid."

Wagstaff pauses for another sip of water, and perhaps to gently emphasise Gemini's failure. Harry sees Deb bow her head.

"In the foreground you see the body of Roman Bebchuk, president of the Crows. He is holding an M4 carbine, which has been discharged. There is a quantity of 5:56 millimetre cartridge cases scattered on the floor and a number of bullet holes in the wall above the opening into the room. Bebchuk had a bullet wound to the upper left chest from which extensive bleeding had occurred, together with a second bullet wound to right chest. A single 9 millimetre case was also found in the

room, similar to those found at the hotel forecourt. Ballistics are working now to establish if they were fired from the same weapon.

"Out of picture to the right is a door from this room leading into a further room built within the factory shed which adjoins the Crow compound. Inside this second room is what appears to be a sophisticated drug laboratory. Forensics are working on it now.

"Okay, our priorities are the following: to identify from cameras on the roads leading to the hotel each and every person who was in the hotel forecourt last evening, possibly as many as sixty bikers according to the hotel staff; to interview all of these to build up a picture of what happened; to seek out witnesses and CCTV records in the vicinity of Mortimer Street; and to identify and interview the owners of the building adjoining the Crow clubhouse. Let's get to it."

The meeting breaks up as case managers set up teams and allocate tasks. Harry watches Marshall have a parting word with Wagstaff then leave. He goes to speak to Deb.

"Sorry, missed the start of that. What about CCTV at the hotel?"

"There wasn't any, not in the forecourt."

"Typical. What's the plan?"

"We're interviewing bikers when they're brought in. But first I want to have a look at that bloody clubhouse again and see what we missed."

On the road over, Deb driving: "I see your girlfriend has moved to the *Times*."

"Has she?"

"You didn't see her latest scoop?" She nods to the paper folded at Harry's feet and he picks it up. It starts on the front page under the headline *New links in Kristich murder*, and continues on page three with the photograph of the Jakarta bar and another of a foolish-looking Potgeiter.

"I don't get her harping on about the Potgeiter bloke," Deb says. "He's only a local councillor. What does she think he's up to? Should we be interested in him?"

"Hm."

"And where did she get that Jakarta stuff from? Why do I get the feeling that she has better sources than we do?"

"Hm."

"What's the matter, Harry? You don't seem to be with us today. Pump up, princess."

With all the police vehicles in Mortimer Street and on the adjoining main road, they have to park some distance away. They register with the scene manager at the barrier formed outside the clubhouse gates, where a few press are waiting, taking their pictures as they enter. Inside the courtyard they have to wait for clearance from the crime scene team who are still working at several locations inside the building. Eventually they are given protective clothing and taken inside along a ribboned route as far as the kitchen, where they can examine the panel door behind the fridge. It's cleverly fitted and hinged so that it is difficult to spot. Harry thinks of some of the ingenious cupboard fittings in Greg and Nicole's house.

But that's as far as they can go. The whole area be-

yond the opening is still being worked over by forensics. Frustrated, Deb leads the way back out. As they make their way down Mortimer Street, she says, "Isn't that your girlfriend?"

Kelly is standing outside one of the little houses, staring up at the windows on the upper floor.

"I wish you wouldn't call her that, Deb."

"Yeah I know. Why don't you charm her into telling us where she got that Jakarta photo from?"

As they approach her Kelly turns and recognises them. "Hello, Inspector, Sergeant. What's going on down there?"

"Seems congratulations are in order," Deb says. "Hope your package covers legal representation. You know, in case you find yourself charged with withholding evidence material to a police investigation."

Kelly smiles at her. "I thought I was trying to support your investigations with my own modest efforts."

Harry says, "We'd like to know where you got that Jakarta photograph from, Kelly."

"I'll tell you if you tell me who murdered Roman Bebchuk here last night," she replies brightly.

"I'm sure you'll be telling us that before too long," Deb snarls and marches on. Harry nods at Kelly as he follows.

When they get back they begin the long round of interviews, trying to tease out fragments of fact from the mainly incoherent accounts of the bikers. Harry is, as always, fascinated and gratified by the variety. There was just the one assailant; or maybe six. He was very tall or almost stunted, dark haired or blond, face covered by a death's-head mask, a scarf or nothing at all. Outside the room, observers are taking notes and passing them on to the information pool where analysts are attempting to place each individual on the ground and map their movements.

By evening everyone is exhausted. A number of bikers have not yet been accounted for, but they will have to keep. There is a meal break and at seven they assemble for another briefing.

Inspector Wagstaff takes charge. He appears to have had a shower and a change of clothes and is the freshest-looking person in the room.

"Right," he says, rapping his knuckles on the table. "Let's get on with it. We have conducted fifty-two biker interviews and taken statements from a further seventeen eyewitnesses. A further six bikers have been identified but not yet contacted.

"Regarding the scene at the Swagman Hotel . . ." He clicks his button and a large plan of the hotel forecourt appears on the screen, covered in numbered circles. "These are the probable positions of our interviewees at the time of the attack. The victims, Capp and Haddad, together with Bebchuk, are here, and the killers are approaching them from the north-east direction here. There are most likely two or three assailants—accounts vary. At least one was armed with a 9 millimetre handgun, another possibly with a baseball bat. The altercation occurred in this area, leaving the victims here, as we know.

"Okay, facial composites. This is Suspect A, the one with the handgun which killed Haddad."

Harry holds his breath as the screen goes blank, before four identikit faces appear, and then he takes a deep breath. It's hard to see himself in any of them.

"We think picture two is closest to our man."

Thanks, guys, Harry thinks. Picture two is a demonic face of vaguely Middle Eastern appearance. Another four images hit the screen, and a chill goes through him.

"This is Suspect B, the baseball-bat-wielding man who clubbed Capp . . ." Two of the faces look very like Tony Gemmell. "Most probably images one and two."

Those are the ones. Harry is gripped by a feeling of dread. He is like an angel of death, dragging people into his lethal wake.

"On the other hand, they look like at least half the bikers there that night," Wagstaff adds, and gets a few laughs, because the pony-tailed, scowling grey-beard looks like everybody's image of an outlaw motor cyclist. "The images for a possible third suspect are too varied to be reliable.

"Now. The camera images. We have a number to choose from of two riders on the M4 eastbound between 20:21 at Penrith and 20:45 at Homebush, the lead rider unhelmeted. He's the lead rider, and here and here. Roman Bebchuk.

"And following him, about a hundred metres behind, is the second rider, who we believe to be Suspect A."

A series of pictures come up, some in enlargement of the head and shoulders. Harry made a point of dipping his head at intersections and camera poles, and the helmet helps to obscure the upper part of his face, but there's still plenty to work on.

"We're getting enhancements made of the best of these," Wagstaff says. Everyone is leaning forward in their seats, intently studying the images. Harry feels his face tingling.

"And now we come to something interesting," Wagstaff says with a grim smile. "A forensics result, at last. It seems that the Crows aren't that hot on housekeeping—plenty of dust on the floor for crime scene to pick up footprints. They've identified fifteen different recent footprints in the clubhouse, one of which is a match for . . ." he pauses for another smile, "a partial print found at the Kristich murder scene in the Gipps Tower, belonging to neither Kristich nor Lavulo."

There is a brief moment of silence as people take this in, then a communal sigh of revelation.

"Forensics are working on a detailed analysis, but they are confident that this footprint at the clubhouse was made by one of the last people to leave the building before the police arrived. In other words, it could well belong to Suspect A, who, it then follows, was in the Kristich office at or close to the time of the two killings there."

Wagstaff nods his head as murmurs of appreciation ripple around the room.

"Hypotheses?" he asks, then answers himself. "Hypothesis number one: the murders of Bebchuk and Haddad, and also perhaps Thomas O'Brian, Benjamin Lavulo and maybe Kristich himself, were the work of a rival gang trying to move in on the Crows' territory and drug market. We can add Capp to that list—the hospital don't think he'll survive. Hypothesis number two: it was the work of a clique within the Crows, perhaps including former members who were ousted when Bebchuk took over. Hypothesis number three: it was the work of a third party.

"Our priorities? Firstly, to identify and apprehend suspects A, B, and, if he exists, C.

"In relation to that, we need to gather more CCTV footage, for example in the Creek area to track Suspect A's movements after he left Mortimer Street.

"We need to re-examine all of the material on the Gipps Tower killings. Strike Force Gemini was never able to establish how Lavulo, and now Suspect A, were able to enter the building and reach the crime scene, and now, in the case of Suspect A, leave again, without leaving a trace on their CCTV and entry systems.

"We need to track down the remaining bikers at the Swagman Hotel and identify from among all those interviewed a priority list of those we can put pressure on to gain information about the Crows and their rival organisations."

He looks around the room. "Anything else?"

A moment's silence, and then, as he begins to gather up his papers, Deb puts her hand up.

"Inspector Velasco?"

"If there was a third man in the Kristich offices that night, it's possible that Kristich's girlfriend might have seen him. At any rate, she knows more than she's told us."

"Yes, yes," he says dismissively, "she'll have to be reinterviewed of course."

"And it's possible that the third man may have removed

something from the office when he left—a file, a memory stick, a camera."

"I suppose it's possible. Why?"

"Because the reporter Kelly Pool appears to have information and photographs that must have come from a source very close to Kristich. She also knew that the name of the person killed with Kristich was Lavulo. Perhaps the third man has been her source. Perhaps he has been in contact with her. Perhaps she has seen him, or heard his voice."

"All right," Wagstaff concedes. "Why don't you follow that up, Deb? Right everyone, a good day's work, but much, much more to do. I don't need to remind you that this is receiving the highest priority. The eyes of the commissioner and the government are upon us."

As the meeting breaks up, Deb says to Harry, "Okay, let's go and have a talk with Pool."

Harry checks his watch. He badly needs to talk to Tony Gemmell, and says, "Let's leave it till tomorrow, Deb. I'm buggered."

"A chat to your girlfriend'll perk you up. Come on."

She gets the number of the *Times* offices and asks for Kelly Pool. When she's told Kelly's not available she asks to speak to the editor. She's put through to Catherine Meiklejohn.

"Can I ask what it's in connection with?"

"We urgently need to speak to Ms. Pool concerning the recent deaths in the Gipps Tower, Ms. Meiklejohn. We believe she can assist us with our enquiries."

"I see. Well, I'm afraid I can't help you. She was due here for an editorial meeting two hours ago and she hasn't shown up, and can't be contacted on her home or mobile phones. We don't know what's happened to her."

"Can you give me her contact details please?"

"I'm not sure that I can."

It takes some persistence on Deb's part, but eventually Meiklejohn relents. Deb tries the numbers herself. No result. Kelly's mobile is switched off and her landline rings out.

"Do you think she's done a runner?"

"Why would she? She's probably hot on some story and'll come bouncing back tomorrow."

Reluctantly Deb decides to let it go for now. They drive back to headquarters and Harry checks out. As soon as he is clear of the building he calls Tony Gemmell.

"Harry. I've been waiting to hear from you. The papers are full of it."

"So you know Bebchuk and Haddad are dead, Capp due to follow."

"They had it coming, mate. You comfortable with that?"

"Yes, but we stirred up a hornet's nest. This is cop priority number one. Today they've been rounding up all the bikers who were there and trying to reconstruct what happened. They don't seem to have anything on your car though. How did you get home?"

"All the bikes screamed straight off down the main road to Penrith and the motorway, so I took the back streets around the town and headed back through St. Marys and Mount Druitt and Blacktown, nice and slow. How about you? Last I saw you were after Bebchuk on some poor bastard's Harley."

Harry tells him, then says, "They've got identikits of us, Tony, and yours isn't too bad. One of their scenarios is that former Crows might've had a grudge against those three, so they'll probably want to talk to you sooner or later."

"Okay. Any suggestions?"

"Trim your hair and beard—nothing so drastic your friends will remember. And get yourself an alibi for last night. Again, nothing exotic, just something you'd usually do."

"Sure."

"And they'll possibly tap your phone."

"I've had practice, mate."

"I know."

"Mate, Rowdy's up there, raising a beer to us. I can see him now."

Harry rings off and tries Kelly on his unmarked phone. No response.

THIRTY-FOUR

WHEN DEB AND HARRY spotted Kelly in Mortimer Street, she was staring at the upper windows of the houses. It has taken her a while to get here, with everything that happened last night, but the whole time she was trying to piece together the facts and rumours around the biker deaths, one part of her brain has been worrying away at the children question. They flit in and out of her mind like little ghosts, just like Phoebe's description. The reason she didn't dismiss it as senile rambling was because of something she'd hardly registered until Phoebe raised the topic. That first time the police were in Mortimer Street, when they raided the Crow clubhouse, Kelly remembers seeing children's play equipment in the Crow courtyard, beyond the flattened gates. It seemed incongruous, comical almost, and she'd thought no more about it until Phoebe. And then, the paedophile allegation against Potgeiter.

Three disconnected references. A very flimsy foundation for any answer to the big question—what the hell has been going on at Crucifixion Creek? But still, the children keep coming back to trouble her, and so Kelly is here now, outside number eleven. Not staring down at the exotic cactus garden but up at the bedroom windows, which are screened by internal grey blinds. And as she looks closer, she sees that the upper windows of the adjoining houses, all along the street, are screened in exactly the same way. Identical grey blinds. A job lot? A group discount buy? The effect is uncanny, like a group of people standing together in the street, all with their eyes closed.

She rings the front doorbell.

Nothing happens for a while, and then she notices a movement out of the corner of her eye. The curtain of the little bay window over to the right of the door. Without turning her head, Kelly slides her eyes to the right and catches a glimpse of a forearm raised as if holding a phone to an ear. Then the curtain closes again.

She waits, and eventually the door opens and Donna Fenning smiles at her, feigning surprise. "Oh, hello, um, sorry, I've forgotten your name . . ."

"Kelly, Kelly Pool. Sorry to bother you again, Donna. Is this a bad time?"

"Um, no, I suppose not. What is it?"

"May I come in for a moment?"

"All right."

Donna has changed since the last time. She was enthusiastic about Kelly's articles, was open and welcoming. Now she's like a different person.

They go into the front room again. Donna seems to rouse herself, and says, "I don't know anything about

what's been happening down the street. I didn't see anything last night."

"Okay. But it wasn't about that. I just wanted to ask
you more about the children."

"Children? There are no children here."

"Here?"

"In the street."

"But last time you said there were biker families here
with kids."

"No, you must have misunderstood me. Years ago I
suppose there were."

"But . . . in the bikers' compound I've seen children's
play equipment, quite new-looking, and a sandpit that
had obviously been used recently—there was a bucket
and spade in the sand."

"I wouldn't know anything about that." Donna is looking at her with a fixed stare, and it seems quite apparent
to Kelly that she's lying. Then Donna blinks a couple of
times and looks away. It is a moment Kelly recognises, the
moment when the interviewee realises they've been
caught out. It is often followed by an admission.

Donna gets abruptly to her feet. "I'll tell you what. I
baked a cake. I'd like some coffee and cake, how about
you?"

"Mm, I'd love that." This is encouraging, it means that
Kelly is being invited to stay. A hospitable interviewee
usually turns out to be a truthful one.

"Good. You just stay there and I'll fix it up in the
kitchen."

As soon as she's out of the room Kelly gets up. From

the sounds, the kitchen is at the back of the house, while the foot of the stairs is directly across the narrow hallway from the living room door. Kelly steps quickly across and hurries up the stairs. On the upstairs landing she tries the doors in turn—a bathroom, a master bedroom with Donna's cosmetics on a dressing table, two smaller bedrooms. These other bedrooms are very spartan, in each of them a couple of bare mattresses on folding bed frames and a clothes rack with wire coat hangers. In one room there is a cheap print of a desert island taped to the wall, and in the other a childish stick-figure has been scrawled with a crayon on the wallpaper, low down near the skirting board.

Kelly returns to the stairs, and as she's halfway down Donna appears below her, carrying a tray. She looks up and Kelly says, "Sorry, I was looking for the bathroom, do you mind?"

"Straight ahead of you at the top of the stairs."

"Thanks." She turns back upstairs.

When she returns to the living room, Donna is pouring from a coffee pot into mugs.

"Black or white?"

"Black, one sugar please."

"It's quite strong. I hope that's all right for you."

"Perfect. I need it."

"Your job must run you off your feet. I feel stressed just thinking about it."

Kelly goes along with the small talk, waiting for the moment of confession. The cake is a well-made sponge, the coffee strong and sweet. She yawns, covering her mouth. "Sorry. Late nights."

"My husband has that, shiftwork at the hospital. Takes him time to adjust."

Kelly wonders whether she should ask about what he does there, but frankly she's not that interested. In fact she's not that interested in Donna. She asks herself how a reporter could think that. Everyone has their stories to tell, and it's time Donna told hers, like about that thing upstairs . . . what was it? She's so tired she's finding it hard to think straight. The child's drawing on the wallpaper, that was it. She yawns again and raises her hand, forgetting that she's holding the coffee mug now.

"Oops." Donna takes the mug gently from her. "Thanks," she mumbles. How did she get to be so tired? Her eyes are blurry, and she tries to focus them on Donna, but it's too difficult. She closes them, just like the blinds in the upstairs windows.

THIRTY-FIVE

THE NEXT DAY, A Sunday, is Harry's rostered day off. He feels suspended once again, waiting for events to unfold elsewhere, for the knock on the door, for Deb's husband and his ninja mates to come storming in for him. He's grateful for Jenny and the steady, determined way she goes about the daily chores, making the bed together, preparing breakfast, writing out a shopping list. She hands it to him and it's not bad. *Cauliflower* goes off the end of the page and *no-fat Greek yoghurt* runs downhill across *my muesli*, but otherwise pretty impressive.

"Fine," he says. "I'll get onto it. You'll ring me if anyone calls on the landline? And don't answer the door."

"Stop worrying," she says, laying a soothing hand on his arm. "If this is our last day of freedom, let's enjoy it." She's teasing him. But is that how she's secretly thinking, that their world may collapse at any moment?

As soon as he's in the car he rings Kelly again. Nothing. What the hell is she doing?

Frustrated, he calls the accountant, Sam Peck. "Sam,

hi, Harry. Listen, I need to talk to you about one or two things, Greg's accounts."

"Jeez, Harry, it's Sunday."

"Yeah, well, I've been busy. Homicide never sleeps."

"Lindy's got people coming over for lunch; she's going nuts. Actually, yeah, maybe I can spare an hour. At the office?"

"If that's where the records are, yes."

He is opening up the office when Harry gets there. "Lindy blew her top when I said I had to go out. I hope this is worth it."

"So do I. I want to look at Greg's records for three years ago, June 2010."

"Three years ago? Come on, Harry, that's ancient history!"

"What if it was the ATO springing a desk audit on you? Come on, last month of the financial year. You should know all about it."

"Mind telling me why? What are you looking for?"

"Humour me."

So Sam, grumbling, pulls files from his cabinet and sits down at his desk, switching on the computer. "Let's see, let's see . . ." He begins flicking through Greg's bulging client file with notes of meetings. "Oh god, yeah," he groans. "He was having one of his crises . . . Then at the last minute a cheque came in, a big one, right at the end of June."

"Who was it from?"

"The council. Greg was doing a lot of maintenance and small works for them. Yeah, I remember now. They'd approached him a couple of months before to do a heap of small jobs. They were in a rush to get them done before their grant ran out at the end of the tax year. It was a godsend for Greg. He put his other work on hold and took on extra people. Course there were big outlays, materials, wages, but the council blokes assured him he'd be paid in regular instalments. Only that didn't happen."

Sam flicks through the pages of the file, notes of telephone calls, meetings. "Yeah, after the second month the bank started getting shirty about his overdraft and he got back to the council. More promises. There was some problem with the finance department's computer or something. Not to worry. But he *was* worried, because the council needed to make the payment before the end of June, before their grant money expired, or he might have to wait months before they found the cash to see him right."

"But they did pay?"

"Yeah, on the thirtieth of June, right at the death knock. But only after Greg had gone to see one of the councillors, who eventually sorted it out."

"Do you know his name?"

"No, no idea. Someone he met at Rotary or Lions or somewhere."

"Did Greg go on doing work for the council?"

"Yes. He called it bread and butter work, not the sort of difficult jobs he liked to get his teeth into, but it was good for the bank balance."

"And were they responsible for his latest crisis?"

Sam frowns. "Not that I know of, but I can't really be

sure. Greg tended not to confide in me until things really went pear-shaped, and this last time was all about the Bluereef loan. And like I said, he didn't consult me on that one until it was too late."

"Okay, thanks."

"Should I be looking into the council contracts?"

"No, don't worry. I might have a word with Peter Rizzo."

"You'll probably find him at the new depot. He told me he's flat out."

"The new depot?"

"Yeah, he's renting one of the empty sheds near Greg's old place."

THE NEW DEPOT IS just one building away from the blackened ruin of the old, and, Harry realises, abuts the empty shed which the Crows had partially colonised with their armoury and drug factory. He remembers Wagstaff's briefing, the direction to find out who owns that building, and it makes him think of the police investigation, continuing while he is still free to drive around.

A single white ute stands outside, beneath a gleaming new sign, *RIZZO CONSTRUCTION, MASTER BUILDERS*. Harry pushes open the door to a small office area. A radio is playing somewhere inside the shed beyond the counter. There is a bell marked *Please ring for attention*, so he does. After a moment Peter Rizzo appears. He seems surprised to see Harry, a little put out, but covers it up with a cautious smile.

"Harry, hi. You're lucky to catch me."

"Sam Peck told me I'd probably find you here. He said you're very busy."

"Yeah, that's true, trying to catch up on things since . . . Come on through."

Harry follows him into a small office. The desk, chairs, filing cabinets, computers, printer and photocopier, all look brand new. Through the window into the working area Harry can see cardboard and polystyrene foam from unpacked equipment. They sit.

"How's it going, Peter?"

"Oh, non-stop, trying to catch up on Greg's contracts. Every day there's some new crisis." He gives a you-know-how-it-is kind of smile.

"And it's worked out with the old clients?"

"Yeah, pretty much. They just wanted to get their jobs finished."

"How about the council?"

"Huh?"

"Greg was doing work for them, wasn't he?"

"Just a bit of building maintenance, nothing big."

"Are they bad at paying on time?"

"No. There are a lot worse."

"Only Sam told me Greg got into a bit of bother with them three years ago—June, end of the financial year. Remember?"

Peter frowns, scratches his neck. "No . . . Sam said that, did he?"

Harry keeps his eyes on Peter's, but he is taking in the body language, the tense posture, lopsided, as if preparing to bolt.

"Yes. He said Greg eventually got onto one of the

councillors, who sorted it out for him. You know who that was?"

Peter looks up at the ceiling. "No-o, can't say I do."

"How about Potgeiter? Does that name mean anything to you?"

"Sorry?"

"Potgeiter. Joost Potgeiter."

"No, no, can't say I've heard of him." He raises his wrist to examine his watch.

Harry rises. "Okay, I'll let you get on, Peter."

Rizzo leaps to his feet. "Any time, Harry. How's Nicole making out?"

"Taking each day as it comes, you know."

"Sure, sure."

ACTUALLY, WHEN HE RINGS Nicole from the car it sounds as if she's making out pretty well.

"Harry! We're planning a barbecue. I was hoping you and Jenny would come over, but I just rang her and she said you needed a bit of peace. You've had a bad week? Those people—bikers—they're animals. Poor you."

"I just wanted to clear something up, Nicole, about Greg's work. Sam Peck was telling me Greg got into a spot of financial bother three years ago, because of some problem with the local council about getting paid. I wondered if you remembered him talking about that."

"Three years ago? No, I'm afraid not. Isn't that ancient history?"

Ancient history, he thinks. Doesn't she remember what happened three years ago? She sounds as if she's already got the cork out. "There was a councillor who helped sort it out, apparently, by the name of Potgeiter."

"Oh him! Yes, I remember him at some charity do we went to, and then another time somewhere. Horrible little man. He was all over me, getting too close, touching me. Really slimy. I told Greg and he said something about keeping in with the right people. Joost! That was his first name. Joost keep your hands to yourself was what I wanted to say to the nasty little creep!" She giggles loudly.

"Sounds as if you're having a better day today, Nicole. I'm glad."

"Oh, Harry, I am feeling better. For the first time I feel as if there's light at the end of the tunnel. Of course nothing will ever be right again with Greg gone, but I've been so worried about the money, and giving the girls a good life. I know how hard you've worked to sort things out for us, but now I am feeling optimistic, for the first time in ages."

"That's good. Has something happened?"

"Oh . . . nothing specific, you know." She is suddenly cautious, sober. "I just feel things will be okay."

"Good. I think you're right."

"And Harry, do talk to Jenny about lunch. We'd love to see you, if you feel up to it."

"I'll do that."

HE STOPS AT A supermarket on the way home to pick up the groceries on Jenny's list. Shoppers with glazed, hung-over expressions push trolleys through bland music, and Harry has a sudden urge to shout at them. *Wake up! Don't you realise how vulnerable you are, how little there is between you and chaos?*

He wheels his trolley out into the car park. The grey sky is clearing, a wintry sunlight glimmering through. He notices a pristine new Mercedes opposite him in the car park, and as he opens the boot a man gets out and comes towards him. He is wearing the sort of casual clothes you might expect in an expensive country club, out of place among the T-shirts and track pants in this suburb, but it is a moment before Harry recognises him in this unlikely context.

"Detective Sergeant Belltree." The man transfers his shopping bag to his left hand as if he might offer his right.

Harry continues to load his boot. "Mr. Horn."

"A strange place for us to meet," the lawyer says with a thin smile.

"We all have to eat."

"True. Actually, I'm glad I've seen you. There's something that I've been wanting to tell you, if I may."

"Go ahead."

Horn comes closer and lowers his voice. "In confidence? It concerns three of my clients, but since they're dead now I feel at liberty to share this with you.

"As a member of the legal profession I was of course very much aware of your father's remarkable achievements, in fact we sparred several times, when he was at the bar and on the bench. I admired his passion and integrity."

As you might admire an exotic plant, Harry thinks, but says nothing.

"The last time we met was outside the courtroom, in his chambers. Not long before he died."

He has Harry's full attention now. "Really?"

"It was on a matter that hadn't been publicly announced but was known to a small circle of people within the profession, myself included. The state government at the time was considering introducing a bill to impose severe—I might even say draconian—restrictions on the rights of members of outlaw motorcycle clubs to assemble and wear identifying clothing. The attorney-general had decided to seek the advice of the profession on the legality of this legislation, and was considering establishing an advisory tribunal chaired by your father.

"My clients, represented by one of the three recently deceased—you may guess the gentleman I mean—were extremely concerned about the proposed new law, and asked me to try to find out where Justice Belltree stood on the matter. Well, I made an appointment to see him, ostensibly on another issue, and went to his chambers. He was very friendly, very open, and our conversation ranged over a number of topics, including the one my clients were concerned with, and it became very clear to me that he was firmly of the view that the proposed legislation was in the public interest. He also believed it could be reconciled with constitutional principles, and in fact he seemed very eager to get the tribunal going—prod the government into action.

"I reported this to my clients, and heard no more on the matter. Two months later your father was dead, and soon afterwards the tribunal and the legislation were quietly abandoned.

"Of course, there may be no connection between these events, but I felt uneasy. To be frank, my client was a violent man with an extensive police record, and it would not have surprised me if he had used lethal force to further the interests of his associates and himself."

Horn falls silent. Stands there in his cashmere sweater and Rockports, waiting for Harry's response. Harry says, "Are you planning to make a statement to the police?"

Horn shakes his head. "Not a word. It would be professional suicide. But I wanted you to know. You may say that I am merely trying to ease my conscience, and you could be right. But I think you have a right to know."

"Thank you."

Horn does his tight-lipped smile again. "I'll get on with my shopping then. Have a nice day, Sergeant."

Harry watches him walk away, then slams the boot and stands for a moment, thinking. He walks over to the shelter of a stunted gum and phones home, using the rogue mobile. He asks Jenny to find out where Nathaniel Horn lives. It doesn't take her long.

"The North Shore," she says, and gives him the address. It is at least twenty kilometres away. Then he tells her he's spoken to Nicole, and suggests that they take up her invitation to lunch. Jenny says she'll ring her.

As he gets back into the car he's thinking that it is impossible that Horn met him by accident. But if not, then how did he know where to find him? Are they tracking his car, his phone? The story Horn told is very tempting, but also very convenient. He has no doubt that Bebchuk and his mates killed his father and mother. The problem is why? For whom? Now Horn has provided an answer. They did it for themselves. Case closed.

When he gets home he sits Jenny down next to the CD player and puts on some music to cover their voices and murmurs his conversation with Horn; also his meetings with Peck and Rizzo. "I think Peter is up to something," he says. "It may just be that he's setting himself up in Greg's business and feels awkward about it, but he's acting shifty. I think it would be good if we could find out more about him."

"Okay, I'll see what I can do."

Once she would have winced, catching herself using the word *see*. Now it doesn't seem to bother her.

"Why did you change your mind about going to Nicole's?" she asks. He tells her about her sister's change in mood.

"I don't think it was the champagne. I think she was celebrating, and I'd like you to find out what's happened."

"Harry, you see problems everywhere, even when people are happy."

IT IS THE FIRST barbecue at Nicole's since the day before Greg died, and although Nicole seems oblivious, Harry finds it uncomfortably poignant—the same tortuous route down to the deck, the same brand of beer in his hand, the same smell of burning meat. He calls the girls over so Jenny and Nicole can talk, and they ask him about the biker killings, about which they seem to have a morbid fascination. "Did they really just shoot each other down in the car park? It's like a western! Anyone could have been killed!"

It's late in the afternoon when Harry and Jenny leave. In the car he turns the radio on and asks her what she's found out.

"It took a lot of probing, but eventually she came out with it. She's had a visit from a lawyer representing the estate of Alexander Kristich, who told her that it had never been Kristich's intention to evict them from the family home. He assured her that that would not happen. She's over the moon about it."

"A lawyer?"

"Yes. She showed me his card. Nathaniel Horn. He made her promise to tell no one about his visit. Said it might prejudice the arrangements he was making for her."

That's it then, Harry thinks. Horn is cleaning up the mess. So they are tracking him, whoever they are.

He uses his unmarked phone to try Kelly's numbers again. No answer.

There is a text message on his phone from headquarters. He is instructed to attend a health and safety workshop first thing tomorrow, no ifs, no buts.

THIRTY-SIX

KELLY BLINKS AWAKE, FEELING cold, thinking there's a frog in her throat. She tries to cough it up and chokes. She is lying on her front on something . . . a mattress. It stinks, she is suddenly aware, of urine. She tries to roll over but her arms are pinned down. And her legs too. She is spreadeagled on the mattress. The frog croaks and she hears a shuffle behind her.

"Ah, Kelly, you are awake at last."

She blinks up but can't see him, though she knows the voice, that South African accent. Potgeiter.

"Water?"

He grips a handful of her hair and pulls her head roughly back, holding a cup of water to her mouth. She gulps, chokes. Much of it spills, running cold over her skin.

"It's *so* nice to meet you again, Kelly," he purrs, his mouth close to her ear. "The last time you and your sweet little friend had the advantage of me. You had fun with me, didn't you?" His grip tightens on her hair and she cries out with pain. "And now I have the advantage of you, and I will have much more fun with you."

"Please . . ." She barely manages to croak out the word.

"Oh, you will please me, Kelly. Without a doubt."

"Why?" she gasps.

"Why? Well, my friends are very keen to learn where you got those photographs of Jakarta and Vanuatu, and who gave you all those interesting titbits of information, and what else you know. Would you like to tell me?"

"No."

He laughs. "I thought not. I told them, 'This will take time.' They are impatient, but I have plenty of time. I'm only sorry that your sweet little friend isn't here too."

He releases her hair and her head flops back down onto the mattress. She feels his hot hand on her shoulder, then sliding down the skin of her back, and she realises that she has no clothes on. She winces as his hand reaches her buttocks, and she cries out, "Don't touch me you disgusting little toad."

He removes his hand, saying nothing, and she feels a moment of hope. Then she hears a thump, and another—two boots hitting the floor—and the snuffling sound of fabric dropping on the floorboards and she thinks NO. There is a sharp crack and a searing pain rips the flesh across her back. It takes her breath away. She sucks air into her lungs in panic and there is another crack, another shocking flash of pain, and she begins to scream.

HE TIRES AFTER PERHAPS an hour, and tells her that he is taking a break for lunch. She lies trembling on the mattress, covered in blood and semen, the stink of it foul with the urine. Alternately sweating and shaking with cold and pain and shock, she gradually subsides into a catatonic stupor. From time to time she is aware of background sounds—a telephone ringing, the pop of a champagne cork, the rattle of cutlery.

In the afternoon he comes for her again, brutalising her in long waves of pain interspersed by sudden shocks of agony.

He leaves her when darkness comes. She hears a shower running, the sound of his voice singing off-key. When he returns she smells aftershave. He tells her that he has an appointment and is going to put her away for the night. He releases her hands and feet and trusses her limp body into—what?—a straitjacket, it seems. Muttering to her words she barely understands. ". . . Safe . . . sink hole . . . deep, deep . . . mustn't struggle or cry or you will fall . . . never found . . . tomorrow more, much more . . ."

As he heaves her over his shoulder she sobs helplessly. He lugs her out of the building into the dark. She smells fresh air, tinged with smoke. The night sky overhead is bright with stars. He drops her, her bruised flesh striking the hard ground, and she sees the outline of a gantry against the sky. There is the roar of a motor kicked into life and he fits a harness around her and she is hauled upright and swung beneath the gantry, swaying, turning.

Then she is dropping slowly into a dark tube. Sounds become muffled, the darkness is absolute. Her descent abruptly stops and she hears a clang from far above which echoes all around her, then fades into total silence. She spins slowly in the chill black, and a dreadful smell rises from the void beneath her feet.

THIRTY-SEVEN

THERE ARE FOUR OF them sitting in a circle around the psychologist, Harry and three highway patrol officers, "cockroaches" as the others call them, because they come out at night. They look much as Harry feels. Long-suffering, wishing they were somewhere else.

The psychologist explains that the subject of the workshop is RESILIENCE—she writes it in large letters on the whiteboard. She gets them to discuss the things that can affect their resilience—appropriate training, health and fitness, nutrition and exercise, feelings of job satisfaction, stress management strategies (other than alcohol).

Harry hardly hears her. He is preoccupied with the progress of the homicide investigations that are swirling around him without his involvement or knowledge. And Kelly Pool—what the hell has happened to her? Last night he phoned the *Times* and spoke to Catherine Meiklejohn again, and she still had no idea where Kelly was. She sounded worried. "It's just possible that she's gone to Indonesia without telling us," she said. "Apparently she discussed it with her colleague."

"Are you with us, Harry?" the psychologist says.

"Sorry, yes, of course."

"Now here's the thing," she goes on, holding up a blank sheet of A4. "In an ideal situation, this is our police officer coming to work, starting a new shift fully rested and resilient. But this is not an ideal situation. He has been unable to sleep properly for the past month after attending a particularly nasty crime scene involving the death of a child."

She has their attention, and they watch as she tears a strip off the side of the paper.

"So his resilience is reduced. Also, his relationship with his wife is not good at the moment. It's been going steadily downhill for a while, she's angry because his work schedule prevented them going to an important family event, and he's worried that this may be the last straw. So he feels he has no emotional support at home." She tears another strip.

"Because of these concerns he has been drinking more than usual lately, and he is suffering now from a pretty bad hangover." Off comes another strip.

"And on top of all this, he has fallen out with two of his workmates, who are giving him a hard time."

She tears off another strip and holds up what remains. "So this is our officer, at the start of another day in the firing line."

They all stare in silence at the diminished piece of paper.

"Jesus," says one of the cockroaches. "He's white as a sheet."

The psychologist looks at him, her mouth quivering, then she starts to giggle. Now they all crack up, roaring with laughter, and the cockroach takes a handkerchief from his pocket and wipes his eyes.

AS SOON AS HE can get away, Harry gets a vehicle from the car pool and drives out to the Creek. He parks in Mortimer Street and goes over to the spot where he last saw Kelly, in front of the cactus garden, staring up at the bedroom windows. What made her come here? What did she see? Like her, he notices the same blinds, all closed, in all of the upper windows of the houses on this side of the street, running down to the Crows' compound at the end.

He goes up to the front door and rings the bell. There is no reply. The whole street seems unnaturally silent. After a minute he makes his way down the narrow covered passage between the house and its neighbour and comes into a rear yard, bare of plants except for a neglected lawn. He knocks on the back door, then breaks the pane of one of its small windows and reaches inside to release the lock. He goes inside, calling out, "Hello? Police. Anyone home?" Silence.

Two cups and saucers stand on the draining board, quite dry. He searches the downstairs rooms and continues upstairs, where he checks the main bedroom—feminine bits and pieces—then the small bedrooms at the front, dimly lit through the closed venetians. He is on the point of turning back when something about the blinds catches his eye—there are no cords to raise or open the blades. He takes a closer look. The bottom strips are screwed to the windowsills.

On the landing he notices something else not quite right. There's a door in the party wall between this house and the next. There is a key in the lock, and he turns it and steps through. This house seems identical to the last, except that there is no comfortably furnished bedroom—all the upper rooms are filled with steel-framed single beds, like dormitories. Beyond them there is another door in the next party wall, locked this time from the other side.

Harry calls Jenny and asks her if she can find out who owns these properties. It doesn't take her long to ring back.

"A company called Pretoria Holdings. Sole owner Joost Potgeiter."

Harry remembers Kelly's text message. *Potgeiter is the key.* "What do we know about Potgeiter? Where does he live?"

"I have an address . . . two actually. He has an apartment in Parramatta, and a property out near Orchard Hills. And I have several phone numbers."

Harry notes the addresses and rings the numbers in turn. The landline to the Orchard Hills property is answered by a man who sounds as if he's been woken from a deep sleep. "Hello? Hello? Who is this?" Harry recognises the vowels and hangs up.

AS SOON AS SHE gets off the phone Jenny remembers the other thing she had to tell Harry. Working through another Kristich file that she has managed to open, she has found more references to payments to "Curly," for larger sums this time, tens of thousands of dollars. She decides to ask the computer for its suggestions, and it comes up with a list of synonyms and associations. Among them are translations of the word into other languages. In Italian, the word for curly is *rizzo*. She rings Harry again but it goes to voicemail, and she leaves him a message.

IT'S A THIRTY-FIVE-MINUTE DRIVE. Beyond Orchard Hills the GPS takes him off the bitumen and onto a dirt road that runs between empty brown paddocks. He reaches the number painted on a post and turns into a long drive leading to a single-storey house with verandas and a tin roof. When he stops no dogs bark. A white Holden Caprice is parked at the front door.

Harry walks around the house, looking through windows. Through one he sees Potgeiter preparing something in the kitchen, through another an unmade bed, and through a third a bare mattress on a bed frame with what appear to be straps attached to its four corners. He peers in more intently, shading his eyes, and sees other things scattered on the floor. Some clothes, a cane, a thick whip. Harry puts on gloves and tries the window, which proves to be unlatched. He climbs in. He smells bacon frying and hears the sound of a radio from the kitchen as he steps among the things on the floor. The clothes are a woman's. There is dried blood on the braided leather lash of the whip, and in patches on the mattress, which stinks of body fluids.

"And who the fuck are you?" The same words that Kristich used when he caught Harry in his office, spoken now with a broad South African accent. Harry turns to see Potgeiter standing in the doorway with a shotgun in his hand. He looks tousled, wearing the T-shirt and boxers he probably slept in. His face clears in recognition, and he cries out in mock affability, "Why, Detective Belltree! How kind of you to call!"

"I don't think we've met," Harry says.

"No, but I know all about you. And about your illustrious black father, of course."

"Why? What was he to you?"

"A bloody nuisance. What are you doing here?"

"I'm looking for the reporter, Kelly Pool. Do you know where she is?"

"Aha." Potgeiter gives a knowing smile and his eyes stray to the bed. "Indeed I do, and I have some further business to conduct with her which you are holding up. So let's take a little walk. Come along." He waves the barrel of the gun, and Harry steps slowly forward.

"That's the way, nice and easy." Potgeiter steps back from the door to keep him covered, but as he reaches it Harry puts out a hand and slams it closed, then drops as the shotgun booms and shredded plywood sprays across the room. He springs up, runs to the window and dives through. Races to the front door, reaching it just ahead of Potgeiter, who bursts out, gun first. Harry grabs the barrel and rams the butt into his stomach. In a moment he has the gasping man back inside, handcuffed on a wooden chair. Eyes watering, Potgeiter sucks in air and stares up at Harry.

"Do you have a warrant, Detective? You don't, do you? You are a trespasser, breaking the law. I had every right to shoot at you."

"There are a number of things I want you to tell me," Harry says. "Let's begin with Kelly Pool. Where is she? What have you done to her?"

"Go fuck yourself. Oh!" He sees the look on Harry's face, and gives a crow of satisfaction. "Are you going to hit me? Well, go ahead! As much as you like. And when you're finished, and I've told you nothing, I shall destroy you. How proud your father would have been of you, threatening a defenceless prisoner."

Harry draws up a chair facing him. He feels weary. Thinks of the psychologist's piece of torn paper. "What do you know about my father's death?"

"Does it bother you still, Sergeant? Didn't Marco Ganis tell you what you wanted to know when you broke into his tow-truck yard? You threatened him too, but of course you didn't really hurt him. I'm not so easily frightened. He told Bebchuk about your visit, and Bebchuk wasn't best pleased. He was a brute, that Bebchuk." Potgeiter chuckles, indulgent. "Didn't Ganis' story satisfy you? Bebchuk ran your father's car off the road."

"I want to know who Bebchuk did it for."

"Oh, those bikers. They did it for themselves. Your father upset them."

"No, I don't believe that."

"Really? Then you'd better be very, very careful,

Detective Belltree. And you can start by getting off my property."

Harry shrugs and gets to his feet. He goes through to the kitchen and starts going through the drawers. From one he takes a pair of large poultry shears, and from another a steel mallet with a serrated face for tenderising meat. He returns and sits down again in front of Potgeiter, who eyes the tools with a sparkle in his eye.

"Ooh, mister detective, please don't hurt me," he whimpers, mocking. Then he snarls, "You want to do to me what Bebchuk did to your old army mate? I was there, you know. I watched it all. Are you no better than Bebchuk? I can hear your father and mother spinning in their graves. No, you won't do it. You won't break my fingers and toes."

"I don't think they're the bits you value most," Harry says, and reaches across to pull Potgeiter's shorts down to his ankles. He picks up the shears and rests them on Potgeiter's thigh. The man flinches, his face grows a little paler, and when he speaks his confidence is less convincing.

"No, no," he says. "You won't frighten me, mister police officer," and he smiles as Harry lays the shears down on the floor.

Then Harry pushes Potgeiter's knees apart, picks up the steel mallet and slams it down on Potgeiter's left testicle, which explodes in a spray of pale blood. The scream rings across the empty paddocks for quite some time.

––––––––

IT IS PERHAPS TWENTY minutes before Potgeiter is capable of speech. He sits there, drops of sweat glistening on his chalky forehead, saliva dribbling down his chin.

"You're an animal," he croaks.

Harry says. "My father. Who wanted him dead?"

Potgeiter opens his mouth but says nothing, just panting, and Harry raises the bloody hammer once again.

"NO!" Potgeiter is trembling, shaking helplessly. "Oldfield! The minister—Oldfield. It's all about him, all of this. Your father, the kiddies, everything."

Harry's lost. "What about the kiddies?"

"He couldn't leave them alone, always calling in at Mortimer Street to be with them."

Harry is thinking of Kelly's last news story. "You all went to Jakarta to get children?"

"It was just business as far as the rest of us were concerned, but Oldfield was obsessed. Look, people are too sentimental. There's no future for them in those slums, and their families were glad of the money."

"They sold you their children?"

"Sure, yes. For adoption, we said. Well, you don't want them to feel bad, do you? At first Mansur brought them back on his boat, but then we used other ways, containers and so on."

"And then you sold them."

"Of course. Just business."

"And my father found out?"

"What? No, no, that was something different, something between him and Oldfield. I don't know what that was. The kiddie business was going well until Kristich got killed. I still don't understand what that was all about.

But after that everything unravelled, and the bikers got out of hand, and we had to wind things up fast. Listen, I'm telling you all this, I'm cooperating, okay? But you've got to help me. I can give you everything—bank accounts, customers' names, everything. But then you need to let me go. A twenty-four-hour start, okay?"

Harry nods. "Keep talking. Did Greg March know about all this?"

"He suspected, I think. That's why he had to go. It was him who got us first involved in Crucifixion Creek. Old-field was looking for a way to get at your father and he found out about a family connection in business down there, having money problems, and Oldfield got me to get him tied up with council contracts so we could put pressure on him for information about your father's movements. March thought it was just to arrange a meeting with the good judge, but later I guess he put two and two together. We kept him in line by promising more work. But we were looking for somewhere quiet to run the kiddie business, and Kristich saw the potential of Mortimer Street. He already knew the Crows through their drug operation so it was a perfect set-up."

"What did you mean, 'he had to go'?"

"Kristich and Bebchuk arranged that. March was asking questions, so they decided to get rid of him. He was short of money again and Kristich tied him up with a loan. Told him he'd sort it out if he ran an errand for him, to deliver a parcel to a kid in Belmore. The parcel contained cash to pay the kid to kill whoever handed it over."

"I see."

"Well, he was a liability. And the other fellow was more use right from the start."

"What other fellow?"

"The other builder, Rizzo. He's taken over March's business now but he was involved all along. Preparing the Mortimer Street houses for the kiddies, making sure March didn't cotton on."

"He knew all about it?"

"Sure. He and Oldfield and Kristich were great buddies. He was just a tradesman, of course, but they took him to parties, showed him a good time."

Potgeiter stops, sits there panting. "Listen, I'm telling you all this and I'm in pain. Get me some water and painkillers from the bathroom, eh?"

"Tell me about Kelly Pool. Where is she? Have you killed her?"

"No! I was a bit rough with her yesterday, you know, but she's fine."

"Where?"

"Out in the paddock. I'll show you."

"Don't try anything. You know what I'll do to you."

"No no! Just undo these cuffs and help me up."

Potgeiter can barely stand, and Harry grips his arm to steady him as he shuffles with whimpering sobs towards the door. When they step outside he points to the steel gantry like a hangman's scaffold, out there across the dry grass. "It's an old mine shaft, deep. I put her down there for the night to loosen her tongue. There were things they wanted me to find out from her."

When they reach the place Harry sees that a concrete slab has been laid across the top of the shaft. It is littered with old bits of machinery and a pair of steel trapdoors are set in the centre. Potgeiter slides back the bolts and Harry helps him heave open the heavy flaps. A taut cable runs from a pulley at the top of the gantry down into the dark hole.

"Kelly!" Harry's shout echoes in the void, but there is no answering sound. A foul stench rises out of the hole and he chokes. "What's that smell?"

"There are dead animals down there." Potgeiter is fiddling with a small engine on the winch mechanism. It coughs into life and he presses a button and the winch turns, hauling the cable up. Staring down, Harry sees a pale shape begin to emerge from the darkness. It rises into the light, a trussed figure dangling from a harness on the end of the cable. He recognises the bowed head, the tangled red hair. Horrified, he grabs her and swings her away from the hole. He unfastens the harness and she flops to the ground and he starts to tear away at the straps of the jacket. He sees the naked flesh beneath, bruised and bloodied.

"Dear God." He looks up at Potgeiter, kneeling beside the winch with a furtive leer on his face.

"Just a bit of softening up, old chap. Nothing like what you did to me, eh? She's alive, isn't she?"

He's not sure. She's so cold. He feels her throat and finds a pulse, and then her eyes blink open, struggling to focus. "Harry?"

"Yes, it's me." He pulls off his jacket and wraps it

around her, then gets to his feet. He grabs Potgeiter, hauling him upright.

"We have an agreement, Detective!" Potgeiter squeals as Harry drags him towards the hole. He is still protesting when Harry lifts him into the air and hurls him down the shaft.

His scream fades into the void, then abruptly stops.

Harry stands there for a moment. He turns back to Kelly and sees her staring at him.

"You didn't see that, Kelly." He takes her weight and begins to carry her back to the house. "You're going to be all right now. You're safe." She grips his shirt, pressing her face into his chest.

In the living room he lays her on the sofa and gets blankets from Potgeiter's bedroom and wraps them around her. He fetches a glass of water and waits, holding her hand, until her shaking subsides, then gets up and cleans the chair where Potgeiter sat, and the mallet, and takes it and the shears back to their kitchen drawers. He returns to Kelly and places the phone beside her.

"I'm leaving, Kelly. I've never been here. Potgeiter brought you back to the other room and left you lying on the mattress and then went out again, you don't know where. You managed to crawl out here to the phone to call for help. You've no idea where Potgeiter's gone, and no one else has been here, okay?"

She nods.

"Give me a minute to get clear, and then ring triple-O. Can you do that?"

She nods again, then whispers, "He won't come back, will he, Harry?"

"No. He'll never come back."

As he heads to the door she calls after him, "But I don't know where I am. What do I tell them?"

"That's okay, they'll trace the number."

THIRTY-EIGHT

AS HARRY DRIVES THROUGH Orchard Hills an oncoming ambulance and police car rush past him with sirens and flashing lights. He continues east, back into the city, to the Creek. On the way he checks his phone, and gets Jenny's message about Curly.

The white ute is there on the forecourt of Rizzo Construction, but this time the door is locked. Harry picks up a brick and smashes the lock and the door flies open. In the reception area he can hear the distant sound of machinery, then the muffled burst of a jackhammer. He opens the door into the shed but there is no one there. The sounds seem to be coming from the far wall. He goes towards it and sees the outline of a door frame set into the wall, barely visible between some shelving and racks of timber. He opens the door and the noise hits him. He is in a section of the shed next to the vacant unit that the bikers had colonised, and ahead of him a small backhoe is digging in an area of concrete floor that has been partially broken up.

The roar of the backhoe engine dies to a rumble, and

a figure wearing safety helmet, goggles and ear muffs jumps to the ground and picks up a shovel. He has his back to Harry, who walks towards him and taps him on the shoulder. The man jumps and cries out, spins round and sees Harry, then drops the shovel and pulls off the ear protectors and goggles. "Shit, Harry!" Rizzo yelps. "You nearly gave me a heart attack!"

"We need to talk."

"Um, okay. I'm kind of busy. Maybe later?"

"This won't take long."

"Well . . . let's go to the office."

"Here'll do. What are you doing?"

"Um, there's a problem with the drains."

"Yes, I can smell it." It's a familiar stink, one he's smelled recently. He looks at the trench Rizzo is digging and sees black plastic but no drains.

"So what did you want to talk about?"

"I wanted to ask you again about Potgeiter."

"Potgeiter? I told you, I don't know any Potgeiter." Rizzo pulls off his helmet and makes a big thing of pulling a cloth from his pocket and wiping his brow.

"That's funny, because he knows you. Curly, isn't that what they call you?"

Rizzo's hand drops from his face. He stares at Harry, quite still. "Curly?"

"Yes. Potgeiter has told us everything—Oldfield, Mansur, the children from Jakarta, how Greg died, and your special role in it all."

"Oh God . . ." Rizzo's voice is a whisper. "I . . . I didn't really know what was going on, Harry, I swear. Whatever he's told you . . ."

"The parties Oldfield took you to, your private work preparing the houses for the kiddies. That's the word he used—kiddies."

Rizzo groans. "I didn't see anything. I mean, I wondered—but those bikers threatened me. I was scared to death."

"Show me what you're doing down there." Harry nods at the trench.

"What? No, it's nothing."

Harry takes a step towards the broken slab and Rizzo leaps for the shovel and swings it up to his shoulder like an axe. "Get back, Harry. I swear I'll . . ." He stops in mid-sentence as he sees the pistol in Harry's hand.

"That's good, Rizzo. You attack a police officer and I shoot you, with the greatest of pleasure."

The shovel slides off Rizzo's shoulder and he drops to his knees, sobbing.

"Get in the hole," Harry says.

"Oh God, oh God."

"Get in the fucking hole, Rizzo." Harry kicks his knee and he stumbles to the edge of the trench and lowers himself down.

"Pull up the plastic. I want to see what's under there."

Rizzo tugs half-heartedly at the edge of the heavy black sheet. "I can't. It's pinned down. There's nothing there, just sand."

Harry cocks the pistol and aims it at Rizzo's head, and Rizzo drops to his knees in the dirt and begins tearing at the sheet. A corner gives way and a gust of foul air fills the hole. Rizzo reels back, gagging, and Harry looks down at tufts of black hair and putrefying flesh.

He bends down and grabs Rizzo's wrist and handcuffs it to the heavy steel reinforcing mesh projecting from the broken concrete slab.

"Who are they?"

Rizzo snivels and sobs. "One of the containers got held up. They were all dead when they arrived. They were going to put them down a mine shaft at Potgeiter's property, but there were already . . . Potgeiter was getting worried about the smell, so they told me to bury them here."

"Now listen to me, Rizzo. The cops will arrive any minute. The others will hang you out to dry without a second thought. You've got one chance to survive this and that's to tell the cops everything. Understand? You ask to become a crown witness and tell them everything. And we will know if you hold anything back, or tell any lies. Do you understand?"

Rizzo nods so hard his whole body shakes. "I had no choice, Harry. I got this girl Jamila pregnant and her family threatened me, then the bikers threatened me. It was a nightmare. I'm only a builder for God's sake!"

"But you knew what was going on—what Oldfield and the others were doing with the children. That's what you tell the cops, it's the only thing that'll save you. In the time that's left before they arrive you must go over everything in your head, every detail, and make a full confession."

"Yes, yes, I want to."

Harry leaves him. When he reaches his car he calls Deb's mobile. "Where are you?"

"On my way out to Orchard Hills. They think they've found your girlfriend."

"Let them deal with that, Deb. I'm at a factory unit in the Creek, Rizzo Construction, next to the Crow compound. Get over here with backup and crime scene. There are bodies here, and a witness, Peter Rizzo. He was involved. He wants to make a full confession."

There is a moment's silence, then she says, "Is this for real? What the hell's going on, Harry?"

"Just get here, Deb, fast as you can." He rings off.

THERE IS MUSIC FAINTLY audible at the front porch of the Point Piper home—Mozart, something poignant from the Vienna years. Harry takes a small plastic bottle of hydrogen peroxide from his pocket and sprays and wipes his pistol, which he wraps and tucks into his belt. He rings the bell and the music fades. Oldfield opens the door and Harry just stares at him for a moment, trying to reconcile the urbane features with the truth he now knows.

"Well, Detective Sergeant Belltree? What can I do for you?" But Harry thinks he can see a flicker in Oldfield's eyes, as if he already understands.

"A few minutes of your time, sir."

Oldfield glances over Harry's shoulder, then shrugs. "Very well."

He leads the way to chrome and leather seats— authentic Barcelona chairs—and they sit, facing each other across the glass-topped Barcelona coffee table.

"I've just come from interviewing Joost Potgeiter," Harry says, and a bleak distance settles upon Oldfield's face. "He has provided details of your role in the illegal importation of children from Indonesia for sexual purposes. Acting on the information he provided, I have also been to premises at Crucifixion Creek, where Peter Rizzo has been found disposing of the bodies of dead children. He also is in the process of making a full confession."

Oldfield stares at him, then his eyes swivel away to a decanter on the sideboard. "I would like a very large scotch. How about you?"

Harry says, "Stay where you are. I'll get it."

He pours one glass and sets it down in front of Oldfield, then draws the pistol from his belt, wipes the butt once more, and sets it down with an ugly clunk on the glass top beside the scotch.

"What's that for?"

"It has one bullet in it," Harry says. "The police will be here in a moment to arrest you. It's up to you what you do with it. I want only one thing from you. I want to know why you wanted my father dead."

"Ah." Oldfield sighs. "The indefatigable Harry Belltree. We've watched your progress with something like awe." He reaches for the whisky and takes a deep swallow, then clears his throat, raising his eyebrows as if contemplating the inevitable. "It was nothing personal on my part, Harry. But, like you, your old man was very persistent. He upset people, friends of mine."

"Who?"

"That I can't tell you."

"Why? How did he upset them?"

Oldfield gives an exaggerated shrug. "It doesn't matter now. Let me give you good advice. Forget it. You can't bring him back. Live your life for the future, not the past."

He cocks his head and Harry catches the sound of a siren. Distant at first, coming closer.

"Your colleagues," Oldfield says. "You'd better go and receive them."

"Why?" Harry insists, but Oldfield just shakes his head. The siren, loud now, abruptly cuts out. The doorbell rings and Harry gets slowly to his feet. He opens the front door and shows the two uniforms his ID. "You'll find him—" but his words are cut off by the crack of a gunshot.

THIRTY-NINE

THE CRITICAL INCIDENT TEAM is led by the same senior officer, a superintendent from North West Metropolitan Region, who interviewed Harry after Greg's murder. He stares balefully now at Harry.

"We may as well make this a regular appointment, Belltree. March, O'Brian, and now Oldfield, in the space of a month. You need your own personal CIT. How do you do it?"

"Just lucky, sir."

"Lucky." He glances at his two companions, who frown. "What were you doing in Oldfield's house?"

Harry tells the story. He went to the Creek to check up on his brother-in-law's business and stumbled upon Peter Rizzo burying bodies. Rizzo said he was doing it under duress from the Crows, who were acting on the instructions of Derryn Oldfield. "I arrested Rizzo, called Inspector Velasco for back-up, then went to Mr. Oldfield's house to question him."

"How did you know where he lived? It's not public knowledge."

"Inspector Velasco and I had been there once before, to question Oldfield about his relationship with Alexander Kristich."

The three CIT officers begin turning the pages of their files, searching for the reference, and Harry gives them the date. "It's a bit complicated."

The superintendent's frown deepens. "Who did you notify, that you were going to interview Oldfield?"

"No one, sir. I was at fault there, I admit. I knew Rizzo would spill his guts to Inspector Velasco and name Oldfield, and that she'd send backup there, as she in fact did, but I should have called it in. I think I was distracted by what I'd seen in the hole Rizzo was digging. Have you been there, sir?"

"Yes." The superintendent clears his throat, as if he can still taste the foul air. "So you went to a murder suspect's home without consultation or backup, to question him without a witness."

"Yes, sir."

"I find it inconceivable that an experienced homicide detective would do such a thing. I can only think of two reasons why you would."

"Sir?"

"One, to intimidate or threaten Oldfield without a witness present. Or two, to warn him."

"No, sir. I wanted to arrest him. I cautioned him and told him he was under arrest on suspicion of involvement in a homicide."

"Did you restrain him, or search him for a weapon?"

"No, sir. I had used my handcuffs to restrain Rizzo, and I was about to search Oldfield when other officers arrived and rang the doorbell. I went to let them in, and that's when Oldfield must have got to his pistol and shot himself."

It goes on like this for some time, the questions repeated and rephrased, details examined.

Eventually, late in the evening, they release him, promising more tomorrow. They order him not to communicate with any other officers tonight. He has already surrendered his weapon and police ID. The double padlocks are back on his locker.

FORTY

HARRY SPENDS THE NEXT morning with the critical incident team before he is finally released and told to go home. He goes back to the homicide suite, where he runs into Deb. She waves him into a meeting room and closes the door.

"Harry, what's happening?"

"Don't ask me, Deb. I've been with the CIT all this time. I don't know what's been going on."

Her eyes are searching his face, trying to read him. "You've really been in the thick of it, haven't you? Rizzo, Oldfield."

He shrugs. "They were panicking, Deb. It was only a matter of time before it all fell apart. What about Kelly Pool? What happened to her?"

"She's in Westmead. She was pretty confused, but from what we can gather, she was drugged and taken to Potgeiter's property out west, where he raped and tortured her, then left her hanging down a mine shaft overnight. The next day he took her back into his house, then he disappeared and she managed to call for help. It's kind of an odd story, isn't it?"

"Yeah. Did he do a runner? Have you picked him up?"

"We found his body down the bottom of the shaft, along with the corpses of four children."

"Jesus."

"There are strange wounds on his body. The pathologist is carrying out a second post-mortem today with another expert."

She's still keeping her eyes fixed on him.

He says, "Anything else?"

"They reckon the gun Oldfield killed himself with was the same one used to shoot the bikers, Bebchuk and Haddad."

"Really? How does that work?"

"Hard to say. We're still trying to figure it out."

"Deb, why are you looking at me like that?"

"Like what?"

"I don't know, like I'm an alien. Or you are." He grins at her and she holds his gaze for a moment, then smiles too and looks away.

"I don't know, Harry. Ever since we met Kelly Pool at the siege . . . remember?"

"Sure."

"Ever since then things have been going haywire, and you always seem to be in the thick of it."

"What are you saying?"

"Is there anything that you've been keeping from us?"

"If I had anything to say, Deb, you'd be the first to know."

"Well . . . Bob Marshall's like he's on hot coals. He reckons when we release all of this it'll bring down the state government."

"What about Maram Mansur? He was the other one in that Jakarta photo that Kelly published."

"Done a bunk by the look of it. His boat left Sydney three days ago. They're trying to track it down."

There is an awkward silence, then she says, "I'd better get on. What about you?"

"They've told me to go home."

"Okay. See you then." She turns away and he heads for the exit.

HARRY DRIVES OVER TO Westmead Hospital. Kelly is in recovery after surgery to repair both internal and external injuries. She grips his wrist and he lowers his head to hear her whisper.

"You saved me, Harry."

"You haven't told them that, have you, Kelly?"

"No, but I want to. I want them all to know."

"You mustn't. You'll get me into a heap of trouble."

"I know. But I'm already writing the story in my head. 'My night in hell.' Is that too lurid? It's true. That's what it was."

He wonders if that's a good idea. Wouldn't it be better to try to put it out of her mind, to think of other things? But she reads his thoughts.

"That's my way of dealing with it, Harry. It's my way of pushing that man into a sack and throwing him away. But I'm sorry I can't tell them how much I owe you."

As he returns to his car, Harry gets a call on his mobile. It is Toby Wagstaff.

"Harry, Deb told me you'd left. I need to have a private talk with you. There are things I need to get straight."

"I'll come in, sir."

"No, I want this completely off the record. The shit is about to hit the fan big time, and I want to bounce a few things off you. Private thoughts, no one else to know, okay?"

"Sure."

What the hell does this mean? Is the squad compromised in some way? Does Wagstaff know something about Harry? "Okay. Where do you want to meet?"

"The Creek. Meet me outside your brother-in-law's burnt-out place. I'm down here now with crime scene at the Rizzo unit. They're removing the last of the bodies, but they'll have cleared the place by tonight and everyone will have gone. I'll stay on. Meet me here at seven."

"Right. No problem."

FORTY-ONE

SHE HAS BEEN INDOORS too much; she needs to get out. She checks the time on her computer and goes to the little hallway. Pulls on her coat and picks up her cane. As she closes the front door behind her she takes a deep breath, relishing the smells of damp brickwork and mould. She makes her way down the lane, taking care with the tree roots that have buckled the footpath, then turns left, up towards Crown Street. The sounds of traffic become louder, the purr of tyres and the growl of engines. She can visualise every building along the way, every cross street, feeling with her cane for the obstacles that are scattered in her path, the lamp posts, traffic signs, litter bins, bus shelters. Ahead of her she hears the bleeping of the pedestrian crossing. It has stopped by the time she reaches it, and she stretches out her hand to the pad, feeling its steady throb, like a little electronic heart. The bleeping starts again and she steps off onto the roadway. Halfway across she hears running footsteps and someone crashes into her, knocking the cane out of her hand. She steadies herself, then bends down to retrieve it. Her fingers can't find it. The beeping is becoming more insistent as the time runs out. At last she feels the smooth tube and grasps it and stands up, but now feels disoriented, unsure which way to go. The beeping abruptly stops and engines begin to rev. She heads for the absent sound, feels a kerb with her cane and steps forward, unsure if she has moved forward or back. She stretches out a hand and feels glass, smells something musty and old—the antiques shop. Good. She takes a deep breath. Panic over. She is on the other side. She turns left and continues.

When she reaches the surgery one of the girls recognises her and shows her to a chair. "We're running twenty minutes behind," she murmurs. Jenny is content, listening to the sounds in the waiting room, the health tips on the TV, the chatter from the girls on reception, a mother arguing with her child.

Then the doctor is at her side, taking her arm and guiding her through to her room. "So how have you been, Jenny?" she asks, and Jenny tells her the abridged version. There is an examination, tests, a conversation. Then the result. "We'll do all we can to help," the doctor says, and Jenny wipes a tear from her eye.

She walks home in a bubble, oblivious to all the difficulties. They have waited so long, almost given up, and now at last. Of course it's very early days, barely begun, but it *has* begun. She replays the doctor's words over in her head. *Yes, I'm quite sure.*

It is a kind of miracle. There has only been that one time, that night when Harry came back from the Gipps

Tower, smelling of gunpowder. She thinks of Shiva, the destroyer and creator.

She imagines with a shiver telling Harry when he comes home tonight.

FORTY-TWO

CRUCIFIXION CREEK IS A dark and forbidding hollow, the silhouette of its buildings barely touched by the dim glow of the surrounding street lights. There is no passing traffic, and as Harry walks down the service road towards Greg's ruined site he sees that Rizzo's shed, its perimeter draped with police tape, has been abandoned for the night.

The bulky figure of Toby Wagstaff steps out of the shadows to greet him.

"Thanks for coming, Harry. God . . ." he nods towards the Rizzo place, "what an abomination. What monsters we are, eh? And they've found heaps more drug chemicals—precursors, reagents, solvents—a regular little industry. The drug squad have no idea where it's all come from.

"This place is the pits." Wagstaff turns and makes a sweeping gesture with his arm. "You know its history, do you, Harry? Lieutenant Perch's expedition?"

Harry doesn't know it, and Wagstaff tells him.

"So those blokes are about here where we're standing

now, up to their knees in the stinking bog, sweating like pigs in their worsted army redcoats in an Australian summer for God's sake, long-suffering grunts like us," he cracks a rueful smile, "just trying to get a job done. And they look up there—there, the trees between those sheds—and see the Aborigines. And Perch gives the order, and they heave up their muskets, Brown Besses they would have been, five kilograms, six foot long, eighteen millimetre bore, and they blast away."

Harry shifts his weight on his feet, wondering when he'll get to the point. Is he trying to draw some parallel with the bodies in the pit?

"So, Harry," Wagstaff says, still staring up at the trees in the little park on the knoll, "did you find out who killed your mum and dad?"

He says it as if it's all part of the same story, and Harry has to blink and take a breath. What does he know?

Wagstaff goes on, "You worked out that Bebchuk and his pals drove them off the road that night, and made sure they were dead. I guess they didn't realise that your Jenny was lying injured in the well of the back seat."

Harry says, "Hang on. Where is this coming from?"

"This is the Bob Marshall theory, Harry. So why'd they do it?"

Harry hesitates, then says, "I know they were acting on orders from Oldfield."

Wagstaff nods.

"But I don't know why, and I don't know who else wanted them dead."

"What makes you think there were others?"

"Oldfield more or less told me as much."

"Did he now. No ideas?"

"No, but I'll keep looking."

"Course you will." Wagstaff turns to face him and now Harry sees the pistol in his right hand.

"Sir?"

"Just have to get the job done, Harry. Nothing personal." And he pulls the trigger. Once. Twice. And watches Harry fall.

Wagstaff moves in to the prone body, the gun trained on his head, when he feels something—Harry's hand?—nudge against his leg. He tries to kick his foot free, but for some reason can't. He crouches down and finds to his surprise that Harry has handcuffed himself to his ankle.

"You bugger!" Wagstaff mutters, almost admiring. "How did you manage that?" He reaches to Harry's throat and finds no pulse. Automatically reaches to his hip pocket where he keeps his own handcuffs, and the key, before remembering that he doesn't have them with him today. Impatient now, he reaches down and starts groping through Harry's pockets, turning them out, one after another. Nothing. There is no key.

He straightens, forcing himself to slow down, to think. His car is up there on the perimeter road, maybe thirty metres away. In the glove box he has a notebook, a pen, a screwdriver, a torch and—a knife, with which he can cut off Harry's hand.

He pockets his gun and bends down to grip the body under the armpits and begins to drag it up the concrete driveway, watching the long dark trail of blood growing behind them. When he reaches the street he stops at his car and takes out his gun again so that he can get at the car keys in his pocket, and at that moment a patrol car swings around the corner and catches him in its head-lights.

The two officers see a man crouching over a body. They jump out of their car and see a gun in the man's hand, and begin shouting together, "Police! Drop your weapon!" The man swings upright, yells something, the gun still in his hand, and they both squeeze their triggers, three rounds each rapid fire, and the man falls.

They run over to the two prone figures.

"This one's gone."

"This one too." The officer shines a light on Wagstaff's face. "Jeez . . . he looks familiar."

FORTY-THREE

JENNY HEARS SOMEONE APPROACH, then seat themselves in the chair at her side.

"Mrs. Belltree? I'm Detective Inspector Deb Velasco. I am . . . I was a colleague of Harry's. I came here as soon as I heard. I'm so sorry."

"You worked with Harry in homicide?"

"Yes."

"Can you tell me what happened? No one seems to want to tell me."

"They're not telling anybody. I'm sorry, I just don't know. Apart from the fact that they found him at Crucifixion Creek."

The woman's voice comes closer to Jenny's ear and whispers, "Do you know what he was doing there?"

"No. He didn't tell me. I'd been expecting him home."

They fall silent, unable to find words. Then Deb says, "We all liked Harry. We all . . . admired his dedication." It's as if she's practising the phrases for a eulogy.

Jenny says, "He's done this before."

"What? How do you mean?"

"In the army, in Afghanistan. Eighteen minutes that time."

"Yes . . . I . . . he . . ." Deb sounds confused.

"This time it took longer—thirty-eight minutes, as near as they can tell." She still feels the numbness that seized her when they told her Harry was dead. It made her close down somehow, and now she is finding her brain only accepts information a little drop at a time. "They call it Lazarus Syndrome, apparently."

"I don't understand," says Deb.

"He was dead for thirty-eight minutes. Can you imagine that?"

"What, they brought him back?"

"They're operating on him now."

"But . . . they think he'll be all right?"

"They don't know. It may be weeks, months, before we know."

"My God."

"But he'd damn well better be all right. I've got something important to tell him."

AFTERWORD

Clearly Harry Belltree is an entirely fictitious character, and his activities in no way represent the real behaviours of the New South Wales police. However I am indebted to a number of people who have helped me to breathe into him whatever life the reader may detect. In particular I should like to thank Detective Superintendent Matt Appleton APM, Alex Mitchell, Dr. Tim Lyons, Lyn Tranter, Mandy Brett and especially my wife, Margaret.